CHINA ROSES

CHINA ROSES

Jo Bannister

SEVERN
HOUSE

First world edition published in Great Britain and the USA in 2021
by Severn House, an imprint of Canongate Books Ltd,
14 High Street, Edinburgh EH1 1TE.

Trade paperback edition first published in Great Britain and the USA in 2022
by Severn House, an imprint of Canongate Books Ltd.

severnhouse.com

Copyright © Jo Bannister, 2021

British Library Cataloguing-in-Publication Data
A CIP catalogue record for this title is available from the British Library.

ISBN-13: 978-0-7278-5065-2 (cased)
ISBN-13: 978-1-78029-804-7 (trade paper)
ISBN-13: 978-1-4483-0542-1 (e-book)

Typeset by Palimpsest Book Production Ltd.,
Falkirk, Stirlingshire, Scotland.

ONE

G abriel Ash waited, and no one came. No good news; no bad. He walked to the window, saw nothing but the grey November sky, returned to his seat. Got up again, fed coins into the coffee machine, added milk and sugar – though he didn't take sugar – and put the cardboard cup on the low table to go cold with the rest. Waited some more.

Finally – *finally* – footsteps in the corridor and, drying his hands on a paper towel, a man pushed through the swing doors. He was a young man, powerfully built, dark-skinned, with a broad face designed for good cheer. But not today.

Ash knew what he was going to say before he said it. His heart turned over and fell, bleeding as it went.

'I'm sorry. We did everything we could. The odds were always against us. There was just too much internal damage.'

'But . . .' Pain made Ash unreasonable. 'I thought you people were the experts.'

'We're good at what we do,' the young man assured him sombrely. 'We're not miracle-workers. Sometimes, in spite of our best efforts, we're beaten. This was one of those times.'

'But . . . she wasn't even all that old!'

The young man, whose name was Diego, kept a diplomatic silence. He had long since learned there was no point arguing with the bereaved. No point observing that all things are comparative, and anyway it's not the years that count so much as the miles on the clock.

'How am I going to manage without her?' wondered Ash. 'She's always been there for me – reliable, uncomplaining. I need her!'

Diego gave a sympathetic shrug. 'You will miss her. But then' – brightening – 'I don't suppose she was your first and she won't be your last. You'll find another that you like just as much. I can help you look, if you like. Showroom condition or been-round-the-block?'

The waiting-room door opened again and a woman came in, stamping liquid mud off her boots. She was wrapped from thigh to chin in a thick padded jacket, slick with rain, and from the eyebrows upwards in a woolly hat with an enormous pompom, currently saturated and drooping over her left ear. The gap between the hat and the collar of her coat was filled with a mass of fair curls, roughly tamed by an elastic band in the nape of her neck.

She took in Ash's expression in a moment and knew that his worst fears had been confirmed. Though she was in general a kind woman, she hadn't a lot of patience with sentimentality. 'I take it she's off to the scrap-heap?'

Ash turned on her with a distress that was absolutely genuine. 'Hazel! Don't be so cruel. I loved that car. She's been part of my family for nearly twenty years.'

'Which makes it time and past time you bought a new one,' said Hazel Best briskly. 'Gabriel, it's been a heap of junk for as long as I've known you. Your mother drove it for fourteen years, it was mothballed after she died, and you've got another two years out of it. It's done. It has gone to that great car-port in the sky. You need a new one.'

Diego the mechanic hid a grin.

Ash sniffed, hurt by his friend's levity. 'She should have gone on for years yet,' he muttered rebelliously. Then he gave Hazel a puzzled look. 'Anyway, what are you doing here?'

'Diego called me. He said you were going to need a lift home. And a shoulder to cry on.'

They were halfway to Highfield Road, to the stone house which Ash also inherited from his mother, when Hazel's phone rang. She pulled over dutifully before answering it. 'Dave Gorman,' she mouthed at Ash as she listened. They were good friends, these three, on first-name terms among themselves, but now Hazel worked for Detective Chief Inspector Gorman she called him Chief in the CID offices at Meadowvale Police Station, and sir in public.

This was business. Ash saw the fractional change in her expression that was his friend Hazel retuning to Detective Constable Best. There was still a part of him that regretted the change, that recalled with nostalgia those simpler days when as a uniformed officer she began and mostly ended shifts at regular hours, could spend time with him and not have her phone constantly interrupting.

She ended the call, rejoined the traffic. 'I'll drop you off. I have to go to the hospital. They've got a John Doe.'

That put Ash's automotive issues in perspective. After a hot, dry summer, the winter had hit hard, steamrollering autumn into the sodden ground; even before Christmas, people without warm homes to go to were paying the price. Norbold Infirmary would have more hypothermic vagrants to thaw out before spring came round, and for some of them the warm bed would come too late. 'Will he be all right?'

'They don't know. He's in Intensive Care. Concussion.'

Ash frowned. 'How do you get concussion from sleeping out in the rain?'

'You don't,' said Hazel tersely. 'You get it from having your head kicked in by someone who wants your coat more than you do.'

PC Budgen met her with a cheery smile in the corridor outside ICU. 'I'm gagging for my breakfast,' he said.

'Where's our John Doe?'

Budgen jerked his head. 'Next to the end, on the right.'

'I suppose you've done all the usuals – checked his clothes for any kind of ID?'

Budgen nodded. 'Nothing. But then, not that much in the way of clothes either, considering the weather we've been having. Shirt and sweater, cords – nothing helpful in the pockets, just a hanky and a bit of small change. No coat or hat. If he had a wallet it must have been in his coat pocket. Unless whoever duffed him over rummaged his poke as well.'

Hazel wasn't sure where Wayne Budgen hailed from – there was a hint of Birmingham in his accent, and a broader hint of somewhere more rural – but his conversation was littered with expressions she needed the context to translate. She concluded that PC Budgen was wondering if the assailant who'd put the unidentified man in ICU had not only taken his coat but raided his trouser pockets as well.

'What's the story?'

The constable gave a glum sniff. 'Thought I was being clever, didn't I? Last patrol of the night, thought I'd head back to Meadowvale the quiet way. Well, nobody wants to stumble on the Great Train Robbery just as he's coming off shift, does he? So I cut back through Siding Street. Well for him that I did. If I hadn't found him, he'd have drowned in the gutter.'

'He was beaten up?'

'Either that, or a herd of buffalo ran over the top of him. And that hasn't happened in Norbold for, ooh, months now.'

She looked at him. He looked back.

'What's the damage?'

'Broken wrist, cracked ribs, heavy bruising pretty well all over, and the concussion. None of the rest of it is life threatening. They're waiting for him to wake up before they commit themselves on the head injury.'

'Where's his stuff?'

'In the locker by his bed. Here, I'll show you.' Budgen led the way. 'You'll need to put them on a radiator for a couple of hours before you bag them up, else they'll go all mouldy.'

If the medical staff were waiting for the unknown man to wake up, Hazel hoped they'd brought sandwiches. He didn't look anywhere close to regaining consciousness. There was no restiveness of his body, no vague movements of hands or head, no fluttering of eyelids. More than that, there was a flatness under the sheet that you don't get with essentially healthy people who've broken a leg. It looked as if the hospital bed was only half-occupied already.

She took out her notebook, made some objective assessments. Height a little less than medium – perhaps an inch shorter than her, around five foot seven; build hard to judge in his current position, but not heavy; age, mid-thirties; hair dark, eyes shut, face black and blue . . .

. . . And familiar. The wild improbability of it startled a gasp out of her, and Hazel moved to the other side of the bed for a better look, to make sure. 'Wayne, I know him.'

'Oh, good,' said Budgen, disappointingly blasé. 'That'll simplify matters. Who is he, one of your lame dogs?' Hazel had a reputation for collecting waifs and strays.

'No. He's not from round here at all. I can't imagine what

he's doing in Norbold, let alone what he's doing getting mugged in Norbold. He's . . .'

How to explain so convoluted a family history before PC Budgen lost interest and wandered off in search of his overdue breakfast? Either a very few words or a whole book. She opted for the former. 'He's an archaeologist. His family owns the big house in Cambridgeshire where my dad's the handyman. His name's David Sperrin.'

Budgen frowned. 'I thought that family were called Byrfield.'

'David's the old earl's by-blow.' Even as she said it, she knew Sperrin himself would have scorned the euphemism, happily admitted to being a bastard. But anything was better than describing a man in his thirties as a love-child.

'Well, what's he doing here then?'

'I can't imagine.'

'Looking for you?'

'If he wanted me, he'd phone. If he hasn't got my number, his brother certainly has. I can't think of any reason for him to come looking for me without calling first. Actually, I can't think of any reason for him to contact me at all.'

Wayne Budgen gave an amiable leer. 'A secret admirer?'

Hazel shook her head. 'I'm too young for him. Two thousand years too young.' A thought occurred to her. 'What about his car?'

'What does he drive?'

'A beat-up old Land Rover. The agricultural version, not the Chelsea tractor. Largely green, although when bits fall off he replaces them with whatever he can find at a scrapyard. Last time I saw it, the driver's door was orange.'

'Well, it wasn't in Siding Street. I couldn't have missed that. I'll tell Sergeant Murchison – the area car can look out for it. It can't be far away. He hasn't staggered far in that condition.'

'No.' Hazel was still looking at the unconscious man, taking in the damage he'd sustained. Whoever had done that to him hadn't meant him to get up afterwards. Not immediately; possibly not at all. Hazel was surprised to feel her stomach twist in a way that it didn't every time she was tasked with cleaning up human wreckage.

There was nothing, nor had there ever been, between her and David Sperrin. Growing up near the village where his mother lived, she'd been dimly aware of him – no more than that. He had left for university before her idea of masculine perfection stopped involving a flowing mane and twinkling hooves; and anyway, David Sperrin had never been anyone's idea of masculine perfection. He was short, spiky and grace-less, often muddy, sardonic by default and widely considered too clever by half. She knew he'd had his eye blackened by a farmer's son who didn't know what Crypto Hominid meant but knew it wasn't a compliment.

She'd got to know him better two years ago, when he had dug behind the big house and unearthed not the expected cist but a family tragedy. She would have counted him a friend, more or less; at least, more than an acquaintance. She wasn't sure Sperrin could have picked her out of an ID parade.

She leaned closer, said his name. There was no response that she could see. 'What happened to you, David?' she asked softly. 'What are you doing here? Who did this to you?'

'So what's he doing in Norbold?' demanded Detective Chief Inspector Gorman. 'And who the hell ran over him in a tank?'

'Muggers?' suggested Hazel weakly. 'His coat, his wallet and his phone are missing, and we can't find his car.'

Gorman was looking at the photographs. It wasn't a pleasant thing, to photograph the injuries of an unconscious man, but it was a necessary part of a criminal investigation. 'That wasn't a mugging. That was punishment.'

'How do you know?' She wasn't arguing, she was trying to learn. Hazel was still a beginner in criminal detection, at least officially.

'There's too much damage,' said Gorman. 'A mugger isn't interested in hurting his victim, only in robbing him. He'll do enough to incapacitate him, then scarper with his valuables before there's any risk of being caught. If he can achieve the same end with a good shove and the element of surprise, so much the better.

'A good shove didn't do all this, neither did a fist. He hit Sperrin round the head with something hard and heavy, then he went on hitting him; and even after *that* it looks as if he put the boot in. You don't need to do half of that to snatch somebody's wallet. You're just wasting time that you need for your getaway. He wanted to hurt Sperrin more than he wanted to rob him.'

'What did he want with his coat?' asked Hazel, perplexed. 'Because in this weather he must have had one.'

'Maybe it's in his car. He might not have had it on, if he was driving.'

'He'd have needed a warmer coat to drive that particular car than if he'd been on foot.'

Gorman gave a shrug. 'So maybe it seemed easier to take his coat than to get his wallet, his phone and his car keys out of the pockets. We'll probably find it in a rubbish skip some-where – have the foot patrols check. And can we for pity's sake find his car? It sounds pretty distinctive, and it's got to be somewhere. Professional car thieves with mobile spray-painting rigs *don't* steal old Land Rovers. If the muggers – I don't know what else to call them for now – took it, it was to do a runner. They'll have dumped it before we knew to start looking. If it isn't on the street somewhere, it's in a vacant lot or round the back of an empty shop or something. It hasn't just vanished into thin air. We need to find it.'

'You think it'll tell us something about what happened?'

'I won't know that it *won't* until we find it.'

'If it really wasn't a mugging,' Hazel said slowly, 'what was it? He's an archaeologist. How does an archaeologist make the kind of enemies that want to put him in ICU?'

Somebody had to say it, and Detective Sergeant Presley was in the next room. So Gorman sighed and said, 'Maybe he's been playing around with somebody's mummy.'

Hazel eyed him reproachfully. 'This isn't funny, Chief. David's badly hurt. Until he wakes up, we're not going to know how badly.'

'I suppose I'd better inform the family. Do you have a number for them?'

'Yes. But I think I should call them. It might be easier for his brother, coming from someone he knows. If I talk to Pete, he can drive into Burford and tell David's mother.'

'All right,' nodded Gorman. Breaking bad news wasn't anyone's favourite job. 'See if they know what he was doing here. You're sure he wasn't looking for you?'

'I can't imagine why he would be.'

'Well, he must have had some reason to come to Norbold. You can get beaten up quite satisfactorily without leaving Cambridgeshire.'

'We'll ask him when he wakes up.'

'Hm.' DCI Gorman was looking at the photographs again. He didn't say, If he wakes up. But Hazel heard it just the same.

TWO

The 28th Earl of Byrfield had no idea what his brother was doing in Norbold. He hadn't seen him for several days; in fact, he hadn't seen much of him for some weeks. He understood he'd been working on a dig in Lincolnshire, or possibly Leicestershire. Roman – or was it Norman . . .? They didn't have a great deal in common – not in interests, not in appearance, not even in the single parent the wider community believed they shared. As David Sperrin was the result of the 27th earl's wanderlust, so Peregrine Byrfield was the product of an indiscretion by the countess.

What they did share, with one another and their two sisters, was a kind of wry, amused, clannish affection, a tolerance of one another's weaknesses and an appreciation of one another's strengths. It didn't strike Hazel as significant that Pete Byrfield – he resolutely refused to answer to his given name – was so vague about his brother's recent activities. Possibly David hadn't told him; possibly Pete had been reading *Farmers Weekly* when he did.

'How bad is he, Hazel? Honestly?'

'Honestly, Pete, we don't know. He has a couple of broken bones, but nothing that won't mend over the next few weeks. The only real concern is the concussion. He's been out cold for several hours now – we're not sure how long – and he's not ready to surface yet. Until he does, until the doctors can talk to him and see how he responds, there's always the chance that he's sustained some lasting damage. Probably not – I don't want to alarm you, Pete, I just want to put you in the picture. So far as I understand it, there's no reason to get seriously worried unless a few hours turn into two or three days. Even after that, lots of people suddenly sit up and ask for a cup of tea, and go on with their lives as if nothing had happened. But I'll be glad when David's back to being his old snide unlovable self again.'

'And you don't know who attacked him? Or why?'

'We're working on it. *I'm* working on it – I'm trawling CCTV footage, looking for some sort of clue. Siding Street, where he was found, isn't much more than a back alley, there are no cameras there, but there's a pub round the corner: we've got the computer geek trying to enhance their footage. Brighten the image, cut out some of the shadows, improve the contrast, that kind of thing. It may tell us something. If we can identify David, we'll know which direction he was coming from. We'll know if he was alone, and if anyone was following him.'

'It won't tell you why someone beat the crap out of him.'

'No,' agreed Hazel. 'But David will. Hold onto that thought, Pete. David will tell us what happened.'

'I'll come over,' decided Byrfield. 'I can be there in an hour forty-five.'

'Not legally you can't,' said Detective Constable Best sternly. 'Anyway, there's no rush. If he wakes up before you get here, that's a good thing. Feed your cows or whatever it is you do at this time on a Tuesday morning, have a cup of coffee and then come. If there's any change in the meantime, I'll let you know.'

Leaving the CCTV footage with Melvin the geek, she made the short trip from Meadowvale to check that she hadn't over-looked other, potentially more helpful cameras positioned to give a better view up Siding Street. But there were none. It wasn't that sort of street. There were no banks, no building societies, no department stores or hotels, only some lock-up garages at one end and a huddle of two-up, two-down terraced houses at the other. There had once been more, but first they'd fallen vacant and then they'd fallen down. Beyond the high brick wall on the other side of the street there were in fact cameras, but they were turned the other way, monitoring activity in the railway yard.

Finishing in Siding Street, disappointed but not surprised to have learnt nothing new, Hazel took the scenic route back to Meadowvale via Rambles With Books. It was a busy morning in Ash's second-hand bookshop: he had two customers at the same time. One was Miss Hornblower, who spent almost as much time there as the proprietor did; the other was a young man with a nose stud. Ash was serving up coffee and biscuits. When he saw Hazel parking outside, he went back into the little kitchen for another mug.

'It's all right,' he said, handing it to her steaming, 'you don't have to keep checking on me. Scrapping my car hasn't left me suicidal.'

'It's not that,' said Hazel.

Her tone stopped him in his tracks. A brief study of her face and he steered her into a quiet corner – the whole shop was quiet, but the quietest corner – and sat her down. 'What's happened?'

So she told him.

Ash's acquaintance with the family was much more recent than Hazel's, but he had been involved in the discovery of the little grave beside the Byrfield lake and everything that followed from it. He liked Pete Byrfield, which wasn't difficult, and also rather liked David Sperrin, which was.

'And how is he now?' he asked after Hazel had finished.

She gave a helpless shrug. 'No one's willing to commit themselves. He could wake up in time for lunch, or next week, or next month, or never. He could wake up with nothing worse than a headache, or with alphabet soup for a brain. No one knows.'

'Laura Fry' – Ash's therapist – 'told me once that no brain injury is so trivial that it should be dismissed or so serious it should be despaired of. Most people who suffer concussion make a perfectly good recovery. It's certainly too early to start assuming the worst.'

Ash had a way of sounding like an expert even on subjects he knew very little about. Sometimes that irritated Hazel; today it was a comfort. 'I'm sure you're right.'

'Did you know he was coming to Norbold?'

'Of course I didn't. What possible reason could David have for coming here? Our Roman villa, our Iron Age hill forts, our mediaeval cathedral?'

Ash looked at her doubtfully. 'We don't have any of those things.'

'Exactly.'

Ash pondered how to put this. 'So the only thing in Norbold which might be on David's radar is you.'

'If he thought really hard, he might remember what town I live in. He could probably get my address, either from Pete or from my dad. But why would he want to? And if he did want to see me, why come here without a word of warning? He'd phone first. That's the normal thing to do.'

'This is David we're talking about,' murmured Ash.

She ignored that. 'Even if he did decide to come on spec, what the hell happened to him between turning off the motorway and ending up in ICU? Dave Gorman isn't buying it as a mugging. He thinks whoever did that much damage didn't just want his valuables, he wanted to hurt him. But why? What did David ever do to earn that much enmity?'

'This is still David Sperrin we're talking about, right?' murmured Ash.

Hazel scowled at him. 'I know what you're saying: he's never set out to win popularity contests. I know he's rude, and arrogant, and clever enough to get right under people's skin and too stupid to stop himself. I know all that. But Gabriel, someone damn near beat him to death. Why? And why here?'

But Ash couldn't even make a guess.

'Listen, I'd better get back to Meadowvale,' said Hazel. 'Pete's on his way, I'll go back to the hospital with him. If he wants to stay over until we know what's happening, he can have Saturday's room.' Hazel would always think of the tiny back bedroom at her house in Railway Street as Saturday's room, although the waif who once occupied it was now a young man with a good job and his own flat in London.

'If there's anything I can do, you will let me know?' said Ash.

'Right now, I'm not sure there's much more any of us can do.'

The 28th Earl of Byrfield came armed with a plastic shopping bag advertising his local supermarket. 'I brought him some clothes. I didn't know what he'd need.'

'Everything,' said Hazel, glancing at the contents with approval. 'His own were' – how to put this tactfully? – 'pretty well trashed, and anyway we've bagged them as evidence. When he comes round, he'll probably be in bed for another day or two, but then he'll be wanting to get up and dressed.'

Pete Byrfield looked nothing like David Sperrin, a fact that caused no surprise among casual acquaintances who didn't know they were supposed to be half-brothers, or really close friends who knew that actually they weren't. He was tall and narrow, with a long mild face and fair hair, already growing somewhat sparse. Their personalities were diametrically different too. Despite the ermine and strawberry leaves, Pete was essentially a farmer, a gentle, methodical man. David, inheriting nothing except his father's stature and his mother's powerful will, had proved ambitious, quick-witted and determined, and had quickly developed a scientist's disdain for the less intellectually gifted.

'He will be all right, won't he?' said Byrfield unhappily as the lift bore them upwards; and Hazel provided the reassurance he sought even though she had no more information now than Pete had.

'I'm sure he will. Concussion always has to be taken seriously, but most people make a complete recovery. Gabriel said so.' She was aware as she said it that Ash was no more a doctor than she was. He'd been an insurance investigator, a security analyst and a second-hand bookseller, but he'd never been a brain surgeon and his knowledge of head injuries was derived from what he'd read and what he'd been told. Only his knowledge of mental illness was rooted in personal experience.

But Byrfield took comfort from his assessment just the same.

The next thing he said was what they were all wondering. 'What was he *doing* here, Hazel? Had he been in touch with you?'

Hazel shook her head. 'The last time I saw David was at your wedding, and I haven't talked to him since. There's been no reason to. And I wouldn't have thought he could find Norbold on a map.'

They stood looking down at the still form in the hospital bed, white-faced, his left arm in plaster, the palette of bruises growing increasingly lurid. There was still no sign of returning consciousness that Hazel could see, although one of the ICU nurses, passing by, gave her a smile and said, 'I think he's looking a little brighter.'

'And who the hell did this to him?' demanded Byrfield thickly. 'And why?'

'We don't know that either,' admitted Hazel. 'Pete, we are trying to make sense of it, but . . .' She shook her head, bewildered. 'And we still haven't found his car. We are looking for the right one, aren't we? He hasn't swapped it for a family hatchback?'

'Good God, no. He'll keep that Land Rover until the scrapmetal police prise the keys from his cold dead hand . . .' Realising what he'd said, Byrfield fell abruptly silent.

Kindly, Hazel diverted his thoughts. 'Gabriel's looking for a new car. That old Volvo of his mother's has wheezed its last. I thought he was going to ask me to arrange a funeral for it.'

Byrfield managed a dutiful smile. But it didn't last. 'What if he doesn't recover?' he wondered in a low voice. 'What if he's never the same again?'

She knew what he was asking. 'Then we'll look after him,' she said quietly. 'We'll find out what he needs, and we'll look after him. But it won't come to that. He *will* recover. It may take a little time, but time is on his side. If you believe nothing else, believe that.'

She offered him the back bedroom at Railway Street, but Byrfield declined. 'I have to get back. As luck would have it, we're TB testing tomorrow – it's an all-hands-on-deck job. I'll come back as soon as we're through. Will you call me tonight, let me know how he's doing?'

'Of course I will,' promised Hazel. 'There'll be better news by tomorrow, I'm sure of it.'

He ran a hand distractedly through his pale hair. 'I feel like I'm abandoning him.'

'Don't be silly. I'm here. Gabriel will look in on him, too. There's nothing you could do that we can't. And no way can you leave Tracy to TB test three hundred cows on her own.'

'Three hundred and twenty-two,' murmured Byrfield with

a hint of pride. 'I know, you're right. I just . . . I hate leaving him like this.'

'Try not to worry too much,' said Hazel.

She was with Gorman when the call came in.

The DCI had wanted to know why, eight hours after Sperrin was found, his car was still missing. 'It's not as if it would be hard to spot,' he growled. 'It's a Land Rover. It's green with one orange door. It's not going to be hiding in plain sight, is it?'

Hazel wasn't sure why he was blaming her for the short-comings of the whole of Meadowvale Police Station, and she was fairly sure that if she challenged him he wouldn't know either. She took it philosophically. If he needed someone to shout at, that was the least she owed him.

But it did make her think. 'Maybe we can't find it because it isn't here. Maybe that's not how he got to Norbold.' Her fair brows knitted in a pensive frown. 'Maybe this isn't where he was attacked.'

Gorman stared at her. 'You mean, he couldn't drive because of his broken wrist, so he got on a train to come and tell you all about it?'

When he put it like that . . . 'It doesn't sound very likely, does it?' she admitted. 'But then, whatever happened to him was pretty unlikely, almost by definition.'

'Did you track down who he was working for? If we can't figure out what he's doing here, can we at least find out where he was supposed to be instead?'

Hazel consulted her notes. 'He was working as a consultant – a sort of Have Trowel, Will Travel arrangement – for the Anglia Archaeology Trust. The last job they had for him was in the Leicester area. But they wrapped that up ten days ago, and David said he was taking a break before he started on anything else. No one at Anglia knows if he was planning a holiday, or had a paper to write or what.'

'He writes for a newspaper?'

'No, a scientific paper. It's what scientists do – they set out their findings in a paper that'll be read by an average of one and a half other people. It's really just a way of putting information into the public domain. I doubt if it's why someone set about him with a baseball bat.'

'It wasn't a baseball bat,' said Gorman, 'it was a monkey wrench. Some kind of tool, anyway. There was machine oil on his clothes.'

It wasn't helpful. 'If he'd come to blows with another archaeologist over carbon-dating methodology,' said Hazel, 'it would have been mud.'

That was when the call from the hospital came in. DCI Gorman gestured Hazel to stay. Her stomach knotted briefly, but she quickly gathered it was good news rather than bad.

Gorman put the phone down. 'They say he's showing signs of waking up. They say it'll be a while before he can answer questions, but if we want to send someone to sit with him he might say something halfway sensible, and it wouldn't do any harm.'

'Can I go? It'll be easier for him, waking up to a familiar face. And I'd like to be able to tell his brother I was with him.'

'Yes, all right.' Gorman had never considered sending anyone else. 'Don't pester him. But – you know – if he *is* making any kind of sense, anything he can tell us would be useful. Starting with where that bloody Land Rover is!'

THREE

She called at the florist's in Windham Lane on her way, not because she thought David Sperrin would appreciate the gesture but because it would make his cubicle look more cheerful – more hopeful – when his brother made the long journey back from Cambridgeshire the next day.

Mrs Kiang tried to sell her roses. 'Beautiful roses – Banksiana roses, very fine – all the way from China. Beautiful lady must have beautiful China roses. Very good price.'

But the flowers were for a friend, not a lover, and beautiful China roses would not have been appropriate. Hazel picked out some carnations. 'Mrs Kiang, can I ask you something?'

The little florist put her hands together and bowed acceptance.

'Weren't you born in England? And isn't your husband's name William King?'

From under the greying fringe, the black eyes shot her an astute glance. 'So?'

'So why the Widow Twanky act?'

Mrs Kiang straightened up abruptly. 'It sells flowers,' she said shortly, in an accent indistinguishable from any other on the streets of Norbold that afternoon. 'Now was there something else, or will you bugger off before you frighten the paying customers?'

Trying not to smile, Hazel held up the carnations. 'I paid, Mrs Kiang.'

'Not enough,' said Mrs Kiang darkly.

They'd moved Sperrin from ICU to an observation ward. One of the nurses brought a vase for the flowers. 'Don't be concerned if he seems disorientated. It's to be expected. Talk quietly to him, and when he's ready he'll start talking back.'

He wasn't ready yet. His eyes weren't open except for the thinnest of white lines under each bruised lid. But his fingers were moving on the bedclothes, plucking vaguely at the fold where the sheet was turned back, and his broken lips were twitching, and a sound that was half a murmur and half a grunt came intermittently down his nose. Wherever he'd been to, he was on his way back. At least, someone was.

Hazel drew water from a handy tap and stood the carnations in the vase. She had no talent for flower arranging, and she didn't think David Sperrin would care if she'd brought him flowers or not. Having satisfied her modest expectations, she hooked a chair towards her with her foot and sat down beside him.

'It's Hazel,' she said quietly. 'Hazel Best – you know, Fred Best's daughter? You're in Norbold, you're in hospital, and you're going to be fine. You've had a knock on the head, that's all. Pete was here a little while ago, but he had to go back to Byrfield. TB testing. He'll be back to see you tomorrow. I'm going to phone him tonight. What shall I tell him?'

She waited then, watching to see if he'd make any response. But nothing changed in Sperrin's inward-turning, self-absorbed expression. Perhaps his eyebrows drew momentarily a little closer together, but the cuts and bruises made it hard to be sure.

Hazel sighed. Perhaps it was asking too much, that he might go directly from hours of unconsciousness to holding an intelligent conversation. 'Oh well, never mind. Maybe you'll feel more like talking later.'

She went to the window. There was a deeply uninspiring view over the car park to the ring road, and it was raining again. She was beginning to think it would never stop. She was beginning to think Ash should buy a boat rather than a new car. She grinned privately to herself. She'd take him to visit some dealerships on her next day off, get him to make a shortlist. The challenge would be to stop him coming home with a slightly less elderly Volvo estate, in that same odd shade between beige and brown, simply because that was what he was familiar with.

She turned back to the bed, and David Sperrin was looking directly at her. She caught her breath. 'David?' And when he didn't reply she added inanely: 'Are you in there?'

She couldn't tell how aware he was of his surroundings. He wasn't looking round him, and although his eyes were still on her she saw no recognition in them, wasn't sure he was actually seeing her at all. She sat down again and, after a moment, took his good hand, the one that wasn't in plaster, with her own and squeezed gently, reassuringly. 'Take your time,' she said softly. 'I'll wait right here.'

His eyes fell shut again.

The nurse Hazel had seen before looked in again. 'Not up to making a signed statement just yet then?' She didn't sound particularly concerned. Perhaps she couldn't afford to be.

'I thought he was waking up a minute ago. But then he seemed to nod off again. Is that normal?'

'Insofar as there *is* a normal with head injuries, there's often a bit of coming and going before people are ready for the real world again. But everyone's different. There's no point trying to hurry things.'

'How soon will we know if there's any lasting damage?'

'You should really be talking to the doctor.' But when she looked around, there wasn't one in sight and she relented a little. 'Probably not immediately. You do see people who bounce back as if nothing had happened, but often there's a degree of confusion. We'd only really get concerned if there was no sign of that starting to dissipate over the next day or so.'

'Would you expect him to remember what happened to him?'

The nurse raised her eyebrows. 'Don't count on it. There's commonly some memory loss around the concussive event – before, after or both. Not always. We had a rider in here a couple of months ago who woke up after two days and knew exactly what had happened, including which side of the horse she'd fallen off. Brains are funny. No two brain injuries are exactly the same, and no two patients recover from them in exactly the same way.'

'And the ones who don't recover?'

She was making the nurse uneasy. 'I really shouldn't be talking to you about this.'

Hazel followed her out to the nurses' station. 'I'm not a

member of his family,' she pointed out, which was accurate if disingenuous, 'I'm a police officer investigating a crime. We can talk generalities if that's less of a problem. I just want to have some idea about what we can reasonably expect.'

After a moment the nurse nodded. 'Generalities: all right. Except in extreme cases, the technology – the X-rays, the CT scans, the EEGs – can be misleading both ways. They can be overly pessimistic or unduly encouraging. You really only know the patient's in serious trouble when they've had time to wake up properly and haven't done. The memory loss may be extensive, even total. There may be loss of cognitive function, or motor function, or both.'

Seeing Hazel's eyes glazing she translated. 'They may have trouble thinking or moving. They may be left in a persistent vegetative state, never more than half awake, for years. Or they may appear to make a reasonable recovery, but the person who returns is not the person who left – the personality is profoundly altered. The only thing you can say for sure about brain injuries is that they're unpredictable.'

At that point she seemed to notice how the colour had left Hazel's cheek, and think that perhaps she should have kept the lecture for other medics, not a rather new detective who also – she'd noticed Hazel's hand on Sperrin's – seemed to have a personal relationship with the patient. She smiled brightly. 'But those are pretty much worst-case scenarios. And usually they follow protracted periods of unconsciousness. When it comes to concussion, being out to lunch for half a day is fairly small beer. I've known patients make good recoveries after weeks of unconsciousness.'

Which was certainly more encouraging. 'I'll get back to him. I ought to be there if he is going to wake up. He just might have something useful to say.'

'Yes, indeed,' said the nurse, plainly unconvinced.

When Hazel returned to his bedside, David Sperrin was making another assault on the gates of the world. His eyes were open again, and this time there was a suggestion of intelligence, of someone looking out of them. He was trying to focus on the vase of flowers. A whisper of a word escaped him. 'Roses . . .'

It wasn't the Gettysburg Address, it wasn't Henry V's speech before Harfleur, but it was a start: it was a recognisable word in an appropriate context. Yes, his grasp of botany left something to be desired, but possibly it always had. Hazel found herself smiling with a relief that might still be premature but was at least semi-justified.

She sat down beside him again, took his good hand in hers, and watched as his gaze moved slowly round from the vase to her face. 'David, it's Hazel. How are you feeling now?'

He gave it some thought. 'I hurt,' he whispered.

'I bet you do. Your wrist's broken, you've sprung a couple of ribs and you've had a knock on the head. But you're going to be fine. Do you know where you are?'

Perhaps he'd been listening earlier; perhaps the white sheets and the flowers were a clue. 'Hospital?'

Every word he managed – every word he said that made sense – lifted Hazel's heart. 'Yes. In Norbold. David, can you tell me why you came to Norbold?'

His voice was a breathy echo. Already he was tiring. 'Norbold?'

'That's right. What are you doing here? Were you looking for me? Had you another reason to come here?'

Again the lengthy pause while he considered. Then he said, 'Where the fuck's Norbold?'

'Not an unreasonable question,' admitted Ash. 'I mean, even those of us who live here wouldn't claim it's the centre of the civilised world.'

'Not really the point, though, Gabriel,' said Hazel impatiently. 'If the very name of Norbold means nothing to him, what was he doing here?'

'Did you ask him?'

'I was going to ask him. He nodded off again before I got the chance. I'll go back in the morning. By then he may be able to stay awake long enough to answer.'

'On the plus side, he seems to be making sense. Surely that's a good sign.'

'Yes, I think so. The staff seemed satisfied, anyway. They reckon he'll be clearer tomorrow.'

'Any sign of his car yet?'

Hazel shook her head. 'It's beginning to look as if whoever beat him up, took it and kept driving until they found somewhere safe to dump it. A gravel pit, something like that. No witnesses, no cameras. It's on the registration number watchlist, so if it was still driving around, the automatic number-plate recognition system should have picked it up by now.'

That made sense. So far, it was about the only thing that did.

Hazel called Byrfield. 'It's good news, Pete. He's been awake and talking – not long and not much, but enough that his doctors are pretty happy with him. He didn't know what he was doing in Norbold, but that was this afternoon. By tomorrow he may remember more.'

'I'll be finished with the vet by lunchtime,' said Byrfield. 'I'll be with you around three.'

'I don't think there's much to worry about now,' said Hazel. 'There's no need to break the speed limit.'

She'd barely ended the call when, halfway to her pocket, her phone rang. It was DCI Gorman. 'We've found Sperrin's car.'

'Where?' She expected him to say a gravel pit, a derelict factory, something like that.

But he didn't. 'It's parked beside a standing stone on a farm lane between Royston and Biggleswade.'

'Where?' It was clear from the tone of her voice that she suspected him of making it up.

'South-east of Bedford,' said Gorman. 'Otherwise known as The Back of Beyond.'

'Who found it? And how?'

'The farmer complained that it was in his way. When the local plods ran the number plate, they came up with our BOLO.' Busy policemen love a good acronym: this one, describing a general request to Be On the Look-Out, saved the DCI from saying four extra words.

Hazel had thought – they all had – that finding the Land Rover would make things clearer. But then, none of them had expected to find it up a farm lane fifty miles from Norbold. 'Could the farmer say how long it had been there?'

'That's the best bit,' said Gorman, with a kind of grim satisfaction. 'Since yesterday afternoon.'

For a moment, Hazel thought she'd actually misheard. Then she thought, and dismissed the idea immediately, that he was pulling her leg. Detective chief inspectors do not waste their time making fools of their new detective constables, a task which the new DCs can safely be left to accomplish by themselves. Finally she said, 'That's not possible.'

'He seemed pretty clear on the subject. He had to squeeze past it at three o'clock yesterday afternoon. He shouted for the owner but no one showed up. When he was still having to squeeze past it this morning, he phoned the local lads to complain. I've said we'll pick it up first thing tomorrow. Take Sergeant Wilson with you – nobody reads a crime scene better.'

'You want me to go?' She couldn't decide if it was an honour or a punishment, didn't think she deserved either. 'I was planning to see David again in the morning.'

'I can send someone else.'

'No, that's all right.' Hazel thought there was more to be learned from talking to Sperrin than by examining his car, but clearly she couldn't be in two places at once.

Nor was it just a matter of turning up with a low-loader. There would be liaising to do with the Bedford police, paperwork to formalise the transfer of the vehicle. There had already been some debate over which CID team should lead the investigation, an argument which DCI Gorman seemed to have won for Meadowvale on the basis that an assault victim in Norbold trumped an abandoned Land Rover in Bedfordshire. Even so, there would be ruffled feathers to smooth and she would likely be there much of the day.

When Gorman rang off, Hazel turned to Ash. She filled in the details he hadn't been able to infer from her end of the phone-call, then asked if he'd mind shutting the shop for an hour the following afternoon. 'I was going to meet Pete at the hospital at three, and take him for a bit of tea after he's seen David. It's a long old drive, to come here from Byrfield and head straight back again. Would you mind standing in for me? You can tell him where I am, and I'll call him after I get back.'

'Yes, all right.' One of the advantages of self-employment

was that Ash could shut the bookshop any time he liked. One of the advantages of running at a minimal profit was that this didn't usually cost him money.

'The chief's going to send someone to take a statement from David. If they turn up while you're there, you might make sure they don't press him too hard. You know, if he isn't up to it.'

Ash raised a doubtful eyebrow. 'How do you propose I do that?'

'You'll think of something.'

Hazel was about to leave and go home. But Ash was hovering in a way that suggested he had another matter to broach but wasn't sure how to start. She waited patiently. When that didn't work she said, 'Was there something else?'

Ash took a deep breath. 'I've been meaning to tell you. I've started divorce proceedings.'

She caught herself staring, made herself blink. 'Have you?' she said levelly.

'You remember, we talked about it . . .'

Actually they'd argued about it. She'd told him it was time he moved on with his life, severed the last remaining link with a woman who'd almost destroyed him, and Ash had reacted as if she was intruding in his personal affairs. Which she was, but that's what friends are for.

'I do,' said Hazel. 'Has your solicitor said how long it'll take?'

'I don't think he's sure himself. Somewhere between long and very long. The fact that Cathy's the subject of a red Interpol notice might speed it up a little. The court might take the view that, however much we advertise, we're not going to find her, and she wouldn't be in a position to defend the action if we did. Either way we're talking years – somewhere between two and five.'

'A bit soon to order the cake, then.'

Sometimes Hazel's caustic side took Ash by surprise. This was one of those times. It was six years since he and Cathy had had a life together. Then she disappeared with their sons, and he'd believed that they were dead and it was his fault. That was when the foundations of his sanity shook. Four years later he'd discovered that they were in fact living comfortably in Cambridge on the proceeds of her crimes. She was wanted for murder and conspiracy.

Ash hadn't wanted to believe it. She had left him no choice. Even so, it had taken him until now to take the steps necessary to bring the marriage to an end. He knew Hazel thought him weak. He could usually count on her natural kindness to prevent her from saying so out loud. But she had always taken a somewhat robust attitude towards Cathy.

'I just thought you ought to know,' he said, rather formally.

'Yes. Fine.' She thought for a moment. 'Don't forget about Pete, will you?'

FOUR

S ergeant Wilson was a legend at Meadowvale Police Station.

He'd been an amiable and reasonably competent police officer for the first half of his career, but no one who had known him then would have expected him to become the Olympian figure he had. At a time when policemen were valued more for their stature than their intellect, he'd been of barely acceptable height and more – sometimes significantly more – than acceptable weight, and he drew more than his fair share of desk duty since it was universally acknowledged that the only criminals he was ever going to chase down were those whose walking frames had a flat tyre.

But what Sergeant Wilson could do better than anyone at Meadowvale, possibly better than anyone in England, was read a crime scene. Detectives grown old and cynical on the job stood in amazed admiration when Sergeant Wilson looked at a room, or a garage, or perhaps a street corner, and absorbed by some kind of osmosis the myriad details of how things had fallen, or how they had been thrown or thrust aside, and calmly related an account of what had happened. These details would often lead to apprehending a suspect who would sulkily confirm them.

When the powers-that-be decided that scenes of crime officers should no longer be police but civilian staff, Sergeant Wilson calmly tendered his resignation, collected his pension, applied for his old job and was back where he belonged without taking so much as a long weekend first. The eagle-eyed observer might have noticed that he no longer turned up in uniform, but since he did all his best work clad in a hooded, top-to-toe white plastic garment that did nothing whatever to flatter his figure, most people didn't realise there'd been a change but kept addressing him as they always had.

Never one to squander an opportunity, Hazel spent most of the drive quizzing him about his speciality. And he was happy to indulge her, even though he'd sooner have been talking football with the young man from the police garage who had come with them to recover the Land Rover.

They found the lane with some difficulty, followed it for half a mile deep into the dormant winter landscape, past a farmyard and up to an open gate. The standing stone was in the middle of the field, but even a Land Rover would have struggled with the churned-up mud of the gateway. This one had been pulled into the hedge on one side by a driver who must have proceeded from there on foot.

Sergeant Wilson approached the vehicle first, carefully, looking around it before he looked into it. He kept the others at a respectful distance until he was quite sure he'd seen, measured and photographed everything he could. Then he beckoned Hazel over. In view of the conditions underfoot he didn't insist on her covering her boots with plastic bags, but he did silently hand her plastic gloves before proceeding.

'In short,' he said, the scalpel-sharp precision of his words contrasting with the nasal burr of his Midlands accent, 'and with the proviso that this is an initial assessment not a final report, nothing happened here.'

Hazel stared at him. 'What do you mean, nothing?'

'Nothing,' he said again, pontifically. 'Not a fight, not an attack, no incident of any kind. The keys are in the ignition, the engine was turned off, Sperrin's coat is on the seat, his wallet and his phone are in the pockets. I've got one set of footprints walking away and not coming back, and another, in wellies, coming up the lane, turning round and going back down the lane. That'll be the farmer. Over there' – he pointed to a bit of mud which seemed to Hazel indistinguishable from the rest of the mud – 'is where he stopped his tractor.'

'So whoever took the Land Rover was acting alone?'

'One set of footprints would generally equate to one person,' said Sergeant Wilson, smiling into the woolly scarf he had tied inside his forensic hood. 'But the person who attacked your friend isn't the one who left the Land Rover here. I think that was Sperrin himself.'

Hazel was staring at him. 'That isn't possible.'

SOCO raised an eyebrow at her. 'On the contrary, it's the

only logical explanation. We know from the farmer that the vehicle was left here at least seventeen hours before Sperrin turned up in Norbold. What do you suppose? – that whoever mugged him took him away in their own car, drove him round for half a day or so, and then chucked him out in Siding Street? Unless of course,' he added with a twinkle, 'they mugged him in Norbold first thing yesterday morning, then drove out here to abandon his jeep the previous afternoon. That would work, if it was a time machine as well as a Land Rover.'

The rumble of a train passing somewhere in the middle distance interrupted his flow of wit. After the sound had diminished and died it took him a moment to pick up again where he'd left off.

'We know that Sperrin got out of the Land Rover meaning to come straight back – he left his parka on the seat, and it's too cold to go far without a coat. If anyone else had brought it here, they'd probably have emptied his pockets and certainly chucked the parka in the back, out of their way – they wouldn't have driven here sitting on it. And the single set of footprints don't go back up the lane and thence to the county road and ultimately civilisation, they head off towards that.' He pointed.

'The standing stone?'

'He's an archaeologist, isn't he? Who else would wade across a muddy field in November to look at a bit of granite?'

'Police officers looking for clues?' Hazel guessed grimly. They splashed their way to the stone.

'Yes, there's his boots again,' said Sergeant Wilson, pointing to a slightly flattened bit of mud. 'He walked round the stone, stopped, walked on again. And then . . .'

Now he stopped, in an attitude as close to that of a springer spaniel as a man of his age and bulk could assume. Hazel followed his focus across the field to the boundary hedge. 'And then he set off again,' said Sergeant Wilson, 'and this time he was running.'

'Someone was chasing him?'

SOCO looked around, shook his head. 'No. So either someone was threatening him from a distance – waving a gun, maybe – or he wasn't running away from anything. Maybe he was running towards something.'

They followed the line Sperrin – assuming it was him – had taken. Beyond the hedge was a tarmac lane. There was a gate, secured by a chain and a padlock long rusted up. Hazel scaled the gate with ease, helped Sergeant Wilson over the corroded top bar. He began casting round, again like a spaniel, then gave a grunt of satisfaction. 'Something stopped here. Not a tractor – maybe a van. Bigger than a car, anyway. People got out – can't say how many, but more than one. One of them was a woman – see, that small print there?'

Hazel looked where he was pointing but didn't see what he was seeing. Sergeant Wilson went on. 'There was some milling around. Then, presumably, they all got back inside and drove away.'

'And David was with them?'

'I'm a scenes of crime officer,' Wilson reminded her, 'not a clairvoyant. I can't see any sign that he walked away, but then there wouldn't be anything to see on the tarmac. But if he got to Norbold fifty miles away, it seems likely he went in the van.'

Hazel's fair brows knitted as she tried to visualise the events. 'So David came to look at the standing stone. He didn't mean to be long or he'd have put his coat on, but while he was there something happened that made him run – not back to his car but away from it. Maybe, like you say, someone pointing a gun at him. It had to be a fairly serious threat: he's not the sort of guy to be easily intimidated.

'Something happened that he didn't want to wait and argue about, or go back for his phone, and he ran. He probably went over the gate the same way we did—'

'Maybe a little quicker,' conceded Wilson.

'Well, maybe just a little quicker,' smiled Hazel. 'And he flagged down a passing van and hitched a lift.'

'Why did the people in the van get out? If your friend was alarmed enough to run, why didn't he tell them to stay in the van and drive off ASAP?' He watched her curiously, interested in her reply.

'Maybe . . . maybe he was already hurt, and they got out to help him.'

Sergeant Wilson shook his head. 'When he was running he wasn't hurt. He was just in a devil of a hurry.'

'Then . . .' Hazel thought some more. 'Suppose there were more than one of them. That David ran from the man with the gun, and flagged down the van only to find it belonged to the gunman's mates. They jumped out to grab him, threw him in the van and drove off to . . . well, God knows where, except that they ended up in Norbold. Where, having beaten the living daylights out of him, they dumped him in Siding Street.' She looked at the legendary Sergeant Wilson almost shyly. 'Would that work?'

'It might,' he agreed kindly. 'And in this job, knowing what could have happened is the first step to knowing what did happen.'

Ash waited at the main entrance of Norbold Infirmary until he saw the tall narrow figure of Pete Byrfield hurrying up from the car park. 'Hazel was called away. She asked me to meet you.'

It was in Byrfield's eyes that he thought there was bad news. 'Has something happened?'

'Not to David, no,' Ash assured him hastily. 'He's awake, he's had something to eat, he's a bit drowsy and disorientated but his doctor's well satisfied with his progress.'

'You spoke to the doctor?' They were heading up the stairs towards the wards.

'I'm not family, they wouldn't talk to me,' said Ash. 'Hazel got an update before she headed out.'

Byrfield reached the top and turned to face him. 'So David really is on the mend?'

'It sounds like it.'

'Then why did Hazel want you to come here and hold my hand?'

Ash smiled. 'Because she worries about her friends. She knew I meant to visit David as soon as he was feeling better, so she suggested I meet you here. I don't think she had any more of an ulterior motive than that.'

'No.' Byrfield sounded relieved, but also as if he wouldn't relax totally until he'd seen his brother.

This was the first visit Ash had paid to Norbold Infirmary

since learning that Sperrin was here. Not because he was uncon-
cerned, but because he didn't think his presence would be of
any consequence to Sperrin, asleep or awake, and he didn't
want to be in the way.

So he was more shocked than Byrfield, who'd been here
yesterday, at how ill Sperrin looked. He was clearly awake
now – he had a magazine open on his knees, though his eyes
made no effort to focus on it – but for a moment Ash found
it hard to associate the small motionless figure under the
sheets with the pugnacious, dynamic man he had known.
Sperrin hadn't been a big man then, either, but somehow the
amount of personality he managed to cram into his compact
frame usually prevented people from noticing. Ash didn't think
he'd ever seen him completely still before.

But Byrfield was grinning broadly, his relief now uncon-
strained. 'David. You're looking better.'

Sperrin's gaze came round slowly, settled on his brother's
face. 'Am I? Than when?'

'Than when I was here yesterday, and you were away with
the fairies. I was worried about you.'

Sperrin seemed to give that some thought, failed to draw
any conclusions. 'Do you know what happened? Nobody here
will tell me anything.'

'I don't think anybody knows anything. We've all been
hoping that you'd tell *us* what happened.'

'Well, *I* don't know,' retorted Sperrin testily. 'Concussion
– yes?'

'What *do* you remember?' asked Ash.

Sperrin thought. 'I remember Hazel. She wasn't making
any sense. She said I'm in hospital in some place I've never
heard of.'

'That was yesterday evening. You'd only just woken up.
The town's called Norbold. It's not far from Coventry, and it's
where she works and both she and I live.'

'So what am I doing here?'

'We really don't know,' said Ash helplessly. 'You were
found unconscious in a back street early yesterday morning.
Your injuries are consistent with a fairly enthusiastic assault.
Do you know who attacked you?'

Sperrin looked indignant. 'Somebody did this to me? Who? Why?' He thought for a moment longer, then his voice hardened. 'And why the blue blinding blazes am I asking you? Why don't I *remember* what happened?'

Byrfield didn't want him worrying about it, at least until he was stronger. 'David, it's too soon. You were out cold for hours – of course there are gaps in your memory. Perhaps you shouldn't try too hard to remember just yet. Perhaps it'll all come back over the next day or so if you just rest and concentrate on getting better.'

But David Sperrin had never been good at waiting. 'I can't have amnesia. I remember who you are, both of you. I remember who *I* am. Why can't I remember what happened?'

That was the moment at which the detective sergeant from Meadowvale CID arrived to ask the questions Hazel had wanted to. As luck would have it, the sole occupant of the office when DCI Gorman went to dispatch someone was DS Presley.

Tom Presley was a sound, reliable, hard-working police officer, but he would never have won an open scholarship to charm school. When the Continuous Training people had wanted to update Meadowvale on interview techniques in cases of sexual and domestic violence, they had used Presley as an example of how not to do it. Presley still recounted this with pride.

He entered the side ward with a desultory flick of his warrant card, nodded distantly at Ash, took the chair that Byrfield had been about to sit on and introduced himself. He pushed Sperrin's plaster out of the way so he could put his notebook down on the bed, peered at the injured man as if he'd already caught him lying, and said with a kind of bored cynicism: 'OK then, so who beat the shit out of you?'

As the people from Continuous Training pointed out, there were interviewees who could be traumatised all over again by such an approach. David Sperrin was not one of them. The day had yet to dawn when, even well below his best, he could be upset by the likes of Tom Presley. His native contentiousness rose in his veins like wine.

'Gee, Sergeant Parsley,' he said, fixing the detective with a hawkish gaze, 'I don't know. And I'm not the one who's paid to find out.'

Tom Presley rolled his eyes. 'This will be a lot easier, sir, if you try to co-operate. And the name's Presley.'

'I *am* trying to co-operate. I'm trying not to mislead you by telling you things which are not true. I don't know who attacked me.'

Presley wrote something in his notebook. 'All right. What are you doing in Norbold?'

'Where?' said Sperrin.

'Norbold,' said Presley. 'As in Norbold Infirmary. What brought you here?'

'No, I don't know the answer to that one either,' said Sperrin frankly. 'Being hit round the head does that sometimes, I'm told.'

The sergeant looked at him in open disbelief. 'You're saying you've lost your memory? Isn't that a bit convenient?'

Sperrin bristled. 'Not particularly. I'd quite like to know who to thank for all this. Never mind, I'm sure you'll get to the bottom of it soon. Won't you, Sergeant Weasley?'

Presley was beginning to breathe a little hard. 'If you don't remember the attack, what do you remember?'

Sperrin made an expansive gesture that usually requires two hands. 'Lots of things. E equals MC squared. The square on the hypotenuse is equal to the sum of the squares on the other two sides. Mares eat oats and does eat oats, but little lambs' – he leaned forward slightly, insisting on the point – 'eat ivy. There is in fact almost no end to the things I can remember. The only thing I *can't* remember is what I'm doing here, in a town named after a lavatory cleaner, and I think I know why that is.'

He beckoned with the forefinger of his good hand. Tom Presley leaned closer.

'It's because I have concussion, Sergeant Grisly.'

Presley straightened as abruptly as if someone had goosed him. He glared at the unrepentant Sperrin. 'That's *Presley*, Mr Sperrin. Detective Sergeant Presley.'

'Presley,' Sperrin told Ash confidentially. 'I think I may have got that wrong. He's De*fective* Sergeant Presley.'

Byrfield thought he should step between them, at least metaphorically, before the policeman exploded. 'I'm sorry my brother isn't being more helpful, Sergeant. He's right: it is partly the concussion. It's also pretty much who he is. Can I suggest you try again later, when whatever medication he's been given has had time to work its way through his system?'

DS Presley, who had never backed down from a criminal in his career, was happy to leave this victim to his own devices. He clearly wasn't going to learn anything useful, and Hazel would soon be back to take over.

After he'd gone Byrfield said wearily, 'Why do you *do* that, David?'

'Do what?'

'Go out of your way to make people dislike you.'

Sperrin sniffed. Deprived of his sport, he'd sunk back on his pillows, tired and ill. 'It saves time.'

Ash found himself grinning. 'But it doesn't always work.' The urge to take some petty revenge on DS Presley had stirred his own soul from time to time. If he hadn't responded to it, that was because he was a nicer person than David Sperrin. He added as a puzzled afterthought: 'Mares eat oats and does eat oats . . .?'

Finally Sperrin had the grace to look a little ashamed. 'Some stupid little song my mother used to sing, when I was a child.'

Ash remembered the difficult relationship Sperrin had with his mother. He remembered the reason for it. 'I can't picture Diana singing to you.'

'Well – not to me, exactly,' admitted Sperrin. 'To my brother James.'

FIVE

By the time Hazel had returned from the wilds of Bedfordshire, changed her shoes, reported to DCI Gorman and heard an abridged but still enjoyable version of DS Presley's vicissitudes, it was early evening. She decided to pay Sperrin another visit on her way home.

'Well, you're looking better,' she said brightly.

'People keep telling me that,' grunted Sperrin. 'It's not a lot of comfort.'

'You'd rather be told you're looking worse?'

'I'd rather be told what the hell's going on.'

Hazel sat down beside him. 'We all want to know that, David. We thought you were our best chance of finding out.'

'Hazel,' he growled, 'I've already had this conversation once today. With one of your colleagues – a long streak of piss with ferret eyes?'

'Detective Sergeant Presley,' she said, deadpan. She might not have coined the description but she recognised it.

'Him, yes. I couldn't tell him what happened to me, and I can't tell you. I don't know. The first thing I knew was waking up here – last night, was it? – and you wittering on about . . . something.'

'All right,' said Hazel calmly, 'then what's the *last* thing you remember? Before that.'

David Sperrin had spent much of the day, when he wasn't either dozing or baiting DS Presley, wondering the same thing. He hadn't come up with many answers. 'I was driving. Yesterday morning?'

Hazel shook her head. 'By eight o'clock yesterday morning you were worshipping the kerbstones in Siding Street, here in Norbold. Whatever happened, happened long before that.'

'So maybe it was the morning before. Which would be . . . .?'

'Monday,' supplied Hazel.

'OK, Monday. I was driving . . . somewhere.'

'Where?'

His brow was furrowed. 'I don't know. Maybe I wasn't going anywhere in particular. I know I wasn't working. Maybe I just fancied a run-out, and set off to see where the map would take me.'

'Could it have taken you to a standing stone in the middle of a field between Royston and Biggleswade?'

A certain intelligence crept into Sperrin's frown. 'The Myrton menhir? It's possible. Why?'

'That's where we found your car. But it had been there longer than you've been in Norbold, so it wasn't dumped there by whoever thumped you here. Is it possible you left it at Myrton and got to Norbold some other way?'

Sperrin's face twisted as he wrung his brain like a wet cloth. Nothing useful dripped out. 'I don't remember. I don't remember being there, let alone how I left.'

'Well, maybe that's not what happened,' Hazel said soothingly. 'Only, with it being an archaeological site, it seems more likely that you wanted to go there than that someone' – she nearly said *normal* – 'who stole your car did.'

'The Neolithic isn't my period,' said Sperrin pensively. 'If it'd been a hill fort, it would have made more sense. But if I saw a signpost then yes, I might have gone for a look. You say the Land Rover was there?'

Hazel nodded. 'And your coat, your wallet and your phone. At least you weren't robbed.'

'Lucky old me,' said Sperrin, unenthusiastically. He was still trying to force the memories. 'So what do you think happened? I saw the sign, followed it, parked the car . . . Then what?'

Hazel shook her head. 'I don't think we should speculate. I don't want to risk your poor battered head making a false memory – confusing a hypothesis with reality.'

'Get me a map,' he said. 'Maybe that'll help jog my memory.'

'Well, all right,' Hazel said doubtfully. 'I'll bring one in tomorrow.'

'Got a date tonight, have you?' he asked nastily.

'That's right,' she replied, hanging onto her patience. 'With my bed. So have you. A good night's sleep will do you more good than staring at a road map.'

'I don't want a road map. I want an Ordnance Survey, around four miles to the inch, with ancient monuments marked on it.'

'I'll see what I can do,' said Hazel. 'Tomorrow.'

Hazel could get all the maps she needed off the internet. But before she let Sperrin loose with her laptop, she wanted to check with DCI Gorman that it was a good idea. She couldn't justify calling him at home: he'd be at his desk soon after eight the next morning. From the hospital, she went to Highfield Road.

Ash had just put the younger of his two sons to bed, was allowing the elder another half-hour's television in the sitting room. He himself was in his study, poring over car brochures.

Hazel let herself in at the back door, gave Patience the lurcher a pat in passing, put on the kettle and made coffee. There was a sign on the study door that said Do Not Disturb Unless Someone Is On Fire. She ignored it.

'How's the great car hunt coming along?'

Ash gave her a harassed look. 'Not well. When did they all get so *complicated*?'

'During the two decades that the Volvo was in your family. What's the problem?'

'All these' – he flicked unhappy fingers at the glossy photos – 'gadgets! Screens. Cameras. Collision avoidance systems . . .'

'Avoiding collisions is a bad thing?'

'No, avoiding collisions is the primary algorithm of the master tactical computer, i.e. the driver. I passed a test to prove I was good at avoiding collisions. Why do I need a system to do it as well?'

'It's not a question of doing it as well,' she said slyly, 'it's a question of doing it better. Gabriel, you're looking at top-of-the-range models. You might do better looking at what the average eighteen-year-old can afford, not what you can afford.'

'I can't seem to get what I need – plenty of space, safe, reliable and long-lasting – without also getting all this stuff that I don't.' He leaned back from the desk with a gesture of defeat. 'I'm beginning to wonder if I actually need another car at all.'

Hazel breathed heavily at him. 'Of course you need a car. You have a shop, two sons and a dog. Even if you and Patience are willing to walk everywhere, how are you going to collect your stock? On the bus?'

It wasn't practical and he knew it. His life was more complex now than when he first returned to Norbold, when he walked Patience, picking up their modest shopping on the way home, and otherwise rarely left the house. He gave it one last try. 'Frankie' – Frankie Kelly, his children's nanny – 'has got her car, if the boys need to go somewhere. And you—'

'I am a police officer, not a taxi service,' Hazel finished for him. 'You need a car. Diego said he'd find one for you. If this is stressing you out, tell him what you need it to do and let him do the rest.'

'I know Diego,' Ash muttered darkly. 'He'll get me something with screens and cameras and computers and things.'

'Then you'll just have to join the twenty-first century and get used to them, won't you?' she said briskly. 'Now, moving on to something that matters . . .'

'How was David tonight?' He sipped his coffee, watching her through the steam.

'He's taken a hammering, he's not going to bounce back in a couple of days, but I think he'll be fine. I'm not sure he's going to be much help in figuring out what happened to him.'

'Some confusion is to be expected with a head injury. He may be clearer later.'

'Later, whoever did this to him will have had time to cover their tracks.'

'Does he know why he came to Norbold?'

She shook her head. 'He doesn't even remember how he got here.' She told him about where the Land Rover was found.

'Well, he didn't walk fifty miles,' said Ash. 'Either someone drove him or he caught a bus.'

'It's pretty much in the sticks,' said Hazel, 'I think you could be waiting a long time for a bus. There's a railway line in the area – we heard a train on the far side of the road somewhere.'

'Was there a station anywhere near?' But she didn't know.

Ash went over to his bookcase, came back with a bound volume of maps of the British Isles. It wasn't new – it mightn't have been much younger than the Volvo – but it was comprehensive. He turned to a double-page spread of Bedfordshire. 'Can you figure out where you were?'

Hazel belonged to the sat-nav generation, but map reading was still taught as a valuable skill for police officers. She found Royston and Biggleswade, traced the route she and Sergeant Wilson had travelled from the A1, then stabbed a triumphant finger on a small brown symbol in a part of the map marked with very little else. 'There's the standing stone at Myrton.'

'David's familiar with the place where his car was found?'

'He knew about it, anyway. Because it's an archaeological site. That doesn't prove it was him who drove there.'

'No,' said Ash. 'Though you'd have to wonder who else would want to, at least in November. I suppose they've dusted the car for prints?'

Hazel nodded. 'They're going over it with a fine-tooth comb. So far they haven't found anything helpful.' She peered at the map. 'This must be the road that skirts the far side of the field.' She pulled out her notebook, jotted down the co-ordinates. 'I'll check in the morning, but I can't see there being a bus service out there. And here's the railway line.' She glanced at the scale printed at the bottom of the page. 'Half a mile away, maybe a little less? Yes, that's probably about right.'

Ash was looking over her shoulder. 'There are no towns or even villages where there might be a station.'

'Not for miles,' agreed Hazel. 'If he was there, it seems likely he left in the van.'

'What van?'

'Sergeant Wilson found tracks where something bigger than a car had stopped and people got out. They must have given David a lift. Or kidnapped him.'

They both considered that for a moment. Neither could think of a reason to kidnap a spiky, smart-mouthed archaeologist.

'Maybe they *did* give him a lift,' proposed Hazel, 'put up with him for ten minutes or so, then pushed him out when he got too lippy.'

'That would be understandable,' said Ash with a smile, 'and might explain his injuries, but it wouldn't explain how he got from there to Norbold. You're sure he wasn't coming to see you?'

'I'm not sure of anything. But I've no reason to think he was, and he doesn't think he was either.' She hesitated then, for so long that Ash thought she'd finished. He got up to take the mugs back to the kitchen. Hazel glanced at him and then away again. 'Gabriel, last time we talked, I think I was a bit . . . off-hand. About what you said. About the divorce. I'm sorry. It rather took me by surprise. I just wanted to say, I think you're doing the right thing. I'm sorry if I seemed uninterested.'

Ash smiled. For a complex man, he had a singularly warm and simple smile. 'I think sometimes – worry sometimes – that I expect too much of our friendship. Of you. I drop my issues on you as if you were my mother, sister, wife and therapist all rolled into one. If you feel like throwing them at my head sometimes, it's no more than I deserve. Do you remember when we met?'

Hazel blinked. 'Of course I remember.' He'd been beaten up in the park by some local tearaways for no better reason than that they thought he wouldn't fight back. Much of Norbold thought at the time that he was mentally defective. At Meadowvale they called him Rambles With Dogs.

'You were one of the few people I'd met in the previous four years who treated me like a human being instead of either a nuisance or a case study. Who listened to what I said instead of assuming it was nonsense. I don't think you've ever understood how important that was to me. It was as if I'd been a small boat tossing around on some chaotic ocean for four years, and finally an anchor had held.'

The smile had gone now, leaving him serious – his gaze intense, his face with the flayed look it took on when he was in the grip of his memories. 'Even as I felt the world steady, I was terrified that the chain would break – that what was my lifeline was just part of the job to you, and when it was done you'd move on to something else and I'd never see you again. That the anchor-chain would part, and the ocean would swallow me down.

'And you didn't. You stayed with me. You were a friend to me, someone I could trust. I didn't understand then, and I don't understand now, why you didn't just shake my hand, wish me well and walk away. Your life would have been so much easier if you had. But mine would have crumbled, and I want you to know there hasn't been a day between then and now that I haven't been grateful to you.'

He managed a slightly broken little chuckle. 'Off-hand? Hazel, I've given you every reason to come after me with a double-barrelled shotgun! I still impose shamelessly on your time and goodwill. However much I tell myself to stop pestering you with the minutiae of my personal life, it's never long before I catch myself doing it again.

'So you don't owe me any apologies. Not about this, not about anything; not now, not ever. When I told you about filing for divorce, I wasn't looking for either applause or sympathy. It just seemed like something you ought to know. Now you do. Since it seems it'll be years before there's anything more to report, feel free to put the information on the longest of long fingers.'

For a moment Hazel wasn't sure how she ought to respond. She didn't think he was waiting for a response; she could just have nodded, said goodnight and gone home. But he deserved better than that. His wringing honesty called for more than polite evasion.

Finding the right words can be hard. But words aren't the only response worth making. She stood up and put her arms round him – given his habitual stoop, she was nearly as tall as he was – and hugged him. 'I'm sorry your marriage didn't work out,' she murmured. 'I know it mattered to you.'

Which, as far as Ash was concerned, were as close to the right words as made any difference.

Railway Street, where Hazel lived, was a double row of dark brick terrace houses close to the centre of Norbold. It was impossible to know now if the bricks were dark when the houses were built for his workers by some Victorian factory owner, or if they'd acquired their patina from close association with the steam trains that rushed his produce to every corner of the country and the globe. It was a mile away, and a world away, from Highfield Road. The first houses in Highfield Road had been built for factory managers, solicitors, bookkeepers and the like, far enough into what was then open countryside to avoid the pall of smoke that gave much of the Midlands the soubriquet of the Black Country.

Now, in a Norbold that was largely post-industrial, Railway Street could fairly be described as cheap and cheerful. Its two-up, two-down houses, each separated from the street by no more than a step and from the ginnel at the back by a yard or postage-stamp garden, were ideal as either starter or finisher homes, so most of the residents were either young singles or older people whose reduced needs they met perfectly.

Hazel could have afforded something rather smarter by now. But she'd grown fond of the little house; it was big enough to put a friend up if the need arose but still small enough to make minimal demands on her housekeeping skills, and she liked the neighbours. They put up with her working shifts and coming in at odd hours, and she put up with Mrs Burden's Alec singing Gilbert & Sullivan on his way home from the pub at chucking-out time.

And at first, drifting comfortably between sleep and wake-fulness in the bigger bedroom at the front of her house, she thought it was Alec Burden who was creating the commotion she gradually became aware of. Someone was calling out – not very loudly, but loud enough for the wrong side of midnight. She heard a couple of sash windows run up, and tired and grumpy householders asking if the author of the disturbance knew what time it was. Finally she heard an alarm go off as someone stumbled against a car, and sighing she supposed she'd have to do something about it. She was halfway into her clothes before she recognised the car alarm as her own.

That focused her mind wonderfully. A few seconds later she flung her front door open, ready to give someone an earful, and the man on her doorstep with one hand raised to knock fell into her arms.

For a moment she wasn't sure if he was drunk, or attacking her, or both. Her training kicked in automatically, and she had his face to the wall and his arm twisted up behind his back before either of them knew it. In his ear she growled the traditional policeman's greeting: 'All right, then, what's all this about?'

'Hazel?'

She didn't recognise his voice, weak and breathy as it was, but a kind of cosmic inevitability told her who it had to be. She turned him round to confirm it, and David Sperrin slid out of her hands and down the wall until he was sitting on her hall floor. *'David?* What are you doing here?'

He looked terrible: white and exhausted, his eyes vast and unfocused, his face drawn in lines as intractable as scars. 'I told you,' he moaned, 'I don't know.'

'No – *here*, at my house. Why aren't you in hospital?'

'I needed to see you . . .'

'It's two o'clock in the morning!' she exclaimed. 'Couldn't it have waited a few more hours?'

'No. It couldn't.' His eyes found hers, and it was not merely exhaustion hollowing their depths but grinding unhappiness.

'What's happened?' she asked, all her impatience vanished. Then, before he could answer, she knew. 'You've remembered something. What?'

He'd gone to a lot of trouble to find her. He hadn't known where she lived: he'd asked people until he'd found someone to direct him. He'd hauled himself out of his hospital bed, broken wrist, cracked ribs and all, and forced his battered body to carry him into town, in order to tell her what he'd remembered. And now he was here, collapsed on her hall lino, he couldn't bring himself to say it.

'David? What did you remember?'

'The menhir,' he managed at last. 'At Myrton. I *was* there.'

'Yes?' He'd woken her at two in the morning for this?

'There was a girl.'

That sounded more promising. 'Yes?' she said again, encouragingly.

Remembering had brought him no comfort, no peace. 'Hazel – I think I killed her.'

SIX

For this, she woke DCI Gorman as well.

Sleep-fuddled as he was, as soon as he understood what she was saying he knew two things, both of them important. That Hazel had put duty ahead of her friend's best interests, without using the lateness of the hour as an excuse to defer the decision. And that she'd called him instead of Gabriel Ash.

Always with the best of intentions, Hazel had raised so many eyebrows and prompted so many questions about her suitability for a police career that she'd finally been seconded to CID almost in desperation, to see if Gorman could tame her excesses. This gave him reason to believe it had been a good call.

The small glow of satisfaction encouraged a certain flexibility in him. They might well end the questioning in Interview Room 1 at Meadowvale, but he was dealing with a sick, confused and probably frightened man, and until he was reasonably confident that a crime had indeed been committed he could justify beginning it in Hazel's living room. Plus, if he took Sperrin to the police station now, the custody officer – otherwise known as the Prince of PACE – would make threatening noises about having him warranted fit by the police surgeon.

Gorman clambered reluctantly out of the warm cave created by his duvet and pulled his clothes on. After a moment he pulled them back off, removed his pyjamas and tried again.

Despite her anxiety to know more, Hazel refrained from quizzing Sperrin until the DCI could join them. Instead she made him comfortable on the living-room sofa with the duvet still warm from her bed about his chilled body, and lit the fire, and made cocoa and toast. Then she called the hospital to let them know where he was.

Some of it was displacement activity. Sperrin hadn't come here for a midnight feast: he'd come to make confession. But Hazel needed time to figure out where that left her. Clearly, if he'd committed a crime – any crime, but murder above all – she was a police officer before she was his friend. But had he? Over the past few years, men with concussion had told her that she was beautiful, that their landlady was trying to poison them, and that messages beamed from Venus were responsible for contraflow systems on the M1. Apart from the landlady story – Mrs Pond's chilli con carne was notoriously unreliable – she hadn't believed them. Without corroborating evidence, why should she believe Sperrin?

Whatever had happened to him had jangled his brain and disrupted his memory, at least temporarily. Why should she assume that this first attempt at reassembling the jigsaw would give an accurate picture? It was clear to her that he believed what he was saying, but that proved nothing. He could have dreamed it. He could have confused real events in a way that totally altered their meaning. He could conceivably be recounting a film he'd watched the night before he went to Myrton. If he lacked the mental competency to drive a car or operate heavy machinery, and she didn't need to be a doctor to make that call, he certainly wasn't fit to confess to murder.

She couldn't ignore what he'd said, and she hadn't ignored it. That was a long way from saying she believed it. She knew David Sperrin. Not as well as his brother, perhaps, but well enough that what he'd said made no sense. He wasn't a violent man. He was a clever man, with the arrogance of clever men: he would have disdained to sink to violence when sharpening his wit on someone's soul was so much more satisfying and you couldn't be jailed for it.

She heard Gorman's car in the silent street and met him at the door. 'He's in here.'

They talked for half an hour. It wasn't the classic police interview of question and answer, of subtle traps laid to catch incautious lies. Gorman was aware that he was tap-dancing on the edge of professional integrity here. If Sperrin had done what he said he'd done, and later changed his mind about confessing, counsel for the defence would wipe the floor with the DCI. But before he set the legal juggernaut rolling, he wanted to form his own opinion of the man and the story he had to tell.

This was the first time he'd met David Sperrin. All he knew about him came from Hazel, from DS Presley, and from Detective Inspector Norris who investigated following the discovery of the sad little grave down by the Byrfield lake. Twenty minutes ago, when the phone woke him, he'd thought Sperrin was the victim of a vicious assault that could have no possible connection with earlier events in his life. Now he found himself wondering.

Warmed up and nursing a mug of cocoa, David Sperrin was looking more nearly human again. At least Gorman didn't feel there was any danger of him turning his toes up in the middle of the interview. And if he was going to retract his confession, he wasn't ready to do so yet. He was as anxious for Gorman to understand what he had to say as Gorman was; painfully so, he leaned forward through the steam rising from his mug in order to drive his words home.

The problem was, there weren't many of them. He hadn't remembered what had happened – what he had done, what had been done to him. At the end of half an hour, the best Gorman could get from him was a snapshot, a moment in time – a girl who cried out and died in his arms – and an over-whelming tsunami of guilt.

When Hazel went into the kitchen to make more toast, Gorman followed her. 'Well, what do you think?'

The face she turned to him was both worried and confused. 'Chief, don't put that on me! I don't know what to tell you.'

Gorman shrugged, not altogether sympathetically. 'You wanted to be a detective: well, this is what detectives do. We make educated guesses. Sometimes our guesses are more educated than others. Then we set out to find evidence to support or contradict them. You know this man and I don't. I need your best guess as to how much faith we should put in what he says.'

Hazel hated to speculate in so serious a matter, but the DCI was entitled to her best efforts. She picked her words carefully. 'I don't think he's lying. What he thinks he remembers is freaking him out. Ordinarily he's a pretty robust character – I've never seen him this distressed, and I was at Byrfield when he found out what happened to Jamie.'

Gorman had not been there, Byrfield was far outside his manor, but he knew the story. 'He shot his brother dead.'

Hazel was quick in defence of her friend. 'That's not what happened, and you know it. He was a child of five! Their father was stupid enough to leave a loaded shotgun lying on the ground while he attended to Jamie. David did what any five-year-old would have done, what the parent of any five-year-old should have known he'd do, and picked it up.'

'And then put it out of his mind for thirty years.'

'Do *you* remember everything that happened when you were five?'

Sometimes Gorman had trouble remembering why he'd gone upstairs. 'I think if I'd shot someone I'd remember!'

'Really? You don't think that's the very thing that your mind wouldn't *want* to remember – wouldn't want to deal with?'

The DCI sniffed. He was aware that some of these younger officers were on firmer ground when it came to psychology. It had been considered very much an optional extra when he was learning the craft. He was a little surprised that his newest DC had no qualms about reminding him of that.

'All right,' he said. 'Then – with your psychologist's hat on – is there a possibility that what happened to him two days ago stirred those suppressed memories, and what he's telling us now is a mixture of the old tragedy and the new?'

Hazel nodded her understanding. 'A confabulation? Hell's bells, Chief, that's one for a real trick-cyclist. You could try talking to Gabriel's therapist, Laura Fry. I've heard the term: she'll have seen the case studies. She could tell you how likely it is, and if we can trust what he thinks he remembers.'

'But why a girl? Why does he think he killed a girl, when it was actually a ten-year-old boy who died all those years ago?'

But Hazel didn't know and couldn't guess.

'So maybe he did,' said Detective Chief Inspector Gorman grimly. 'Maybe what he's telling us is the truth.'

'What about dogs?'

Gorman glared at her. 'What *about* dogs?'

'If something happened in that field where we found his car – if somebody died there – even though the body's no longer there, dogs might pick up the scent. Mightn't they?'

He didn't know either. 'It's worth a try. I'll get onto it in the morning. Er' – glancing at his watch – '*later* in the morning.'

'Shall I take Sergeant Wilson again?' There was an assumption in there that she hoped he wouldn't notice until he'd already agreed.

Gorman shook his head. 'Anything he could see he'll already have seen. I'll come myself.'

Hazel's heart gave a little skip, because he'd said *come* instead of *go*. It might have been careless syntax, but she hoped it meant *come with you* rather than *go instead of you*.

'In the meantime,' he continued, unaware of her mental gymnastics, 'what are we going to do about him?' He jerked his head at the living room door.

Hazel thought for a moment. 'Unless you want to arrest him, I'm going to throw another duvet over him and hope he'll get off to sleep.'

'Don't the hospital want him back?'

'Funnily enough, they didn't seem too bothered. It almost sounded as if they were glad to be rid of him. They said I could probably look after him as well as they could now.'

'Not if you're in Bedfordshire you can't.'

'I'll ask Gabriel to come round.'

Perhaps too much time had passed. Perhaps too much rain had fallen – it was falling again as Hazel Best and Dave Gorman huddled against the leeward side of the standing stone for what little shelter it provided. Or it was perfectly possible that the dog supplied by the Bedford division wasn't picking up any traces of blood because no blood had been spilt there.

Even when he was insisting on his guilt, Sperrin had been unable to say how he committed the murder he claimed. There had been no blood other than his own, and no gunshot residue, on his clothes. He might conceivably have strangled this unknown girl, though it's harder than the movies make it look, or suffocated her, or hit her hard enough to break her skull: he could not remember. They had watched him almost literally squeezing his brain to make the memories come, but the how and – perhaps even more puzzling – the why remained elusive.

The detection dog was a springer spaniel, red and white, a bundle of energy; but eventually the weather and the lack of success sapped even its enthusiasm. Its tail drooped in the rain and Hazel, watching it, swore it looked back at her with an apologetic shrug. The handler threw its ball a couple of times as a reward anyway, and the dog pretended to be pleased, then with an air of shared relief they both got back in their van and drove away.

'So much for that,' grunted DCI Gorman. He tugged the collar of his coat into his neck and looked out across the field. 'Tell me again what SOCO said.'

Hazel consulted her notebook, though she remembered clearly. She pointed. 'The Land Rover was parked over there. Sergeant Wilson said David – at least, whoever got out of it – walked as far as the stone, and then ran to the far end of the field and climbed over the gate. The lane runs on the far side of that hedge. Something bigger than a car had driven onto the verge and stopped. People got out – he couldn't say how many, but more than one. Either David drove off with them, or he headed up or down the lane – there were no signs SOCO could follow on the tarmac.'

'I suppose I'd better have a look.' Gorman sounded as keen as the spaniel had looked.

They scaled the gate – slick with rain, it was more of an obstacle than it had been the day before – and looked both ways along the lane. There was no traffic.

Gorman nodded at the little humpback bridge three hundred metres to the right. 'What's that?'

'That must be the railway line.' She pulled out the map, sheltering it as best she could from the weather. 'There.'

He glanced at the map, back at the bridge. He started to walk towards it. Not sure why, Hazel kept pace with him.

'Useful things, maps,' the DCI observed conversationally. 'Sat-nav's good at what it does too, but it can't give you an overview of the landscape. This lane, for instance, I can see

from the map it runs pretty much south-west to north-east.
Which means the railway line runs pretty much . . .'

'. . . South-east to north-west,' Hazel supplied. She waited.
When nothing more was forthcoming she said: 'So?'

'So what direction, approximately, would you say Norbold
lies from here?'

She had no idea. 'North?' she hazarded. And then, intuition
giving her a glimmer of what was passing through his mind:
'North-west?'

Gorman nodded. 'North-west.'

They had reached the little bridge. It was only a little bridge
because the line below ran through a deep cutting. The stone
parapets on either side were old and weather-worn.

'What can you see?'

Hazel looked around anxiously, wondering what she'd
missed. Surely to God he hadn't spotted a body that had been
here all along? 'Er – nothing . . .?'

'Of course you can,' said Gorman impatiently. 'Tell me
what you can see. *Everything* that you can see.'

'Well – the lane. It narrows a bit where it passes over the
bridge. Underneath is the railway line. There's nothing on it
at the moment, but it is in current use – a train passed when
I was here with Sergeant Wilson, and anyway there's no grass
growing between the sleepers.' She raised her gaze. 'Fields
on both sides, as far as the eye can see. Hedges and trees. I
can see some sheep . . .'

'Closer,' said Gorman.

'Closer? What, on the bridge? I can see . . . oh.'

'Yes,' said the DCI, with a kind of contained smugness.

Immediately adjacent to where they were standing, in the
middle of the bridge, for perhaps half a metre the stones of
the northern parapet looked different to those on either side.
The rain shone more slickly on them. Hazel frowned and bent
nearer. They were shinier because they were cleaner. Years of
accumulated grit and leaf mould and bird shit had been brushed
away, recently enough that the difference was still noticeable.
'Someone was sitting here,' she said.

Gorman gave a disappointed sigh. 'You reckon? Fishing,
perhaps?'

Hazel felt his disapproval like a hangnail: uncomfortable and impossible to ignore. 'No, probably not.' Her eyes widened abruptly. 'You think someone went over here, onto the line? David's girl? Dear God – you don't think he pushed her?'

Gorman looked a little taken aback. 'Well, anything's possible. But no, that's not what I was thinking.

'Look at what we have evidence for. The Land Rover was parked on the far side of the field, and someone walked across to the standing stone. David Sperrin is an archaeologist. Then he ran from the stone to the gate and went over it onto the lane. Another vehicle stopped nearby and people got out. Someone was on the parapet of this bridge within the last few days, and the line underneath heads off towards Norbold. And Sperrin was found in Siding Street, which runs – the clue's in the name – along the back of the train yard.'

'Then . . .' Hazel was trying to follow his logic. 'He came to look at the standing stone. The rain must have stopped for a while, because he left his coat in the car. While he was in the field the other vehicle, probably a van, stopped here in the lane. What David saw next made him run in that direction. To help someone? To intervene in what was happening? If he was the one who'd done something wrong, wouldn't he have run back to his car, to get away?'

'Good,' said Gorman. 'And then?'

'The girl – the one he thinks he killed – maybe it was her who went off the bridge. Jumped – suicide. Maybe that's why he feels so guilty, because he couldn't reach her in time to stop her.'

'Again, it's possible. But it wasn't her who turned up in Norbold, was it?'

'No,' said Hazel thoughtfully. 'So . . . David saw something he wasn't meant to. The people in that other vehicle thought they were miles from anywhere and there wouldn't be anyone around. And that mattered because they were doing something they really didn't want witnesses to. Something that resulted in a girl's death. Not suicide but murder. When they realised David had seen them, they grabbed him. That's when he got beaten up.'

She caught the faint murmur of disagreement, amended

her scenario accordingly. 'No – the beating he took, he couldn't have got away from them afterwards. So . . . he took off up the lane, and found himself trapped on this bridge. Maybe they'd split up and cut him off; maybe they'd gone back for their van so it was only a matter of time before they ran him down.

'However it was, he was desperate enough to try anything. When a train came up the track he climbed onto the parapet and dropped down onto it. It was more of a fall than he was expecting – that's how he got hurt – but the train carried him away towards Norbold and safety. Hours later, with the train now in the yard, he managed to stagger out into Siding Street before collapsing.'

'And that,' said DCI Gorman with some satisfaction, 'is what we in the trade call a working hypothesis.'

SEVEN

The first thing they did was get the Norbold dispatcher to check what trains had come up from Bedfordshire three days earlier and then spent the night parked up in his yard. He quickly narrowed the possibilities down to a goods train heading north from London with a mixed freight of timber and agricultural machinery.

The three of them walked for quarter of a mile through the busy yard to where four flats of farm equipment had been uncoupled. They were still there, at the top end of the shunting yard: a confused nightmare of growling, lumbering machinery and unfenced rails to the police officers, a scene as familiar as his back garden to the dispatcher. It never occurred to him to point out where the visitors should avoid putting their feet. He assumed everyone with a brain would know.

The four trucks were about as far from the station buildings as it was possible to be and still be in Norbold. Hazel was fairly sure they'd passed her house a hundred metres back, which meant Siding Street was on the far side of the black brick wall. The wall had once been continuous, but time had taken its toll and now there were a number of gaps blocked, more or less effectively, with corrugated-iron sheeting.

'What are we looking for?' asked the dispatcher.

Gorman began to tell him, but before he could finish a sentence Hazel said, 'This.' They looked round and she was on top of one of the flats, leaning over the chained machinery.

Dave Gorman was a strong man but he hadn't Hazel's agility and he was out of breath by the time he joined her. He looked where she was pointing.

It came in the category of a minor miracle. The rain that had belaboured Norbold for days should have washed away any blood. But the strong north-easterly wind had created pockets of shelter under the heavy equipment, and dried blood was still plain to see in two places, one tucked away among the machinery, one down the side of the bogey.

When they do this in the movies, it's always an enclosed carriage with a roof to jump onto, and the hero never falls off. It was a lot further down to where a couple of telescopic handlers were chained onto the truck and there was no open space between them to aim for. Sperrin had landed in the tangle of machinery, and the wonder was not that he'd injured himself but that he'd ever got up again.

But he had, and maybe it was hours later and maybe he was still barely conscious, but somehow he'd extricated himself from the load and dropped down onto the tracks, leaving a smear of blood down the sheltered side of the wagon. Thirty metres away they found, marked by a snaggle of wool the same colour as the sweater he'd been wearing, where he'd crawled under the curled-back corner of a sheet of corrugated iron. Soon after that he'd gone down and stayed down, and taking a short-cut back to Meadowvale PC Budgen had found him in the closing minutes of his night shift.

'That's how he got hurt?' asked Hazel. 'A fall, not a beating?'

'I'm not a forensic medical examiner,' Gorman pointed out, 'but that would be my guess. We couldn't figure out what he'd been hit with. Nobody thought of a train.'

'How scared would you have to be to take a risk like that?'

'Shitless,' said Gorman judiciously. 'You wouldn't do it to avoid a black eye, or even a good kicking. He must have known, when he went off that bridge, there was a good chance he was going to die. The only reason you'd do that is if you knew you'd die for sure if you didn't.'

'If you knew that the people chasing you had killed someone already,' suggested Hazel. In her voice was a kind of thrill that was part adrenalin and partly the hope that David Sperrin hadn't after all done what he believed he'd done. 'Maybe that's what he saw. He didn't kill this girl he talks about. He saw her killed.'

'Unless, of course . . .' Struck by a sudden impulse of charity, Gorman didn't finish the sentence. He was finding it hard to remember who he was talking to: a detective constable on his team, or a friend of the man who might be a witness but still might be a killer.

Hazel watched him, puzzled, until understanding came. Her heart, which had been rising as they elaborated on their theory, sank again. She finished the sentence for him. 'Unless he did in fact kill this girl, and that's why people were chasing him. He jumped off the bridge rather than face a life sentence for murder.'

'Look,' Gorman said with a cumbrous attempt at kindness, 'we're not going to know who did what to whom until Sperrin is able to tell us. We haven't got an allegation against him, or a missing person report, or a body. The dog couldn't find any evidence to give credence to what Sperrin thinks he remembers. All we have right now is an isolated memory of a girl, his fear that he may have harmed her, and the possibility that something scared him enough to make him jump off a bridge onto a moving train.

'I have no reason to arrest him, let alone charge him. If he can't give us any more information, and no one steps forward to accuse him of murder, we may have to accept that we're never going to know exactly what happened.'

It was far from satisfactory, but Hazel could see that with nothing to go on there was little more they could do. 'His brother's going to want to take him home. What should I tell him?'

Gorman thought a moment. 'I don't want to have to drive to Cambridgeshire if he remembers something else. Can he stay with you for a couple of days? I know it's an imposition, but . . .'

Hazel had spoken to the ward's lead nurse, who'd expressed – in fairly forthright terms – the view that someone who could evade his carers and make his way into town from the ring road probably didn't need to be taking up a hospital bed. 'That's probably the best solution.'

'If there's still nothing for us to work with by the weekend, his brother can have him, and welcome.'

By afternoon, having caught up on lost sleep, David Sperrin was more recognisably himself. Regrettably, this included his characteristic contentiousness. Ash wasn't interested in arguing with him, was only waiting for Hazel to return so he could go home. But Sperrin seemed to take his reserve as a challenge.

'Why don't they believe me?' he wanted to know. 'What possible reason could I have for saying I'd killed someone if I hadn't?'

'And yet people do,' Ash said mildly.

'Loonies.'

'Well – possibly. Sometimes.'

'Is *that* what they think? That it isn't just concussion I've got, it's brain damage?'

'Concussion *is* brain damage. The fact that people very often recover from it doesn't make it trivial.'

Sperrin was eyeing him speculatively. 'Of course, you'd know.'

Ash sighed. 'Would I?'

'Weren't you sectioned once?'

Ash didn't lie about it: he had nothing to be ashamed of. It still felt like someone rummaging in his sock drawer. 'Yes, I was,' he said patiently. 'And if you know that, you probably know why.'

'Someone put a price on your head,' said Sperrin, watching him speculatively from the sofa. 'And your wife decided she'd rather have the money than you.'

After a moment Ash said, 'Another symptom of concussion is having difficulty distinguishing between appropriate and inappropriate behaviours.'

Sperrin barked a gravelly little laugh. His laugh, like his voice, was gruff from too many hours digging on exposed hillsides. 'That's not concussion. I've always had that problem.'

'I used to have a problem with long division,' said Ash. 'Problems can be tackled.'

Making himself a better person had never been high on David Sperrin's list of priorities. 'When do you think Hazel will get back?'

'Soon, hopefully.' There was no mistaking Ash's sincerity.

'What happens next?'

'That'll depend on what they find at Myrton.'

'They're not going to find a body, if that's what you mean,' said Sperrin shortly. 'Hazel was there yesterday. She found the menhir, she found the Land Rover – I think she'd have noticed if there was a body there too. It must have happened somewhere else.'

'What must have happened somewhere else?'

Sperrin's eyes flickered hotly at him. 'I killed someone. You know that. A girl.'

'I know that's what you believe. I don't know if it's true. I don't know why you believe it.'

'I can see her,' said David Sperrin. His voice fell low. 'All the time. I can see her face, and the life going out of her eyes. Her face was so close to mine, she must have been in my arms. I held her, and she died.'

'How did she die?'

'I don't know.' He shook his head, dark unkempt hair flying.

'Did you have a gun? A knife?'

'What in hell would I be doing with a gun?' demanded Sperrin.

'That was going to be my next question.'

'I've never . . .' He amended that. 'I haven't touched a gun in thirty years. I don't carry a knife. I carry a scalpel, and a small paintbrush, and a trowel in the car.'

Ash blinked. 'A scalpel?'

'For winkling artefacts out and cleaning the dirt off them. I'm an archaeologist, yes?' He gave a savage grin. 'What, did you think I was doing unlicensed surgery on the side?'

'Go back to the girl. What can you tell me about her?'

'Nothing! I don't know who she was. I don't know her name.'

'Do you feel that you should remember? Or that you never knew who she was.'

About to dismiss the distinction angrily, Sperrin found himself reconsidering. 'I don't know. I can't be sure. But I think – I *think* – she was a stranger. There's no echo of familiarity anywhere in my head.'

'All right,' said Ash, 'good. That's something. Describe her.'

'She was . . . young. Twenty, twenty-two – something like that. Dark hair. Dark eyes.'

'Long hair or short?'

'Long,' said Sperrin, after a moment's hesitation. 'Only . . .' His good hand sketched in the air beside his cheek.

'She had it tied back?'

'Yes, probably. Yes.'

'What was she wearing?'

But Sperrin couldn't force the iris of his memory to widen. All she was to him, this nameless girl, was a face. A dying face.

'Suppose you're right,' said Ash. 'Suppose she did die in your arms. Does that necessarily mean you killed her?'

Sperrin stared at him. Ash saw the moment in which hope kindled behind his eyes; and with that hope, the fear that it might yet prove unjustified. 'Doesn't it?'

'Could she have been injured when you found her? Could you have been trying to help?'

It was extraordinary, the change that came over David Sperrin. Although his only memory of these events was that one moment, that one image, he'd thought he knew what it meant, the only thing it could mean: that the worst imaginable thing had happened, and all he was waiting for was confirmation. The baiting, the arguing, the determined unpleasantness, were his shield against an unbearable reality. Now another possibility had been mooted, it was as if that last defence had fallen, leaving him hopeful but also vulnerable, anxious and afraid.

'I don't know,' he said yet again, and this time a kind of desperate yearning caught in his voice. 'I suppose so. I don't know!'

'No, I know,' said Ash, immediately contrite. 'I'm sorry, I don't mean to grill you. I'm just making the point that, until we know what happened, we don't know it was your fault. In fact, there's some reason to think it wasn't.'

Sperrin stared at him. 'What reason?'

'If a girl died, and we can't find a body, that's because someone hid it. Either to protect you, which seems unlikely, or to protect themselves.'

'Maybe I hid the body.'

'You weren't disposing of bodies with a broken wrist. So

it wasn't just you and this girl: there was someone else there. Why didn't they go to the police?' Ash took a moment to consider. 'David, you and I haven't known one another very long, and I wouldn't say we know one another well, so I could be wrong. But Hazel's known you half her life, and she doesn't believe it either. She thinks there must be another explanation.'

David Sperrin crushed the heel of his good hand into his eye socket in a gesture of agonised impatience that Ash could not believe was a good idea. 'Why can't I *remember*? Only that – only her face. I must have seen more than that. Maybe a lot more – maybe everything. Maybe everything we need to know is locked up in my head, and I can't get at it. Maybe I never will. Maybe I'll grow old and die, and never know if I was responsible.'

A thought occurred to him. 'They can do something with electrodes, can't they? To jog your memory?'

Ash winced. 'Electro-convulsive therapy? I don't think it's used any more. I'm not sure it was ever used for amnesia.'

'It might help break the log-jam.'

'It might fry your brain.'

'It might be worth it.'

Ash doubted it. 'Let's look at it logically. Just suppose for a moment that you killed this girl. That something happened to make you act in a way that people who know you consider wildly out of character, and instead of turning your customary sarcasm on her, you killed her.

'Your next move would have been either to hide the body or to flee the scene. The Land Rover would have been your best bet for either. But you didn't even go back for your coat and your wallet. Somehow you ended up in Norbold, looking as if you'd been through a meat-grinder. If someone else was there, and he considered beating you up a higher priority than calling the police, isn't it at least credible that it was he who was responsible for the girl's death? That you were not the murderer but a witness?'

Sperrin's longing to believe was almost tangible. 'You really think so?'

'It makes at least as much sense as the alternative.'

Outside in the street there was the sound of a car pulling up. Ash glanced out of the window: Hazel was back.

On an impulse, perhaps remembering something he'd been told or had read, perhaps venturing a little ingenuity of his own, he said off-handedly: 'What did you say she was called, this girl?'

Immediately, without thinking, Sperrin answered, 'Rose.' Then his eyes stretched wide as he heard what he'd said. He said it again, in a tone of wonderment. 'Rose. Her name was Rose.'

EIGHT

'Her name was Rose,' said Hazel. 'I think some part of him knew that all along. In the hospital, when he was starting to come round, he said something about roses. I thought he was looking at the vase of flowers. But it was that, wasn't it? Rose was the girl's name.'

DCI Gorman gave a disapproving sniff. He could get more disapprobation into a sniff than most people can into a sentence. 'If he knew her name, he knew her. That wasn't just a random event he stumbled across.'

Hazel couldn't argue. She'd already realised that the snippet of information was significant not only because it might help identify the victim but also because it made Sperrin more than a casual witness to a crime. She was sorry, but it didn't alter the job she had to do. She would regret it forever if these events put an end to her friendship with the Byrfield family, but her first loyalty had to be to the victim of a murder.

'I had another go at Missing Persons,' she said. 'The name didn't raise any flags. All the dark-haired, dark-eyed, twenty-something women who've been reported missing in the last month were called something else. Not a Rose among them.'

'It may not have been the name her family called her.'

Hazel hadn't thought of that. 'A pseudonym? A working name? Maybe she was a working girl.'

'A prostitute? Would he be a frequenter of prostitutes, your friend?'

'Your guess is as good as mine. I've no reason to think so – I've also no reason to think he isn't. Ask him.'

'Maybe he's forgotten that as well.'

Hazel frowned. 'You're not starting to think there's something suspect about his amnesia, are you, Chief?'

'I didn't think that,' said Gorman. 'He certainly had the head injury to explain it. Now? – I don't know. It's a bit convenient, isn't it?'

'We were never close so I could be wrong,' said Hazel. 'But as far as I can see, *he* doesn't think it's convenient. He's trying to remember. If he's putting it on, he's a better actor than I gave him credit for.'

'How is he today? It's about time I stuck him in Interview Room 1 and did a bit of serious digging. Is he up to it? It's four days since he went off that bridge.'

'Ask a doctor,' said Hazel promptly, 'that's not my call. Speaking as his friend, I wouldn't be too concerned. He definitely seemed better this morning – clearer, more focused. He's still on painkillers for the ribs and his wrist, but if they're powerful enough to affect his mind I haven't noticed. Do you want me there?'

Gorman considered. There were pros and cons. After a moment he nodded. A familiar face might make Sperrin relax. If he was telling the truth, that might be helpful; and also if he wasn't, because he might be less guarded. 'Unless Tom Presley wants to do it, of course.'

They traded a sly grin.

'How did the interview go?'

Expecting to work well into the evening, Hazel went out to buy sandwiches at five o'clock, calling in at Rambles With Books to share them with Ash. There were also biscuits in the tin on the long table. Miss Hornblower knew this too: she was leaving as Hazel arrived, discreetly brushing crumbs from the collar of her Harris tweed coat.

Hazel gave a disconsolate shrug. 'I think David was doing his best. At least he didn't set out to be difficult, which I thought he might. But nothing came of it. I'd hoped that having a name to pin the face to would help him remember some more, but it didn't seem to. In fact, the longer we talked, the less convinced he was that Rose was her name anyway.'

'It came from somewhere,' said Ash. 'I didn't tell him that: he told me.'

'That's what I said. The trouble is, he's thought about what might have happened and been asked about it so much now he doesn't really know what he's remembering and what he's piecing together. I told him he'd come up with the name Rose on two separate occasions now. He just shrugged and said he thought he'd been mistaken – that he didn't know her long enough for them to introduce themselves.'

'He could be lying,' murmured Ash.

Hazel wasn't blind to the possibility. 'He could. But he's not behaving like someone who's trying to cover up a murder. Halfway through the interview, he started getting tetchy with the chief for not making more progress. Wanted him to put more people on the case. We told him Meadowvale CID can't actually field a full football team, but I don't think he believed us. He said if we'd more important things to do, maybe he should see what he could find out himself. I told him not to be silly. The chief told him if he interfered in his investigation he'd find himself behind bars whether he'd killed anybody or not.'

She ate her sandwich, weary and discouraged. 'Plus, if David hadn't told us there'd been a murder we would never have known. It would have been the easiest thing in the world to keep his mouth shut. Even if a body turns up at some point, we'd never have made a connection to him if he'd just kept quiet. It makes no sense for him to confess, and then not tell us everything he can remember.'

'It might make sense,' Ash proposed reluctantly, 'if the confession was genuine – if at some point that night he remembered what he'd done and needed to tell someone – but by the time he'd recovered his wits a bit more he realised he didn't have to admit to a crime no one knew had happened. Clamming up at this point could be a way of extricating himself.'

'I suppose. But in that case . . .' She recounted the conversation she'd had with Gorman on the bridge at Myrton. 'So if he killed the girl, and jumped onto the train to escape from these other people, why didn't *they* report the murder?'

'That's certainly suspicious,' agreed Ash. 'Which has to be good news.'

'Good news?' Hazel put her fair head on one side, eyeing him quizzically.

'I'm not a police officer,' Ash said firmly, 'I'm allowed to be partisan. Until I have a reason to be something else, I'm on David's side. I want you to find out what happened, as much for his sake as anyone's.'

Hazel took comfort from the fact that, if she couldn't go in to bat for Sperrin, Ash would. 'Maybe we can't be sure that he's innocent' – it seemed an odd word to use of a man like David Sperrin, but she was damned if she was going to apologise for it – 'but if someone got killed, someone else removed the body. Whatever happened at Myrton – whether David's telling the truth, lying or remembering wrong – someone else had to have been involved. Someone who didn't want us to know anything about it. But who that was, we have no way of knowing.' Hazel blew out her cheeks, disconsolate.

'What will you do next?'

'I'm not sure there's anything we can do. Unless someone comes forward with an accusation, or reports a missing Rose, or David remembers something more, I think we've hit the buffers. The chief says he can go home as soon as Pete can pick him up.'

'It's not very satisfactory,' frowned Ash.

'Of course it isn't. But it's fairly typical. Most of the crimes reported to us do not result in charges. The ducks never line up.'

'I thought an hour, less advertising breaks, was enough for a decent detective to solve even a complicated crime,' said Ash, straight-faced.

'Imagine my disappointment,' sighed Hazel.

That was when Ash's phone rang. He hunted through his pockets and turned it up at last with a surprised expression as if at a loss to know how it had got there. It was Gilbert.

'Dad, are you on your way home?'

Ash glanced at the clock over the kitchen door. 'It's a bit soon to shut up shop. I'll be another half-hour or so.'

'Dad – you should really come home now.'

All Ash's warning signals went off at once. 'What's happened? Are you all right? Is Guy?'

'We're both fine.'

'Have you burned the house down? Flooded the bathroom? Where's Frankie?'

'The house is fine, and Frankie's' – the least hesitation – 'busy. I just really think you should come home now.'

'I'm on my way,' said Ash.

He didn't have to ask: Hazel had the car running by the time he'd locked the shop. The four-minute drive was a twenty-minute walk when he'd come down with Patience that morning.

Gilbert was watching the street, met them at the door. He looked warily at Hazel – they had a somewhat guarded relationship – which Ash intercepted. 'Can you wait for five minutes while I find out what's going on?'

'Sure,' said Hazel. She went to follow him inside.

Gilbert Ash was a slender, dark child of ten with an introvert personality and secretive ways. Hazel could see much of his father in him: particularly in his intelligence, which was undeniable, and in the streak of adamantine stubbornness which lay at Ash's core and much closer to the surface of his son. Looking somewhere around Hazel's knees he mumbled, 'It's family . . .'

Surprised and displeased, Ash frowned at him. 'You don't tell my friends that they are not welcome in our house,' he said plainly.

Gilbert looked up at him, found no comfort there, turned to Hazel. All he said was, 'Please . . .' But it so obviously mattered to him that she nodded.

'It's time I was heading back. I want to put in a couple more hours before close-of-play. Call me if you need anything,' she told Ash, and she pulled the door shut behind her.

Ash turned back to Gilbert, about to demand an explanation, when voices reached him from the sitting room. Not quite an argument; more than a conversation. He immediately recognised Frankie's, that he knew as well as his sons', not loud but firm, unyielding. A second later he recognised the other as well, and every vestige of colour fled from his face.

The sitting-room door opened abruptly and a woman came out. Her hair was no longer short and light brown but shoulder-length and dark red; it altered her appearance dramatically. She'd also put on a little weight in the last two years. Of course, last time he saw her it had suited her purposes to appear drained and careworn.

'Hello, Gabriel,' said Cathy Ash.

There were other crimes under investigation in the upstairs offices at Meadowvale Police Station. Hazel spent a couple of hours trawling through security camera footage for a young man in a navy-blue anorak who was making a good living scamming old ladies out of their savings. By the time she was heading home, hopefully for the weekend, she'd come to the conclusion that everyone in Norbold owned at least one navy-blue anorak.

David Sperrin was waiting for her. 'Any news?'

'And a good evening to you, too, Mr Sperrin,' she said coolly, 'and how was your day?'

He looked at her uncomprehendingly. 'What?'

She sighed. 'I don't suppose you've so much as got the kettle on, have you?'

'I didn't know when to expect you.' This was reasonable enough. 'Do you want to eat out? I got my wallet back.'

It was a nice offer – at least, Hazel assumed he was offering to treat her; it might have been an assumption too far – but she was tired. 'Another day, maybe. I've been looking forward to putting my feet up.'

'All right. Then I'll cook. Oh.' He looked at the plaster. 'Er . . .'

Hazel barked a little laugh. 'That'll have to be another day too. Sit down, I'll make something in a minute. What do you fancy? You can have anything you like as long as it's spag bol.'

Sperrin appeared to give it some thought. 'Spag bol?'

'Good choice,' said Hazel.

She left the kitchen door open, talking to him over her shoulder as she stirred the pans. 'Did you get your phone too?'

'Yes.'

'Then call Pete, let him know you're ready to go home.'

There was a long pause. Frowning, Hazel was about to ask if he'd heard her; then Sperrin said in a low voice, 'I'm not.'

'There's no point waiting for your car – we'll hold onto

that until we're sure it's told us everything it can. Which actually doesn't matter since it'll be a while before you can drive it anyway. Unless' – she gave a secret grin – 'you want to take the train.'

'I'm not going back to Byrfield,' he growled, 'until I have some answers.'

She turned to face him. 'David, you may not get those answers. Unless you remember enough to make sense of what happened, we may never know any more than we know today. I'm sorry but that's how it is. Not every puzzle has the solution printed on the back of the box. Sometimes there are no viable lines of inquiry.'

'You're giving up?' He sounded startled; more than that, he sounded angry. 'A girl died!'

'You don't know that. I know it's what you think, but you could be wrong.'

'Then prove it!'

Hazel took a deep breath. 'Think for a moment what it is you're asking. You want us to investigate a crime – a murder – that you might be responsible for. Right now there's no evidence that anyone died. As a friend, I should probably advise you that's a boat you shouldn't be rocking.'

'Never mind me,' he cried, 'what about her? What about' – he could do no better than the name they'd settled on – 'Rose? Whoever killed her, they're going to get away with it. Someone's going to get away with murder, and there'll be no justice for her unless you make it happen! Treat her death as seriously as you would if it was an English girl who died.'

Hazel frowned. 'What?'

'What?'

'You said she wasn't English. That's something you haven't told us before. She was a foreigner? A tourist, an overseas student, an immigrant – what?'

But he didn't know. The comment had come out of the disorganised bottom drawer of his mental filing cabinet, where memories disrupted by his close encounter with a telescopic handler had become hopelessly entangled with the everyday detritus of recollections that hadn't been pulled out for decades, that would probably never be wanted again, but couldn't be thrown out in case they came in useful one day. He dug down into the pile but couldn't find where the information had come from.

Hazel tried again. 'In fact, it doesn't alter anything. There's still no evidence that Rose existed anywhere except in your head. And your head just lost a nutting contest with a piece of agricultural machinery.'

'You think I imagined it? I dreamt that a girl died in front of me, closer than I am to you now? That it might have been me who killed her?'

She refused to be cowed by his furious indignation. 'I think that's a possibility, yes. People have imagined stranger things as a result of head injuries.'

'Then why did I jump off the bridge? I didn't do that because I was concussed – that's how I got the concussion. What possible reason could I have to jump onto a moving train unless I was on the run from something worse?'

Suddenly Sperrin fell silent. He wasn't waiting for her to answer: his focus had turned inwards. Hazel thought for a moment that another memory had surfaced, and was careful not to interrupt; but that wasn't it. After half a minute he looked up again and his expression had changed. The anger had gone, replaced by a kind of hollow-cheeked comprehension. 'This is about Jamie, isn't it?'

Hazel pretended not to understand. 'In what way?'

'You think I'm on some kind of a delayed guilt trip. Because I killed my brother, and never paid any penalty for it.'

'David, you were five years old! What kind of penalty do you *think* you should have paid?'

'I don't know. But *something*. Even at five years old, you don't do something like that – something that monumental – and then just go home and forget about it for thirty years. Not if you're in any way normal. And you think – the police think – that's what this is about. Don't you? That maybe something happened at Myrton, but it could have been anything: a fight, an accident, anything. That it only turned into a mystery because it happened to *me*, and I'm an unreliable witness.

'My head's full of unresolved guilt, and sooner or later it

was always going to spill out and make a mess on the floor. That's why nobody's listening to me – why you're happy enough to send me home and write off a girl's murder as a figment of my imagination. You think I'm using some random event to work through my feelings about Jamie. You don't believe anything I've told you is the truth.'

Seeing the pain racking his battered body and sounding the depths of his eyes, Hazel wished she could deny it. Almost wished she could tell him that DCI Gorman thought he *had* killed someone. Bizarrely enough, it was what he wanted to hear. The alternative was that he'd lost his grip on reality, and given a straight choice he would rather face the rest of his life as a murderer than a madman.

She tried an appeal to common sense. 'David, we can't take everything we're told, even in good faith, at face value. There has to be *some* evidence to support it. People get things wrong, people who've suffered head injuries most of all. No one thinks you're lying about this, but we can't find anything to corroborate it. Nothing. No body, no witnesses, no missing person report – nothing. That's pretty unusual. We can't always make sense of the evidence, but there usually is some. Not this time. And if we can't find any trace of what you say happened, we have to consider the possibility that you've got it wrong. For whatever reason: the concussion, some unresolved feelings about your brother, whatever.'

'Jamie has nothing to do with this!'

'No, he hasn't. But your feelings about him may have. I'm sorry, I don't know what else to tell you. We have nowhere else to take this investigation. If the situation changes – if we get a lead on who this girl was, or if you remember something else – we'll follow it up. Without that, I don't see how we can.'

Sperrin was staring hotly at her. But perhaps the inevitability of what she was saying sank in, because after a moment he blinked and swallowed. 'You want me to go back to Byrfield?'

'There's no point you staying here. If there are any developments, I'll let you know immediately. I promise.'

'I'll call Pete.'

NINE

Ash took his wife's elbow and steered her to his study. The sign on the door had never been more pertinent than now.

'Why, Gabriel, how masterful you've become!' Her tone was provocative; her pale blue eyes, the colour of faded denim, mocked him.

Ash's jaw was clenched tight: he had to make a positive effort to free it before he could speak. 'What are you doing here, Cathy?'

She widened her eyes at him. 'This is my home!'

'This was never your home. Your home was in London. You turned your back on it; and on me.'

Cathy declined to argue the point. Perhaps she recognised it was a restrained way of putting it. 'My sons' home, then. I'm here to see my sons. Surely you can't object to that.'

He gaped at her. 'Of course I object! You're a fugitive from the law – you're going to get yourself arrested. I don't need the boys to see that. I wouldn't have thought you'd want it either.'

She shrugged that off with a negligent gesture. 'No one knows I'm here. Only you. Are you going to turn me in, Gabriel?' She smiled at him impishly, as if confident of the answer.

She had no right to be that confident. Gabriel Ash had good reasons to want to see his wife jailed. Natural justice was one: she'd put him through hell. She was responsible for one death that he knew about – that he'd witnessed – and, to some extent, he wasn't sure how great an extent, for others. And then, having her behind bars in England rather than out in the wider world would resolve any question as to his sons' future. He couldn't imagine a court taking them away from him and returning them to their mother, but a life sentence would put the matter beyond doubt. It ought to simplify his divorce, too.

He should, and he knew he should, have been reaching for the phone right now.

And he didn't, and he went on not doing. Cathy's smile was slowly spreading. A lot can change in six years. But Gabriel Ash hadn't changed that much.

'Well, if you're not going to turn me in, perhaps you'd make me a cup of coffee.'

At least he retained enough presence of mind not to do her bidding. That was a one-way street, and it didn't lead anywhere he wanted to go. 'I need you to leave.' His voice was low.

'Gabriel,' she said reproachfully, 'I've only just got here. I've barely said hello to the boys. Who's the Chinese girl, anyway?'

'Ms Kelly,' Ash said carefully, 'is the boys' nanny and the mainstay of our household. She knows who you are, what you've done. And she never promised to love and honour you. Maybe I haven't the moral courage to turn you in. But she hasn't an ounce of sentimentality in her: the moment she thinks the boys' welfare is at stake, she'll do it for me.'

Cathy shot him a piercing look. She was inclined to believe that he meant it. 'I'm no threat to the boys. You know that. What I did, I did for them.'

Outrage darkened his face and he went to protest. She forestalled him. 'Maybe not all of it, but at the start. We *were* abducted, and it *was* because of the work you were doing. They were deeply dangerous men, and their only interest in me and our sons was to get you off their backs. I made a deal with them to keep us safe. I'm sorry I hurt you, but the boys mattered more. I kept them safe. They're here now, with you, because I supped with the devil.'

'You shot Stephen Graves! You shot me.'

'Stephen Graves was a criminal. And you' – she gave a cool shrug – 'not for the first time, my dear, you got in the way.'

All of which was true. Ash couldn't contradict a word of it. But he knew she had been a much more willing participant than a plain statement of the facts suggested. He knew she'd seen a chance to escape from a marriage which bored her and had no compunction about reaping the harvest of her betrayal.

Hazel had warned him once that Cathy might persuade a jury she did it all under duress, that she was not a villain but a victim. This, he understood with a shock of foreboding, was how she would do it. If he forced her to defend herself in court, she could win. He could lose his sons to her. Again.

Then too, there was still a part of him that didn't want to see her brought down. That . . . didn't care for her exactly, it was too late for that, but retained a nostalgia for what they had once had together. Or possibly, what he'd thought they had. He *had* promised to love and honour, and absurdly enough that promise had stood and still stood between him and any number of things he could have done. One of them concerned Hazel. He knew now, as perhaps she had always known, that he'd never managed to commit to Hazel because Cathy had always come between them. Not because there was any comparison between his feelings about the two women – the faithful friend who'd saved his life, his soul and his sanity, and the wife who'd sold him to his enemies – but because he'd given an undertaking. Forsaking all others, he'd said, and he was a man of his word. It wasn't a source of any particular pride to him, least of all now; it was just who he was. If he could have been someone else, he would have been.

He said, 'What do you want?'

'Apart from coffee?' She eyed him, weighing him up. 'I told you, I want to see my sons. I haven't seen them for two years.'

'I didn't see them for four.'

From somewhere, incredibly, the faded denim eyes conjured a little hurt. 'I have apologised for that, Gabriel. I found myself on a pathway that left me very little choice. Surely it's time to forgive and forget.'

Ash stared at her in disbelief. 'Cathy – why would you even *think* that's possible?'

She raised a shapely eyebrow. 'I hoped we could behave like grown-ups, if only for the sake of the boys. It can't be very nice for them, having their father wishing their mother was dead.'

'I have *never* said that!' exclaimed Ash, appalled. 'Not to them. Not in my innermost thoughts. I have never wished you harm. I just want you to leave us alone. To go back to where you came from, and get on with your life, and not contact me or them again.' Then he remembered. 'Except . . .'

'Except?'

He took a deep breath. 'My solicitors have been trying to find you. I'm filing for a divorce. You could make it easier, on all of us, if you're prepared to.'

'Hm.' She sounded more thoughtful than either surprised or angry. 'So you want me to consent to ending our marriage, then to disappear, and never see or hear from my sons again, and never know if they're well or if they're happy. Tell me: just how does that differ from wishing I was dead?'

Gabriel Ash was an intelligent and articulate man, but he'd never been a master of the sharp retort, the pithy put-down. He was still trying to formulate a reply when Cathy, bored, turned away. 'Still got this old thing, then.' She was looking at the china cabinet.

It took Ash a few seconds to change tack. 'It was my mother's.'

'Yes, it was, wasn't it,' she said flatly. She turned the tiny key, opened the door and took out one of the exhibits. You'd have to say they were exhibits because they weren't useful for anything but gathering dust. 'I don't think I've seen china roses since the last time I was here.'

'She used to collect them. Auctions, antique shops, charity shops, jumble sales. No box of contents was safe if she thought there might be a china rose lurking at the bottom.'

'Why?'

Ash shrugged. 'She thought they were beautiful. She liked the fact that they did absolutely nothing but please the eye. And she admired the skill that went into making them.'

Cathy nodded slowly, turning the pretty thing in her hands, studying it. 'Hours of work,' she agreed. 'Probably years of learning how to do it: bent double over a workbench, ruining your back and your eyesight. And after all that, it's so fragile. One slip, and all you're left with is sherds of porcelain all over your floor. After that, there isn't enough skill in the world to make it whole again. Makes you wonder if there isn't some kind of moral in there, doesn't it?'

For a sickening moment, Ash thought she was going to show him what she meant, and his stomach turned over. Not because the trinket meant much to him, or even because it had meant more to his mother, but because an act so crass would demonstrate – if any further demonstration was necessary – how little was left of the woman he'd loved. A cheap gesture of that kind would have been entirely alien to her once.

And perhaps it still was, because she returned the porcelain flower carefully to the cabinet and closed the door. All the same, she couldn't leave the subject without some kind of jibe. 'There's no law, you know, that says you have to hold onto everything your mother ever bought. Who are you saving them for – the boys? I doubt they'll thank you. You should get rid of the roses, replace them with something a bit more masculine.'

'What do you suggest,' he asked, nettled. 'Guns through the ages? The hand-grenade as art?'

She laughed, that merry tinkling laugh that had once charmed him utterly. 'At least that would be something they wouldn't be too embarrassed to show their friends. Really, Gabriel, what does a collection of china roses *say* about a man?'

Ash sighed. 'Cathy, we both know you do not give a toss, and never have, about the contents of my late mother's china cabinet. I haven't seen you for two years. There must be something more important we could be discussing.'

She turned abruptly to face him. 'You want to talk about the divorce? Fine, we'll talk about the divorce. But don't expect me to give up my claim to my sons just because it would be convenient for you. I carried them for nine months each. I gave birth to them. I raised them for more than half their lives. They are my sons at least as much as yours. I'm not going to pretend they never happened.'

'If you want,' Ash said slowly, 'you can leave a forwarding address with me. A bank or post office if you don't want me to know where you live. When they come of age, I'll let them have it. They can contact you if they want to.'

'You're talking of the best part of a decade,' Cathy pointed out tartly. 'Not two years, not four. Gilbert won't be eighteen for another eight years. Guy won't for another ten.'

'In all the circumstances, joint custody isn't really an option.'

'It could be. If I cleared my name.'

So that was it. Blackmail. He wished he could be surprised. He said again, 'What is it you *want*, Cathy?'

Hazel planned to spend Saturday evening in the bath. A long, hot one. Bubbles, holiday brochures, glass of wine. Well, half-glass: you never knew when the phone would ring and there'd be a juicy corpse to draw a chalk line round.

She'd been out much of the day after all, her weekend eroded by the exigencies of the service as they so often were. She'd done her week's shopping, and on her way home she'd stopped at Meadowvale to check her messages.

One of the old ladies had been in to say she'd spotted the young man in the navy-blue anorak hovering outside the Post Office. So – nipping back to Railway Street just long enough to put her frozens into her freezer – Hazel had gone to the Post Office and viewed their security camera footage, only to find that the young man in the navy-blue anorak was a young woman in a dark green anorak with a baby in a sling.

Informed of her error, and over a cup of tea – the best china, more roses – the old lady was deeply apologetic. 'It's these glasses, dear. I don't know what it is but the optician can't seem to get the prescription right any more.'

Hazel was reassuring. 'We'd much rather check out a possible lead than not hear about an actual one.' More tea arrived, and cake. And by then it was somehow, unaccountably, early evening.

The moment she got home she knew she had the house to herself again. Luxuriating in the peace and quiet – she liked David Sperrin, but there was nothing restful about his company – she shut the bathroom window against the winter's chill and watched the rising steam mist up the mirror and billow along the ceiling.

Her head was nodding over her brochure, her long fair hair dipping its ends in the bathwater, her weary limbs soaking up the heat, when the phone rang.

It wasn't a nice juicy corpse. It was Pete Byrfield, full of worry and apologies. 'We've had a reactor. Did David tell you?'

'What?' She was still groggy from the bath, didn't make the connection right away. And then, though she'd spent her formative years in the country, the Bests weren't a farming family. No farmer's daughter would have heard those words and thought of Sizewell B.

'Only the one,' said Byrfield, 'but we're just as locked-down as if it had been a dozen. I don't understand it. She wasn't a recent arrival – we haven't *had* any recent arrivals; the last time we bought something in was the Fleckvieh bull, and he tested clear. But there's no doubt about it – it wasn't an inconclusive response, she was a clear reactor. We've spent the whole day dividing up the herd, trying to isolate the ones that would have had most contact with her from those that hadn't. Tracy's practically in tears. She wants me to sell the lot and replace them with sheep.'

Hazel had met the new Countess Byrfield. She doubted if tears were in her repertoire, and she'd always preferred her sheep to the Byrfield cattle anyway. But they'd clearly had a shock, and a horrible, exhausting day, and if Pete needed a shoulder to cry on, Hazel didn't begrudge him the use of hers. 'What will you do?'

'There's not much we can do,' said Byrfield glumly. 'APHA – the animal health people – will pick up the cow. And the vet'll be back in a couple of months to retest the whole herd, then again two months later. Till we've had two clear tests we can't move anything, so we're stuck with feeding a couple of dozen bullocks that were market-ready, knowing that by the time we're released from restrictions they'll be overweight and the butchers won't pay top whack for them.'

'I'm sorry,' said Hazel feelingly. 'You could have done without this, couldn't you?'

'We could,' agreed Byrfield. 'But it happens on the best regulated farms, so they tell me. Anyway, I just wanted to apologise again. Tomorrow won't be so manic: I'll hit the road after milking, pick him up about noon.'

It must have been the bath, or possibly the wine. Hazel didn't understand. 'Pick who up?'

'David, of course.' Byrfield sounded surprised. 'I meant to

be there this afternoon, but – as I say – I couldn't make it. Surely he told you?'

The effects of both the hot bath and the cold prosecco were dissipating fast. 'I haven't seen David since before lunch. He wasn't here when I got home an hour ago. He isn't here now. I thought you'd been for him.'

'Er . . .' Ninety miles apart, they both glanced at the time. 'Could he have gone to the pub?'

'Of course he hasn't gone to the pub,' snapped Hazel. 'He's got his wrist in plaster and his ribs strapped up: it's only the painkillers keeping him on his feet. I know where he is. Well, I don't know *where* he is, but I know what he's done. He's gone to ground. I told him it was time he went home, and he didn't want to. He wanted to stay here until we could figure out what had happened. I explained that might not be a realistic option, but you know what David's like – you've a better chance of knocking some sense into an active volcano! He's sloped off while I was at work and found somewhere to hole up – a small hotel or a B&B somewhere. He knew I'd assume he was with you, and you'd assume he was with me. When did you talk to him?'

'About ten this morning,' said Byrfield. 'He said you were out, he didn't know when you'd be back. Hazel, we need to find him. He's not well enough to be fending for himself.'

Privately, Hazel suspected that Sperrin – who'd survived a fall onto a moving train, had scrambled under the shunting yard fence, had walked into Norbold from the hospital out on the ring road and had now outmanoeuvred both of them – was rather tougher than his brother gave him credit for; or if not tougher, at least more determined, which could get you as far. He'd been in the living room when she dropped her shopping off. By then he'd already spoken to Byrfield, knew his ride home wasn't going to materialise. Not telling her had been a deliberate choice.

'Wherever he is, he'll be fine for tonight. I'll track him down tomorrow. He must have called a taxi – there are only a couple of local companies, I'll talk to them in the morning. They'll remember where they took him. If they don't want me going over their licences with a magnifying glass, they will,' she added darkly. 'I'll have him rounded up by the time you get here.'

'You're sure?' asked Byrfield, clucking like a mother hen. 'This is David we're talking about. You take your eyes off him for five minutes and anything can happen.'

'Pete, I was in the bath when you called. I'm standing dripping on the lino right now. I am *not* climbing back into my clothes to go looking for your idiot brother. Whatever happened to him, it happened fifty miles from here. He's as safe in the second-floor-back at the Elite Guest House' – she pronounced it *e-light*, not as a joke but from habit, because Mrs Semple the proprietor had only ever seen the word written down and that was how she said it – 'as he is in my spare room. Make yourself a hot drink and go to bed, and we'll sort this out tomorrow. Either I'll call you or David will.

'And don't worry,' she added. 'This is Norbold – nothing ever happens here.'

TEN

Hazel was wrong about the Elite Guest House, but only by a dozen metres or so. The taxi had deposited Sperrin, with nothing more than the clothes he stood up in, on the steps of Beaufort Lodge, Mrs Semple's next-door neighbour in Utility Street. Norbold didn't have a grand parade of tourist hotels in the way that Brighton and Bournemouth do. There was a motel on the ring road, and the faded and over-priced Midland that was built in the heyday of the railway, and there was Utility Street. The general feeling was that if you couldn't find something to suit you in Utility Street, you could take your airs and graces up the motorway to Coventry.

Mrs Semple's neighbour Mrs Warburton knew immediately who Hazel was looking for. 'You mean the gentleman who can't pronounce Beaufort.' She said it to rhyme with Newport.

Hazel gave a tired sigh. 'Let me guess. He then went on to give you a lecture on how he was right and you'd been saying it wrong all these years.'

Mrs Warburton sniffed. 'I see you know the gentleman.'

Sperrin was in the residents' lounge, poring over a week-old copy of the *Norbold News*. Hazel watched him for a moment through the open door, fighting the urge to throw something at him. 'David, what are you doing here?'

He tapped the newsprint with the fingers emerging from his plaster. 'Cars for sale.'

'I don't mean *here*, in this room, I mean . . .' Hazel heard the echo of what he'd said and changed direction. 'You have a car.'

'*You* have my car,' he pointed out acidly. 'No one can tell me when I'll get it back. And the car-hire people don't trust me not to wreck their shopping special by driving with a broken wrist.'

'You may find your insurers take the same view,' retorted Hazel. 'You're not fit to drive. You're only just fit enough to be a passenger.'

He ignored that, returned his attention to the small ads. Hazel took the paper out of his hand, folded it and put it down on the table beside him. When Sperrin scowled up at her she said, 'You didn't tell me Pete couldn't come.'

'No.'

'Why not?'

'I didn't want you to know,' said Sperrin.

'Because?'

'Because if you'd known he couldn't pick me up, you'd have driven me back to Byrfield yourself. And as I said before, I'm not ready to leave yet.'

Hazel sank into one of the armchairs. 'I don't know what you think you can accomplish here. Whatever happened to you – whatever you did or didn't do – happened fifty miles away. It was just the luck of the draw that you ended up in Norbold.'

'That's probably true,' he acknowledged. 'But this is where I started picking up the threads again. I can't remember – by definition, I suppose – where I lost that chunk of my memory, but I do know this is where it started coming back. Yes, only bits of it – a shape, a name, fragmentary snippets of information dredged up from the bottom of the black lagoon. But here, in this stupid little town with its stupid little people, is where I started to catch hold of them.

'If I leave here – if I go back to Byrfield, where everything's familiar and every face belongs to my life before any of this happened – maybe I'll lose that thread. It's not very strong, and when it does pull something up it makes no sense, it doesn't fit any kind of a pattern. But it's still the only connection I have to those lost hours. I won't risk breaking it. If I can't do anything else, I'll sit here in the Beaufort Lodge' – he pronounced it as Mrs Warburton did, with a savage mocking grin – 'and wait for the next piece of the jigsaw puzzle to surface. And if it takes weeks, it takes weeks; and if it takes months, well, it's not as if I've anything better to do.'

'You're determined?' She saw that he was. She sighed. 'Then you'd better call Pete and tell him. He's got enough to worry about right now without making a four-hour round trip for no good reason. He told you about the TB test?'

Sperrin nodded.

'Do you want to stay here? You can come home with me if you want.'

'Yeah, all right.' For a moment he looked furtive. 'Will you tell Mrs Warburton?'

'That you're not going to be staying? Do you know,' said Hazel wearily, 'I don't think she'll mind a bit.'

Sperrin had nothing to pack, and it was barely a quarter of a mile from Utility Street to Hazel's house in Railway Street. They should have been there in under a minute. But as they drove round the corner, Sperrin saw the street-sign.

'Siding Street. That's where . . .'

'Yes,' said Hazel. After a moment's hesitation she turned into the back street and slowed the car. 'Wayne Budgen found you lying just about here. You'd crawled through that gap under the fence.'

'Can we stop?'

Hazel frowned. 'There's nothing to see.'

'Stop anyway.'

He climbed out, slowly, hissing in his teeth as the pain caught in his ribs, leaning on the car door for support. He looked up the road and down it. There was indeed nothing to see: not just no evidence of his being here, but no other vehicles, no one on foot, no indication of anyone watching from any of the tired little houses. It wasn't because it was Sunday morning. It was because it was Siding Street. 'It doesn't look familiar.'

'I don't suppose it does. You were unconscious when Wayne found you.'

'I wasn't unconscious when I crawled through the fence.'

'Pretty close to it, I think. On autopilot, anyway. That was a bad concussion you had. You're lucky that a few missing hours is all you have to show for it.'

'Lucky,' he echoed, tasting the word. 'Do you know, I don't feel all that lucky.'

Hazel shrugged. It wasn't that she was unsympathetic, although there was little enough about David Sperrin to invite sympathy. But her sympathy could do him no service. If the memories didn't come, somehow he would have to find his way forward without them; if they did, right now it was impossible to predict what that would mean. So far as Hazel could

see, all he could realistically do for now was pack away
everything that had happened to him in the last week and stow
it in some mental attic where the rest of his life wouldn't keep
tripping over it.

She said, 'Whether or not you remember, nothing significant
happened here. If you're looking for something to jog your
memory . . .' She stopped there, abruptly, appalled at her own
stupidity, but it was already too late.

'. . . I need to go back to Myrton,' finished Sperrin. 'Yes.
Now?'

Hazel stared at him. 'What do you mean, now?'

'I mean, will you drive me to Myrton now? This morning.
Or do I need to phone up about some of these cars?' He'd
torn the car ads page from the *Norbold News*, had it folded
in his pocket.

Hazel breathed heavily at him. 'What about Pete? He'll be
leaving Byrfield just about now.'

'There are these wonderful inventions,' explained Sperrin,
'you can talk to someone even if they're miles away, they're
called *telephones*. I'll tell him not to bother. Look, Hazel, I'll
make a deal with you. Myrton's halfway to Byrfield – if you
want to get rid of me, you can take me the rest of the way
after we've been to Myrton.'

Hazel was conscious that if she started shouting at him, she
wouldn't be able to stop. Also, his deal had its attractions.
She gave him a stony look. 'I'll have to OK it with my chief.'

Sometimes Sunday was a day of rest for DCI Gorman,
sometimes it wasn't. As it happened, though, he was not at
Meadowvale when Hazel called but enjoying the luxury of
breakfast at the Swan Inn, overlooking the canal. Hazel heard
him ordering more coffee as she explained.

Slightly to her surprise, he agreed to the excursion. 'Give
it a try. Show him the bridge. If anything's going to trigger a
memory, that should.'

'Do you think it will?'

'Not really, no. But I could be wrong. If I am – and Hazel,
this is not a suggestion, it's not a request, it's an order – do
not attempt to follow up on your own. Call me. And don't let
Sperrin out of your sight.'

This was the third time Hazel had travelled out to Myrton. It took well over an hour: very fast on the motorway section, very slow through the miles of rural lanes. Her first thought was to drive straight to the little humpback bridge and avoid the muddy lane and the tramp across the field. Then it occurred to her that those were the very things that might strike chords in his memory: that it was important for Sperrin to return to the scene the same way he had approached it the first time.

So she drove up the farm lane, giving the grim-faced farmer a cheery wave as she passed his tractor and trying not to mind the way the ruts were shaking her suspension and the mud was splattering her gleaming sapphire paintwork. She parked where they'd found Sperrin's Land Rover.

She had her seat-belt off and was halfway through the door before she realised Sperrin was making no attempt to follow. For a moment she thought he was too sore, his cracked ribs jolted by the same ruts that had bludgeoned her springs, but that wasn't it. He was staring ahead at the granite fingerpost that was the Myrton menhir. She raised an interrogative eyebrow at him.

'I don't want to do this,' he said in a low voice.

Hazel slid back into her seat. After a moment she said quietly, 'You don't have to do this. We can leave now and go on to Byrfield.'

Sperrin glanced at her. Out of the corner of her eye she saw him swallow. 'And never know?'

Hazel nodded. 'Whether you do this or not, you may never know. Or we might leave here only to have it all come flooding back. I don't know what's the best thing to do, David. We're here because you wanted to come. We can leave for the same reason.'

'And waste what's left of your weekend?'

'I'm a public servant, you help pay my wages. You can waste as much of my time as you need to.'

For a minute he said nothing more, just stayed where he was and stared through the open gate and across the field to the standing stone. 'I thought,' he said eventually, 'it would mean something to me. Coming here, seeing it. I thought . . . it would mean something.'

'And it doesn't?'

He gave a fractional shake of his head. His dark hair was unruly. But then, it always had been. 'Nothing. I have no recollection of being here.'

Hazel considered for a long moment. If she chose to take that as the final word, she thought he'd let her turn the car and drive back down the lane, away from Myrton and its enigmatic stone, and never ask to return. She thought that if she made no response, in another minute he'd suggest the same thing himself, and in all likelihood this would be where it ended. Whatever had happened to him, whatever he'd done or seen, would be buried in his mind forever, with only a megalith hewn from the granite bedrock six millennia past to mark the spot; and perhaps that would be best.

But Hazel was not just a private person. She was not just a friend of this man's family, someone who knew his tragedy and had hoped the misfortunes of Byrfield could be consigned to the past. As a police officer, she had obligations higher even than friendship. She didn't know if a crime had been committed, by David Sperrin or anyone else. But if it had – if a girl really had been killed, and the murder tidied away so successfully that the only lingering trace of it was a handful of disjointed memories in an injured brain – here and now was the best chance of getting justice for the victim. This was probably the crime scene, and the man sitting beside her was probably either the perpetrator or a witness. If she turned the car now she would always wonder if, at a seminal moment in her career, she had shirked her duty.

She said softly, 'But here – right here – isn't where it happened. This is where you left the Land Rover. And you never came back.'

Sperrin never took his eyes off the stone. 'I walked over to the menhir?'

'According to Sergeant Wilson, who is the oracle in these matters. And then you ran from there to the lane. There, where the gate is.' She pointed.

Reluctantly, he shifted his gaze to the far side of the field. 'Where's the railway line?'

'Three hundred metres to the right.'

He said, very slowly, 'I suppose we should go and look.'

In a perfect world Hazel would have had him retrace his steps from the car to the stone, from the stone to the gate, from the gate to the bridge. But Sperrin wasn't up to the trek. He might, with difficulty, have crossed the field, but she wasn't going to let him climb the gate. She drove back the way they'd come and worked her way round to the lane, the railway line and the bridge. It took ten minutes.

He got out of the car and looked at the mossy stones, the stone where the moss had been rubbed off, and down to the track below. 'I jumped down there?'

'That's what we think, yes.'

Again the fractional shake of the head, as if he almost didn't believe it. 'What the hell was behind me, that *that* seemed like a good idea?'

Hazel didn't know. 'We could walk back to the gate,' she suggested. 'Where the van stopped. If it was a van.'

There were no signs now of the activity Sergeant Wilson had described on the verge beside the gate. Of course, even four days ago the signs had been unclear to Hazel. She told Sperrin what SOCO had told her. She wasn't sure if it was a good idea or a bad idea, only that if it triggered a flood of memories it would seem like a good idea.

Sperrin looked at the standing stone from this different angle. Perhaps it was an archaeologist thing: a Neolithic menhir was more real to him than the death of a half-remembered girl. 'Nothing,' he said, disappointed; then again, with the roughness of despair, '*Nothing.*'

Hazel waited a little longer, just in case; but finally she had to concede that the long shot had, in defiance of every narrative convention, failed to hit its target. She sighed. 'Well, we gave it our best try. Let's get out of here. See if Pete's cooked enough lunch for four . . .'

That was when she realised Sperrin was no longer with her: not in person and not in spirit. She glanced round. He'd fallen half a dozen steps behind and was now rooted to the crumbling edge of the tarmac lane, eyes great with shock, staring at the vacancy where Sergeant Wilson had envisaged a vehicle.

'David?'

He blinked rapidly; and though he turned his white face

towards her, his gaze stayed fixed where it was. 'There was
. . . a van. You told me that, didn't you?'

Hazel nodded. 'I did.'

'I know you did. I didn't remember it then. Now I do.'

Well, perhaps, thought Hazel doubtfully. 'What colour was it?'

'Grey,' he said after a moment. His voice was hollow,
breathy. 'Or off-white, or maybe cream. Light-coloured,
anyway. With . . . something on the side.'

'A badge, a logo? A name?' Miracles do occasionally happen.

'I don't know. Maybe. And . . . people. They must have got
out of it. There.' He pointed an unsteady finger at the verge.

Hazel felt her interest quickening. He could still be piecing
together things she'd told him and things that Gorman had
said. But she thought Sperrin believed he was remembering.
'What were they doing?' He hadn't run across a muddy field
because he saw some people standing around on a grass verge.

'I don't know. Arguing? There was this girl. She was afraid,
but she was angry too. The men were shouting at her. No, one
of them was – there were two of them. She shouted back.'

Increasingly Hazel believed that he was remembering real
events. 'What did she say?' She kept her voice quiet, encouraging. The last thing she wanted to do now was derail his
train of thought.

But the wisps of memory slipped through his fingers.

'It's all right, don't worry about the gaps. We'll fill them
in later. What happened next?'

'She saw me. She started to run towards me.'

He had the heel of his good hand pressed against his forehead, trying to force the memories to coalesce. But it was as
if the snapshots had been taken from an album and dropped
on the floor, and some of them were in the wrong order and
some of them had got kicked under the sofa. Reassembling
them was taking all the strength he had.

'I must have climbed the gate, because then I was in the
lane and she was still running towards me. She had her hands
stretched out.' Unconsciously he echoed the gesture, reaching
out with his good arm and his broken one. 'She was asking
for help. She was afraid, and she thought I could help her.'

'In English?'

He had to think about that. 'It must have been, or I wouldn't have understood her.'

'So why do you think she was a foreigner?'

He didn't know. Hazel waited, but Sperrin just shook his head helplessly. At length she said softly, 'And then?'

'And then they shot her,' said David Sperrin. His voice was hollow. 'The man from the van. He shot her in the back. The force of it threw her into my arms. She died in my arms, Hazel, and I didn't even know her name.'

'Her name was Rose. Wasn't it?'

He thought about that, shook his head. 'I don't think so. There was no time for her to tell me. I don't know who she was, or what she was doing there, or who killed her or why. But oh, Hazel' – finally he looked at her, and she was at first startled and then touched by the relief mingled with the excoriating grief in his eyes – 'they shot her in the *back*. She died in my arms, but I didn't kill her.'

'No,' said Hazel; and then added, and it was only the snowiest of white lies, 'I never for a moment thought you did.'

She went to steer him back to the car. Still he hesitated, looking up and down the lane. 'And then I ran.'

'Of course you ran!' exclaimed Hazel. 'People were shooting guns at you. What else were you going to do – stay and remonstrate with them?'

'But what if she wasn't dead?' Sperrin had escaped one nightmare only to stumble into another. 'I can't know that she was – there wasn't time to make sure. I dropped her and ran. What if I left her to them? What if I was her only prospect of help, and I let them have her?'

'David, don't torture yourself,' she said insistently. 'You did all you could to help her, and when it was too late for that you tried to save yourself. You have nothing to reproach yourself for. In all probability you're right: she did die in your arms. So her last thought was that someone was trying to help her. That's got to be worth something.'

She got him back in the car. If she'd parked any further away he wouldn't have made it. But there was no longer any question in her mind of taking him back to his brother. When she reached the main road she turned north, towards Norbold.

ELEVEN

Hazel drove directly to Railway Street, shovelled Sperrin into the armchair in the living room, then called Gorman from the kitchen. She told him what had transpired. 'I should probably have taken him straight to Meadowvale. He just seemed so shattered, I wasn't sure I could keep him on his feet long enough. Will you come here and talk to him?'

'No,' said Dave Gorman slowly. Hazel couldn't see his expression, but she could tell from his voice that there was something else going through his mind. 'No, I'll meet you at the hospital.'

Hazel blinked. 'I didn't mean literally shattered. He's just tired: it's all caught up with him. It was a long drive for someone not long out of his sick-bed. But I don't think he needs to be back in hospital.'

'I'm not thinking of Sperrin,' said Gorman distantly. Then, relenting: 'All right, we don't need him collapsing in the corridor. Let him put his feet up for a couple of hours and I'll see you there at three o'clock.'

'There where? It's a big hospital. A&E? Intensive Care?'

'The morgue,' said Gorman.

So Hazel had some idea what to expect. Sperrin didn't. Hazel just told him they were meeting the DCI at Norbold Infirmary, and no, she didn't know why; and she parked hard against the back wall by the unmarked door and took him the shortest way. A late lunch and a rest had restored some of David Sperrin's colour. But Hazel wasn't sure that, even if she managed to get him to the morgue without incident, they'd let her take him out again.

Gorman was already there, waiting in the corridor. 'I understand you had an interesting morning.'

He might not have spoken. Sperrin had spotted the sign on the door. His brow creased. 'This is the morgue.'

'That's right,' said Gorman. 'There's something I want you to look at.'

For almost a week now David Sperrin's brain had been working at less than peak efficiency. But no great leap of intuition was required. 'You've found her?'

'You tell me.'

They went through to the anteroom, a space furnished with just a few chairs and no windows. Gorman tapped the glass panel in front of them, and someone pulled back the curtain.

Hazel had seen people faint in this room, had caught them as they fell. Ordinarily she would not have thought Sperrin the fainting kind, but after the week he'd had it was hard to be sure. She stuck close, just in case.

In retrospect she realised that was naive. Archaeologists confront death every day. Death is how they make their living: dead civilisations, dead people. Every time David Sperrin scrubbed his fingernails, he probably washed traces of dead people down the plughole. Death *per se* held no fears for him, and not much mystery.

This was different. This slim, golden-skinned girl, the white sheet turned back to her long throat, her glossy black hair tidied by a mortuary attendant who couldn't do much to ease the pain of those who came here but did what he could, was as far removed as could be imagined from the fragments of bone left in a rectangle of earth undisturbed for hundreds of years. Only a few days ago she was a living soul. Someone's daughter; perhaps someone's wife. Breath stirred in her breast; a beating heart sped blood to flush the translucent flesh; thoughts and feelings and powerful emotions animated the expressionless face. She felt love, and fear – certainly fear – and hope and anger. She died a long way from home, a long way from those she cared for, and whatever her story had been, whatever her dreams, she had deserved better than to be here, stared at by strangers.

'That's her,' said David Sperrin. There was no emotion in his voice.

Gorman wanted chapter and verse. 'The girl you knew as Rose?'

Sperrin shook his head. 'I never knew her name. But that's

her. That's the girl who died in my arms. Shot in the back, yes?'

Gorman nodded.

'I didn't do that.'

After a moment Gorman said, 'No, I don't think you did.'

Sperrin glanced sideways at the file he was holding. On the cover, in black felt-tip pen, was written: *Doe, Rose – Chinese?* He looked up at Gorman sharply, as if suspecting him of something discreditable. 'And she wasn't Chinese.'

The DCI considered the dead girl beyond the glass. 'She looks Chinese.'

'She looks oriental,' said Sperrin, with some asperity. 'Do a DNA test. There are as many oriental races as there are European ones. She wasn't Chinese, and she didn't like people thinking that she was.'

'David,' said Hazel quietly, 'how do you know that?'

How indeed? For a moment he didn't know. It was one of the snapshots that had been kicked under the sofa. But then, stretching full length on the metaphorical carpet, he managed to reach it with a metaphorical fingertip and pulled it out. 'She said so. No – she shouted it.'

'She ran towards you, shouted "I'm not Chinese", and somebody shot her?'

He would have elaborated if he could. He couldn't; at least not yet. 'I think so. Pretty much.'

'In English?' prompted Gorman.

'Must have been,' said Sperrin, 'I don't speak Vietnamese.'

'But she did?'

Again, he'd pulled out new information without realising it. He marshalled the scraps of memory like someone blowing the dust off treasures. Like an archaeologist. His brow furrowed with the effort, he said, 'Yes. That's what she said. "I'm not Chinese, I'm from Vietnam."'

'If she was shouting in English,' said Gorman, 'that's because she could speak English and whoever she was shouting at couldn't speak Vietnamese.'

That made sense. Sperrin nodded cautiously.

'The men who got out of the van. What can you tell me about them?'

Sperrin considered, then shook his head. 'Nothing. I think there were two of them, but I don't remember anything about them. I was looking at her.'

'Someone produced a gun and you didn't look at him?'

'I don't know,' gritted David Sperrin.

'There's a lot you don't know, Mr Sperrin,' said Gorman, his tone critical.

'Yeah?' Sperrin's chin rose pugnaciously. 'Well, there's a fair bit you don't know either, Detective Chief Inspector. And my excuse is better than yours.'

Gorman didn't deign to answer that. He turned to Hazel. 'Take him home. Maybe another night's sleep will help – his manners if not his memory. Is he staying with you?'

Hazel rolled her eyes. 'Looks like it, for now.'

'Drop him off, then, and meet me back at Meadowvale. You and I need to talk.'

It wasn't until she'd left Sperrin at Railway Street and was turning into the car park behind the police station that Hazel had her *What is wrong with this picture?* moment.

Not so much built as cast in concrete, Meadowvale was part of the 1970s redevelopment of Norbold town centre. An overly optimistic town council had thought to improve on the no-nonsense Victorian street names like Railway Street and Siding Street, but found it easier to gentrify the street signs than the town's essential character, which remained one of weary pragmatism relieved by a resilient strand of self-mocking humour.

Hazel didn't so much park as abandon her car by the back steps, racing up them two at a time, thinking with a kind of thrill that she might be able to tell Dave Gorman something he hadn't already figured out for himself.

But he had. He'd left his door open, waved her inside as soon as she reached the upstairs corridor. 'Well?' he demanded. 'Aren't you going to ask me what she's doing in our morgue instead of one somewhere in Bedfordshire?'

'Er . . .' Hazel was both taken aback and disappointed. 'That's exactly what I was going to ask you. Where was she found?'

'You're going to love this,' growled Gorman. 'Some anglers pulled her out of the Clover Hill dam.'

Hazel stared. 'But that's . . .'

'. . . Our back yard. I know.'

It was also, and both of them knew this too, where Hazel's last car had met its end and for fourteen hours it was feared that Hazel had too. Neither of them referred to the fact. But it added piquancy to their discussion.

'But . . . she was killed fifty miles away!'

'Nearer forty to the dam, but yes. It's a long way to cart a dead body, even in a van.'

Hazel was trying to get her head round it. 'I suppose she *was* dead.'

Gorman raised a bushy eyebrow. 'She looked pretty dead to me. In fact, if she isn't, she's going to be seriously pissed about the autopsy.'

Hazel glared at him. 'I *mean*, I suppose David's right when he says she died in his arms. Maybe she didn't. Maybe that's why they took her with them.'

'She was shot in the back. They must have *wanted* her dead. If they'd found she wasn't dead enough, they'd just have put another bullet in her. Dead or dying, they took her with them because they didn't want anyone to know that she or they had ever been there.'

'David knew.'

'They'd just seen him jump off a railway bridge as a train went by. They must have assumed he wouldn't be telling anyone what he saw, except possibly St Peter.'

'So just as the train was heading towards Norbold, so the van was too? When it came to Clover Hill they spotted the dam; there was no one in the car park, so they drove down to the reservoir and dropped her in.' She hesitated before adding timidly, 'Dead or alive?'

Gorman sniffed. 'By then she was certainly dead. There was no water in her lungs.'

Hazel felt a brief surge of relief. She'd been afraid she was going to have to tell Sperrin that, in running, he'd left the girl to her killers when she might still have been saved.

Gorman was looking at her a shade oddly. She raised an interrogative eyebrow.

'What I wanted to ask you,' he said, 'and what I didn't want to ask you in front of Sperrin, was if you think we should trust him. I know he's your friend, but that makes you a better judge than the rest of us, if you're able to take a step back. Is he telling us everything? Everything he knows, everything he remembers. Or is he holding something back?'

Hazel thought for a moment. 'He *is* my friend – at least, I can't think of a better word. In spite of which, if I thought he was lying to us, I'd have no problem telling you. Now, I seem to have left my crystal ball in my other jacket, but I don't think he's either lying or holding something back. I've watched these memories resurface, and they've hit him like a sledge-hammer every time. Or nearly every time: once or twice they've sneaked in under his guard, and he hasn't even realised until someone pointed it out. It *could* be an act, but I don't think it is. If you want my opinion, that's it: that David's telling us what he remembers when he remembers it.'

'It's just' – Gorman gave an impatient grunt – 'things should be beginning to make some sense by now. Some kind of pattern should be emerging. Instead of which, everything he says seems to add another layer of complexity. If he was trying to confuse us he could hardly do a better job.' He stretched in his chair and rubbed the back of his wrist across his eyes. 'Maybe I'm getting old.' He was forty-one.

Hazel gave a sympathetic grin. She was used to dealing with these male menopause moments: Ash had them too. Contrary to received wisdom, her male friends seemed to worry more about the passage of time than her female ones did. Perhaps because losing one's fertility brought certain compensations, whereas losing one's hair did not.

'It *will* make sense,' she promised. 'Tomorrow or the next day you'll be pinning some snippet of information to the murder board, and you'll see that pattern staring out at you. It's there now, we're just not seeing it. But at some point, one bit of information or one comment or even one fleeting thought bumping into another inside someone's head will tip the balance, and we'll be on our way.

'We've got a body now,' she added. 'At least we know that a crime was definitely committed. We also know that what David remembered was accurate. She *was* a foreigner, and she was shot in the back. When we get confirmation that she was from Vietnam, you'll have all the reason you need to trust him.'

She never knew what it was that set off the mental chain reaction. You never did know, any more than you could know which uranium atoms were the first to get up close and personal and start a chain reaction. Thinking about it afterwards, she wondered if it was the word Vietnam. To people older than either of them it meant an unnecessary war played out on tiny black-and-white TV screens; and then waves of refugees crowded onto inadequate boats. To people of Hazel's generation, it meant thirty-nine people in search of a better life suffocating in the back of a lorry.

Whatever the cue, the chemistry took over, and she watched almost as a bystander while her synapses juggled the pieces and found a few with straight edges and a couple of corners, and began to arrange them into the very beginnings of a picture. Stripped of all the weird imponderables, some of which might be explained by Sperrin's injuries, those facts that could be asserted with a degree of confidence dictated the shape that picture had to take. The dead girl with the bullet in her back; the van which stopped in the quietest of rural lanes where the presence of a chance observer had been so unlikely; the effort made to remove every indication of the tragedy enacted there; even the fact that whoever took her away from Myrton had driven for an hour in order to hide her body in a reservoir rather than leaving her where she fell . . .

'Chief,' Hazel said uncertainly, 'are we dealing with human trafficking here?'

Gorman stared at her. 'That's a bit of a quantum leap, isn't it? Because Sperrin says she's Vietnamese? Even if he's right, she could have been here for any number of perfectly legitimate reasons.'

'Of course she could. But people going about their lawful business don't get shot in the back on quiet country roads nearly as often as people living on the fringe of society.' It was a generalisation but it was also true. Young men selling drugs in back alleys are far more likely to die violently than old ladies walking their dogs.

At least he paid her the courtesy of considering it. As an

experienced detective, he thought it was a big structure to erect
on flimsy foundations, but if he'd learnt one thing about Hazel
Best it was that her instincts were good. Not foolproof, but
good. 'All right,' he said. 'Make your case.'

She sifted around for her strongest piece of evidence. 'They
didn't want her to be found. Not soon, and preferably not at
all. They could have left her at Myrton. Or they could have
dumped her as soon as they were out of the immediate area,
in case someone hearing a gunshot came to investigate. It
would have been much safer than driving for an hour with a
dead girl as a passenger.

'They didn't want anyone to know that she'd died. So it
wasn't a punishment shooting, and it wasn't gang related – if
she'd been killed to make a point, they'd have wanted her
found. They didn't want anyone to know she was ever here.
If David had hit that train just a bit harder, we'd have had no
reason to connect her death with his, even when she turned
up in the Clover Hill dam.'

Hazel thought for a few moments before continuing. 'She
spoke English. More than just a few words – well enough to
shout at someone who was threatening her. "I'm not Chinese,
I'm from Vietnam." As if someone was making an assumption
that annoyed her, and she could only tell them so in English
because, whoever the traffickers are, they're from our end of
the pipeline, not the Asia end.'

Gorman was moved to defend his adopted town. 'We don't
know they're from Norbold . . .'

'No, we don't,' agreed Hazel. 'But I don't suppose Norbold's
immune to what seems to be a growing trade. Or at least, one
we're increasingly aware of.'

'Assuming you're right,' he growled. But his heart wasn't
in it.

'Assuming I'm right,' allowed Hazel. 'Maybe I'm not – maybe
Rose had some other reason for coming to England. She was
young, she was clearly well-educated, she was attractive, she
was healthy. And she travelled from her home to the far side
of the world, which would be an expensive undertaking, which
means she or someone close to her had disposable income. Why
do people come here?'

'For the sunshine and the endless golden beaches?' hazarded Gorman. 'Well, maybe not. They come as visitors, as students, as refugees or economic migrants, or to work. Myrton's a long way off the tourist trail. She could have been a student – that would explain her speaking the language. The international rules that apply to refugees make it quite hard for them to reach England. They're required to seek refugee status in the first safe country they come to, so anyone coming through Europe should do that in Spain or Greece or Italy or – er – France.' That was the furthest extent to which his grasp of geography could be stretched.

'She doesn't look as if she was fleeing from poverty. I know' – Hazel fended off his objection with a raised hand – 'appearances can be deceptive, but she seems to have enjoyed a certain standard of living. Maybe she thought she could improve her prospects, or maybe she wanted to see the world. If she was a student, shouldn't someone have reported her missing by now? Tutors, halls of residence, fellow students – *someone*. I think she came here to work. She'd already learned the language, and she thought she was coming to the kind of job where it would improve her career prospects. Only when she got here, she found that someone had lied.'

Gorman was following her argument closely now. He'd asked her to defend her theory and she was doing exactly that. 'Well, that's how these things work, isn't it?' he glowered. 'The traffickers say there are jobs waiting for nannies and nurses and secretaries, only when it's too late to turn back the girls find themselves offered a different kind of employment. Except it isn't employment in the sense that they can take it or leave it: they're in hock to the people smugglers for more than they or their families can repay any other way. There's no way out. To all intents and purposes, it's slavery.'

'Chief – had they . . .?'

He looked again in the file. 'No. She was a virgin.'

Whatever she'd already been through, this girl they could only refer to as Rose Doe, it hadn't included selling her body five times nightly. *Lovely Oriental girls for the discerning gentleman – fresh, modest and obedient; not argumentative like Western girls!* Perhaps what had happened on that back road by the Myrton menhir was that she'd finally realised the kind of employment she was heading for.

Hazel frowned. 'Why Myrton? What were they doing *that* far off the beaten track? I can see why they'd avoid the motor-ways – cameras, patrols – but how the hell did they end up in rural Bedfordshire?'

'An excellent question,' conceded Gorman, 'but nowhere near as pressing as the next one, which is, Why the hell were they heading for Norbold? We thought it was just the random coincidence of which train Sperrin jumped onto that got us involved. But if that girl was dumped in the Clover Hill dam, the people who killed her had some reason to be in this area. On my manor. And that makes me very unhappy indeed.'

Hazel left Meadowvale with her head still buzzing with possi-bilities, and the need to talk them through with someone less directly involved than either Gorman or Sperrin. She turned, as she always did on these occasions, up the hill towards Highfield Road.

It was dark, and no one saw her draw up at the kerb or climb the steep footpath to the front door. She had to ring the bell. Eventually, when she was on the point of ringing again, Ash opened it. Hazel had one foot on the doorstep, expecting him to usher her in, but he remained stubbornly in the half-open doorway. She looked at him in surprise, saw a guilty flush travel up his cheeks.

'Er – this is a really bad time. The boys have got a . . . a friend over, and they're bouncing off the walls. Can I give you a call in the morning?'

Hazel stepped back, startled and hurt. 'Sure. Call me tomorrow. Or not,' she added pointedly. Head still buzzing, she returned to her car. She heard Ash's door close before she could get in.

She didn't, because of the sound of her engine, hear it open again, or a quick step on the pavement. The first she knew was someone rapping on her window. It was Frankie Kelly.

Hazel had never been close to the Ash boys' nanny. Somehow the opportunity had never arisen. Invaluable a part of the household as she was, Frankie had never wished to be part of the family. She was Ash's employee: his friends were not her friends. A professional to her fingertips, she had no difficulty drawing the line between those aspects of life at Highfield Road which were her province and those which were not. Hazel respected her choices and admired her skills; they were always happy to see one another but never aspired to a social relationship.

This was different. Surprised as she had been to be denied entry to her friend's house, Hazel was astonished to have his nanny come running down the path after her. To explain – to apologise? Could either be part of her duties?

'Frankie? Were you looking for me? Do you want to get in the car?'

Frankie shook her head. Her long dark hair was folded tightly in the nape of her neck. Controlled; professional. 'I mustn't be a moment. I don't want to be missed. I just wanted to say . . .'

But perhaps she didn't know exactly what she wanted to say. Anxious and embarrassed, she ran out of words. Hazel could see her wrestling with her conscience that she was here at all.

'What's the matter, Frankie? What's happened?'

The small Filipino woman shook her head, almost in despair. 'This isn't my place. I just wanted to say . . . To say, Mr Ash needs to see you.'

Which made nothing any clearer. 'I've just seen him. He was busy. He said he'd call tomorrow.'

'Tomorrow? Yes. Talk to him tomorrow.' Her head dipped. 'Please.' Then she was gone.

TWELVE

'Has she gone?' asked Cathy Ash negligently. 'Your persistent little friend?' Hazel was both taller and more sturdy than Ash's wife: Cathy called her that because she knew it annoyed him.

'Of course she's gone,' said Ash shortly. 'What did you think was going to happen? I'd invite her in for supper – a cosy threesome round the kitchen table?'

'As you keep pointing out' – he didn't – 'it's your house.' She smiled maliciously. 'Any friend of yours is a friend of mine.'

Ash stared at her in disbelief. 'Cathy, Hazel is a police officer. There's an Interpol alert out for you. If she had any reason to suspect you were here, you'd certainly be spending tonight in a cell, and I dare say I would as well.'

'Oh, I don't think she'd do anything that would get you into trouble, Gabriel. She's besotted with you.'

'Now you're being absurd,' he frowned.

Cathy laughed out loud. For the first time Ash noticed a kind of artifice about it, as if she knew that, in spite of everything, her laugh was still a potent weapon, at least against him. 'You're not telling me you hadn't noticed? Dear God, she couldn't make it clearer with a sign around her neck! If it came to a straight choice between you and the Queen's Shilling – do they still give you that, do you know? – the Queen would get her shilling back.'

'Don't judge everyone by your own standards. Most people are more honest than you, and Hazel is more honest than most people. She'll do her duty even when it hurts. I've seen her do it. And I'm not going to ask her to make that choice.'

'Oh Gabriel,' Cathy chuckled, 'you're such an innocent. Perhaps I should give you that divorce. It would be worth it to see what you'd do with your freedom. Would you really want to marry her? She's – what? – fifteen years younger than you?' She studied his face for a moment. 'But I do believe you would.'

'Sign the papers and find out.' He didn't think she'd do it, but he doubted he had anything to lose. She had always been a creature of impulse, mercurial – there was just a chance that she would do it merely to see how he'd react.

'Maybe I will. But I want something in return.'

'You still haven't told me what.'

'I need your help.'

'What sort of help?'

'Does it matter? If it means I leave here without my sons, and you get your divorce, is there any kind of help you *wouldn't* give me?'

It was surprising to Ash that she still had the power to hurt him. He forced himself to ignore the pain, ignore the fear, and concentrate. Dealing with Cathy, he needed all his wits about him.

'Actually, yes,' he said. 'I won't bring the weight of the law crashing down on your head. Not because you don't deserve it, but because I don't want our children to have to deal with that. But Cathy, that is all the help you're going to get from me. If you try to take the boys, I'll fight you in the courts. I'll spend every penny I have, and every penny I can borrow, fighting you. And I'll win.'

'That's possible,' allowed Cathy negligently. 'But then, as you know, I don't have to do my fighting in the courts.'

He did know that. Once before he'd thought she'd sent men to take the boys by force. The fact that he'd been mistaken was no guarantee she wouldn't do exactly that at some time in the future.

'If it's money you want,' he said tersely, 'I can find you some.'

'How much money?'

Never in his wildest dreams had he imagined anything so vulgar coming from her lips. It grieved him more than many of the much worse things that she'd done. 'How much money will I give you to abandon your claim to our sons? Do you really want me to answer that question, Cathy?'

She gave a derisive little snort. 'This is no time to be coy,

Gabriel. You want me to remove myself from your life, totally and permanently. Well, how much do you want it?' She looked around her speculatively. 'I imagine the house is paid off?'

'You know it is.' But in spite of all the evidence, Ash thought – he could not have explained why – that she was once again playing with his emotions. He wouldn't have put it past her to put a price on her co-operation, but somehow this was not how the conversation would have gone. He knew her well enough, now, to know that his wife would never turn her nose up at any money coming from any source; but he didn't think that was the reason she was here. What that reason was, he was at a loss to guess.

'Half a million? No, probably not – this is Norbold. Still, a significant amount. I presume you could mortgage it?'

Ash thought for a moment, breathing long and slow. 'No,' he said then, 'I couldn't.'

She seemed surprised. 'Why not? You have a pension, haven't you? It wouldn't break you.'

'I'm not buying you off with my mother's house,' he said quietly. 'Because we both know that, whatever it's worth, it would never be enough. In another year, or two years, or five years, we'd be having this conversation again. If you need money to get safely out of the country, that I can find. I'll go to the bank tomorrow. For anything more, you've come to the wrong shop.'

Her smile spread. So he'd been right: it wasn't about the money. At least, not only about money. 'You mean, you'd rather hang on to your sons' inheritance than your sons?'

He managed a thin smile of his own. 'This isn't about either the house or the boys. Is it? Are you going to tell me what it is about? Or do you want to play games for a bit longer first?'

Cathy sighed. 'I wish I could say you've got boring as you've got older, Gabriel. But you haven't really: you always were horribly prosaic. All right, if you want the truth, I find myself wrong-footed in a business matter. I thought I could slip into the country, tidy up the mess and slip out again without anyone being any the wiser. But things have gone very slightly pear-shaped, and I need somewhere to stay for

a few days. I thought it would be a good chance to see the
boys, catch up on all your news. You know – family stuff.'

Ash was staring at her as if she'd pulled a rabbit out of a
top hat and proceeded to eat it. 'You can't stay here!'

'I could go to a hotel,' she said, almost as if she hadn't
heard him, 'but I'd rather not have to produce my ID. It's fake,
of course; and though it's pretty good, you can never be quite
sure it's not on a watch list somewhere. That's why I didn't
fly in through Coventry: I'm safer coming in, shall we say,
under the radar. I'll take your room.' She smiled at him. 'But
I don't mind sharing.'

Gilbert helped him lug the old studio couch down from the
box-room to his study, and move his desk under the window
to make room for it. With commendable, even remarkable,
restraint for his age, the boy asked no questions and offered
no observations until they were finished. Then he said in a
low voice, 'Is Mum staying then?'

There was no point denying the obvious. 'For tonight,' said
Ash firmly.

'She isn't coming back to live with us?'

Ash lowered himself into the office chair, looking his son
in the eye. 'Gilbert, she can't. You know that. It isn't safe for
her here.'

'Are the police still looking for her?'

'They'll always be looking for her. They don't stop. You
know what she did – what she was a part of.'

'I know.' He said nothing more for a couple of minutes.
But Ash knew there was more to come. 'We could hide her.'

Ash nodded. 'For a day or two. But sooner or later they'd
find her. Someone would notice. Or one of us would say
something – let something slip.'

'Guy,' said Gilbert disdainfully.

Ash managed a thin chuckle. 'Well, maybe. He's the family
chatterbox, isn't he? You and I ration our words as if we'd
paid cash money for them.'

Another pause for thought. 'When she leaves here, where
will she go?'

'I don't know,' Ash said honestly. 'I don't know where she's
come from, and I don't know where she'll go.'

'Dad . . .' A note of supplication had crept into the boy's voice. 'She won't make us go with her, will she?'

Gabriel Ash regarded his first-born and resisted the urge to grab him and hold him tight. 'Over my dead body,' he said.

Gilbert was an intelligent and – for a ten-year-old – literate boy, and he knew what a figure of speech was. And he saw the resolution in his father's eyes, and knew that wasn't one.

Hazel had her phone in her pocket all Monday morning and knew she hadn't missed any calls. She took an early lunch and headed round the corner to Rambles With Books. Clearly something was going on with the Ash household, and she thought she would get to the bottom of it sooner face-to-face than by phoning him.

But the bell jangling on its circular spring as she opened the door brought not Ash but a middle-aged woman in a tweed jacket, who smiled at Hazel's evident confusion. 'Mr Ash couldn't come in today. He asked me to mind the shop.'

Miss Hornblower was one of Ash's most faithful customers; it didn't surprise Hazel that he would ask her to help out, nor that she would agree. She *was* perplexed by the timing. 'When?'

The woman gave her a faintly aggrieved look down her aristocratic nose. 'He phoned me this morning, in fact. Does that matter?'

It did, or at least it might, but Hazel wasn't about to explain. 'He had your number?'

'He looked me up in the phone-book. With a name like mine, I'm not hard to find.'

Hazel wasn't hard to find, either, particularly when her number was usually top of Ash's calls list. If he could call Miss Hornblower, he could have called Hazel as he'd promised.

She gave a slightly forced smile. 'I'm sorry. I'm just a bit puzzled – I've been trying to talk to him since yesterday. I think he must be avoiding me.'

Miss Hornblower had already forgiven Hazel her sharpness. But she still looked concerned. 'He didn't sound entirely himself,' she admitted.

'What did he say?'

'Not very much, only that some sort of family crisis had blown up. I didn't like to quiz him but I said, Nothing serious, I hope, and he said, No, just something he had to deal with. But he did sound anxious. And . . . distracted.'

Ash often seemed distracted. But Miss Hornblower had known him almost as long as Hazel had, she knew that. If she thought he'd seemed troubled, she was probably right.

Hazel thanked her, and left her to the packed lunch she could see laid out on the little kitchen table. In the shop alone, Ash often forgot to eat in the middle of the day. Miss Hornblower had brought smoked salmon, cream cheese and cucumber sandwiches, with the crusts cut off.

A glance at her watch told Hazel there was time enough. She turned up towards the park and, beyond it, to Highfield Road.

She never knew, afterwards, what inspired her to park at the corner instead of where she always did, in front of Ash's house. Perhaps a little bird told her. A bird of ill omen. Feeling foolish even as she did it, she left her car at the corner of Highfield Road and walked the last hundred metres. Or rather, she walked ninety of the last hundred metres.

The big stone house that had been Ash's mother's was built at a time when good workmanship came cheap. The main rooms on both storeys had bay windows. Bay windows illuminate a room wonderfully, and make it possible for those inside to see up and down the street as well as across it. And also for those in the street to see anyone in the embrasure of the window. Hazel stopped dead when she saw two forms cross the window of the master bedroom upstairs. The light was wrong to see much more than the outlines, shapes without detail, but she was as sure as she needed to be of two things. One of the figures was Ash. The other was a woman.

Rooted to the spot, Hazel could not have found words to describe what went through her head then. Astonishment – perhaps more astonishment than she was entitled to. And certainly more outrage than she was entitled to. Ash owed her no fidelity. They were friends – good, close friends – and there had been moments when the possibility of something else had seemed to tread on the heels of that friendship. That it had never been formalised, even by the most tentative of proposals, was due at least as much to her ambivalence as to Ash's.

She'd been too afraid of losing what they had to risk moving the goalposts. She had known – well, believed – that if she'd taken the initiative she could have coaxed a commitment out of him, even if it was contingent on the eventual dissolution of his marriage. The fact that she'd been no more willing than he to make that first move left her on shaky ground as far as a sense of betrayal was concerned.

Yet a sense of betrayal was what she felt. Betrayal, and hurt. Her body rigid, her visible expression carefully neutral, from inside herself she watched with open-mouthed indignation as the two figures moved behind the bedroom window. So the cunning dog had got himself a bit on the side! No wonder he was avoiding her. What offended her most of all wasn't even the fact that, when he'd been ready to move on, it wasn't Hazel he'd been ready to move on with. It was the secrecy, the tacit lies – the hole-in-corner evasions that cheapened both their friendship and this new involvement.

Who was she? Not that it mattered: whoever she was, she had as much reason as Hazel to be upset by Ash's lack of candour. If he'd had the guts to ask Hazel round to Highfield Road and introduce them, she'd have wished them well – regretfully, but in full acknowledgement of his right to a life richer than anything she had come out and offered him. But to turn her away from his door without a word of explanation – to say he'd call her, and then fail to – it was the kind of retreat employed by teenage boys, not grown men! Not a strategic withdrawal but a shifty, shuffling rout. If he finally gave her the glad tidings in a text, nothing on God's earth would prevent her from storming into his shop and feeding him his own entrails.

But for now, she turned quietly on her heel and returned to her car; and didn't slam the door, and didn't drive off in a flurry of grit and exhaust fumes; and didn't have a name for the pain in her heart.

Ash and his wife were arguing. They were doing it in the front bedroom because, rather than risk a careless remark proving infinitely costly, Ash had kept the boys at home today and they were playing in the back garden.

'I'm sorry, Cathy, I'm not going to change my mind about this,' he said – and a part of him was amazed to hear him say it. 'I don't want you here. It isn't safe, for any of us. You, because you'll go to prison if you're found here; me, because I'll be charged with aiding and abetting; and the boys because you've already done your best to break them in pieces, they don't need you kicking those pieces down the wind! I won't stand by and watch you do it.'

'You're over-reacting,' she complained drily, 'as usual. I just want somewhere to stay for a few days: is that really asking so much? You said I could always count on you.'

'That was before you took my sons away and let me think you were all dead! Before you decided I was worth more to you in a straitjacket than as a husband and father. And incidentally, before you shot me!'

'Well . . .' She couldn't deny it. She also couldn't hide the impish little smile. 'All families have their little ups and downs. Look,' she tried again, her tone reasonable, 'I stayed here last night and the sky didn't fall in. It won't fall in if I stay here another few days. I won't go out, I won't answer the door – no one's going to know that I'm here. Even your little friend.'

'I lied to her,' Ash said thickly. 'That's the second time I've lied to her. The first time was for your benefit as well. There isn't going to be a third.'

Cathy sighed. 'Why does everything have to be such a drama with you, Gabriel? Everyone lies sometimes. It's what keeps the world turning. Tell her the boys have come out in spots and you don't want to risk her catching them. That'll keep her at bay for a week. Just, stop looking so god-forsaken guilty! If you go about looking like that, it won't take a detective to figure out that you're hiding something.'

'What have you got yourself involved in this time?' asked Ash in a low voice. 'What can possibly be worth taking such risks?'

She gave a careless shrug. 'There are always risks. Success in life is about risk management.'

He stared at her in disbelief. 'You think you've made a success of your life?'

She looked away from him, deliberately. He followed her gaze down to her hands, palm-down in front of her. She had always liked jewellery. Almost every finger carried a stone of some kind. Ash was no expert, but none of it looked like costume jewellery. Only the plain gold band he'd given her, twelve years ago now, was missing.

He looked back at her, appalled. 'That's how you measure it? By the number of diamonds you own? Cathy – what you did cost you your sons!'

'No, Gabriel,' she said tartly, 'what *you* did cost me my sons. For now. Don't worry, I shan't forget about them. I know where they are. I shall always know where they are. A time will come when what I can offer them will look a lot more interesting than a draughty old house and a second-hand bookshop.'

'When they're old enough to choose, I won't stand in their way. I won't have to. They have values. They're eight and ten years old, and already they know that working for what you want costs less, in the long run, than stealing it from someone else. I'm proud of them. Perhaps you'd find them something of a disappointment. I do hope so.'

That seemed to touch a nerve. It was as if she could deal with the possibility that he hated her – she'd given him reason enough, after all; and she believed that any hatred he was capable of would only ever be a veneer, that underneath it he was still and would always be helplessly in love with her. What she couldn't deal with, could neither accept nor ignore, was being despised. It didn't fit with the image she had of herself. She had come to think of herself as a romantic figure, something between a pirate and a tightrope-walker. It struck at her self-esteem that he saw her as a glorified shoplifter.

'So where do you want me to go?' she demanded nastily. 'The sort of motel where they don't ask for ID and you pay by the hour? How do you suppose I'm going to get there without being seen?'

'The same way you got here without being seen,' growled Ash.

'Friends brought me. The friends who're going to be in as much trouble as I am if I'm picked up. So I don't think setting your mind at rest is going to be top of their priorities, do you?'

Ash breathed heavily at her for a minute. The alternative was to start shouting loudly enough that the boys would hear, even from the back garden. That people would hear him as far away as Whitley Vale.

'All right,' he said eventually. 'Three days. You don't go out, and no one comes here. Then you leave, and you never come back. Do you agree?'

Since it was exactly what she wanted, Cathy had no difficulty agreeing. 'I knew you'd see sense in the end,' she said smugly.

'Three days. If you're still here on Friday, I'll call the police myself.'

THIRTEEN

Through all her adult life, Hazel Best had dealt with reverses at work by seeking consolation with her friends, and vice versa. If her relationship with Ash had foundered on the rocks of time and expectation, there were successes to be had elsewhere. Including one very close to home.

As she left for work on Monday morning, she'd thought Sperrin was looking stronger. She hadn't allowed for the fact that, expecting to see her, he had his game face firmly in place. Coming in unexpectedly at quarter to one, she found him asleep in the living-room armchair, all his defences down, and he looked broken and old. All that had kept him going this far was sheer bloody-minded determination, and now he was paying the price for it.

Seeing him like that, not so much resting as exhausted, his broken arm wedged in the only position that gave him some respite and his face the colour of old concrete, Hazel went through to the kitchen, meaning to make herself a sandwich and leave without disturbing him. But either she made more noise than she intended or some part of his battered brain remained on anchor-watch, because she heard a cough and then his gruff voice saying her name, and she stuck her head back through the door.

'Sorry, I didn't mean to wake you.'

'I wasn't asleep.'

Ash did this too, so did Dave Gorman: you caught them taking forty winks, and they denied something that would have been obvious to a short-sighted man wearing long-sighted glasses. As if there was something reprehensible about sleeping; as if they'd been caught doing something they wouldn't have wanted their mothers to know about.

'Yeah, right,' she said, smiling. 'Do you want a sandwich?'

He shook his head, dark hair tangled from . . . not . . . sleeping. 'I'll have coffee if you're making it.'

It turned out he'd have a sandwich too, if one was available and not nailed down. Hazel let him have it, returned to the kitchen to make another. They munched companionably.

'Do you usually come home for lunch?' asked Sperrin.

'Not usually, no.'

'So?' As if he had a right to some kind of explanation. As if this was his house, and she was the uninvited guest.

Hazel eyed him speculatively. Well, if he wanted to talk . . . 'Why are you here, David?'

His gaze turned mulish. 'You know why.'

'You're expecting to find some answers here. Not at Myrton: here. But why? This is just where the goods train stopped long enough for you to fall off.'

'It's also the nearest town of any size to the reservoir where they dumped the girl's body. Is that a coincidence? Maybe it is. Maybe they set off to follow the train, and that's as far as they got before they lost it. I don't know. I just . . . feel . . . this is where I need to be. That leaving would be too much like giving up.'

'On the mystery?'

'On the girl.'

Hazel pursed her lips. 'Suppose you're right, and these people have some connection to Norbold. That means this isn't the safest place for you now. You witnessed a murder: there could be people here who need to silence you. And they'll know you if they see you, and you won't know them.'

'Maybe I *will* know them. Maybe seeing them will unlock everything.'

'That's possible,' agreed Hazel. 'In which case you're going to feel really pleased with yourself, for as long as it takes one of them to pull a gun. They shot Rose in the back, they're not going to get sentimental about shooting you. Go back to Byrfield. Pete wants you home, and I'd be happier too. I don't like leaving you here alone.'

She half expected that, in the obstinacy born partly of frustration, partly of being who he was, Sperrin would dismiss her concerns: laugh them off. He didn't. He managed a little half-haunted smile. 'I know you're looking out for me, Hazel, and I'm grateful. But I can't walk away from this. It's too big. I can't get on with my life without dealing with this first.'

'We'll deal with it for you,' she promised. 'Meadowvale – CID. It's our job now.'

'But you weren't there, and I was. I need to know what happened. I need to know' – the unbearable possibility – 'if there was something more I could have done.'

'You could have died,' said Hazel simply. 'You still could.'

He thought for a moment before answering her honesty with an honesty of his own. She saw him digging deep for it. It wasn't in his nature to bare his soul. 'You think I haven't thought about that? Of course I have. I'm not stupid. I don't *want* people shooting at me. I'm an archaeologist, for God's sake! – I only venture onto battlefields when I know that all the combatants, on both sides, have been dead for a thousand years. I'm nobody's idea of a hero.

'But that girl thought maybe I could be, just a little bit, just for a moment. The moment that mattered. She thought, if anyone could save her, I could. Well' – his jaw clenched – 'I didn't. Maybe nobody could have. But I don't *know* that. I know I was there, and I know that she died, and I know that I ran. Because she was already beyond any help I could give her? Or because I was too scared to stand my ground and fight for her?'

'Would it be so terrible,' asked Hazel softly, 'if that's what happened? Is it so wicked, to want to live?'

'Wicked?' He seemed to think about it. 'No. It's the common instinct of all living creatures: to stay alive. To do what it takes to survive. But . . .' She could see him struggle to put his feelings into words. 'Everything comes with a price. Every little meanness chips a sliver off your soul. Every petty barter; every squalid little deal you make with fate. Let me succeed: someone else's failure will restore the balance. Let me have respect, my health, the freedom to live as I choose – someone else can put up with being ignored, sick and beaten down.

'And you can do that – maybe we all do it, all the time – because you never get to meet the other half of the equation. The one who drew the short straw. Except this time I did. I met her face to face, closer than you and I are now. And she died, and I lived. And if that was because of a choice I made

– if it was her or me, and I chose me – then the price was too high.'

'David' – Hazel reached a hand out to him – 'how can you say that? You have family, you have friends. It matters to us that you didn't die in that field, on that lonely lane.'

'She had family too. Somewhere. Who don't know that she's dead, and maybe never will know.'

'We'll find them,' she promised. 'We'll find out who she was, and where she came from, and we'll find her family. When we do, it'll be some kind of a comfort to them that at the end there was someone who cared enough to try to help her.'

'If I did.'

'Of course you did,' Hazel said stoutly. 'You could have hunkered down behind the standing stone and no one would have known you were there. We know you didn't do that.' She gave a little pensive frown. 'David, what you said to my boss . . .'

'About what?'

'About him trying harder to find the people who killed her. About thinking you could do a better job yourself.'

Sperrin gave a rough laugh. 'Don't worry, I'm not going to go vigilante on you. I wouldn't know where to start. I was just getting a bit irritated with all the questions. I suppose I mean, with not knowing any of the answers.'

'He is doing his best,' said Hazel. 'My boss. If the inquiry has run out of steam for the moment, it isn't because he isn't trying. He'll go on trying. Any information he gets, he'll follow up. Whether you're here or not.'

'I keep telling you,' gritted Sperrin, 'I'm not leaving. Not until either I have some answers, or it becomes pretty clear I'm never going to get them. I know I'm a thorn in Gorman's side: well, maybe that's the best reason for staying right here. There'll be other cases, easier to solve; there'll even be other murders. But while I'm here, haunting him, your chief inspector won't get the chance to forget about this one. Maybe that's all I'm good for now – to be the burr under the saddle. Well, fine. I can prickle with the best of them.

'And if there's some risk involved in being in Norbold, I'll take it. I owe it to her. I may never know if I let her down before, but damn sure I'm not going to let her down again. Doing that would' – he flicked her the little smile again, exposed and oddly vulnerable – 'finish what the train began.'

He paused, marshalling his thoughts. Hazel held her silence.

'You know about Jamie,' he went on after a moment. 'My mother won't talk to me about him – well, she hardly talks to me at all, but never about him. About the fact that I fired the gun that killed him. Pete says I have nothing to feel guilty about – that no child of five can be blamed for anything, whatever the consequences. You've said the same thing.'

'Of course I have,' murmured Hazel. 'And I'll say it again, any time you need to hear it.'

'I know,' he said. He flicked her the tiny, fleeting smile. 'Thanks. The fact remains, there's a . . . a shadow on my soul because my brother died as a result of something I did. If this girl died because of something I *didn't* do – because I was too scared to help her, or too stupid or too slow – it doesn't actually matter if someone starts taking pot shots at me. Because I don't know how I'd live with history repeating itself like that. I don't think I'd *want* to live with it. That's why I need to know. I need to *know*, not just to hope, there was nothing more I could have done.

'And here – Norbold – is the only place I'm going to find out. Don't ask me how I know that: I just do. Maybe there is a reason, but it's buried along with all the other stuff I've forgotten. Something I saw, something I heard; something that makes sense of everything. Or maybe it's just wishful thinking: I have to believe that the key is here because there's nowhere else I can look. I don't know. I just know there's no point going anywhere else.'

Hazel met his gaze – flayed, desperate – and knew that he was right. He couldn't pick up his life as if nothing had happened until he had the answers he hungered for. If no one could give him those answers, he'd waste his life looking for them: in Norbold, in the bottom of a whisky bottle, in a line of cocaine. He would never break free of the dying grasp of the girl they called Rose. Ultimately her death would consume him.

'All right,' Hazel said, a touch unsteadily. 'So you're staying here. House rules: I need to know where you are. When you're up to going out, don't do it without telling me. I don't want anything to happen to you, David. Anything else.'

His grin was a shadow of its old sardonic self, but it was better than nothing. 'Hazel! I didn't know you cared.'

'I don't,' she sniffed. 'Pete does, and I care about Pete.'

When she'd recognised Sperrin in ICU, Hazel had given her own name as next of kin, partly for convenience and partly because she didn't want the hospital phoning Byrfield to tell him his brother had died before she'd had a chance to prepare him. So it was her number they called when they wanted him back for a check-up. She undertook to take him the following morning.

Predictably, Sperrin was dismissive. 'I'm not spending half a day in Outpatients in order to be poked and prodded and finally told what I know right now, which is that I'm mending just fine. Tell them I'll come in when it's time to get the plaster off.' He brandished his arm at her.

'Another of the house rules that I forgot to mention,' said Hazel calmly, 'is, Don't argue with people who know what you need better than you do. I'll take you in on my way to work. When you're finished, get a taxi straight back here. Don't try to walk it again.'

'I'm fine,' grumbled Sperrin.

'Of course you are. Humour me.'

She fully expected to have the same argument again over breakfast on Tuesday. But by then Sperrin was resigned to doing what was good for him, perhaps in payment for his board and lodgings. Hazel pulled into the hospital car park as the first of the day's appointments were being called.

Still suspicious of his uncharacteristic docility, Hazel wanted to see Sperrin as far as the waiting room, for fear he'd go AWOL once he was out of her sight. They still had ten minutes in hand, so she wasn't concerned when he ground to a halt beside the sweets and magazines kiosk inside the front entrance. 'They won't keep you waiting long enough to need something to read.' She'd clearly inferred from the phone-call that the quicker his medical team could do their duty and get rid of him, the happier they'd be.

He made no reply. When she looked, she saw why not. He was rooted to the spot, staring at a bucket of cut flowers.

'David?'

'China roses,' he said thickly.

These weren't roses either. 'No,' Hazel said, hearing herself sounding like a schoolteacher, 'some of them are chrysanthemums, or possibly dahlias, and those white ones look like Michaelmas daisies . . .' They didn't teach much botany on Police Studies courses either.

'No, *look*,' he insisted.

She did, and still she didn't see what he was seeing. And then she did. The cellophane wrapping each bouquet was printed with the legend 'China Roses'.

'I've seen that before,' said Sperrin. He was breathless, as if someone had punched him. 'Rose wasn't her name. I saw it written down somewhere.'

'China roses?'

He managed to combine a nod with a bewildered shrug. 'China roses.'

She phoned DCI Gorman. By the time she had his full attention and was explaining what had happened, what Sperrin had seen and the effect it had had on him, the revelatory nature of the moment was already slipping from her grasp and she thought he wouldn't understand its significance. But – not for the first time – she'd underestimated him.

Gorman heard her out, only interrupting with a couple of pertinent questions. 'It was the words he recognised, rather than the flowers?' And: 'Could it have been printed on the side of the van? Or maybe as a badge on the men's jackets? Ask him.'

But Sperrin didn't know. He just knew that he'd seen those words somewhere, about the time his world turned inside out. Seeing them again filled him with unexpected terror. It was carved into the lines of his face, intractable as scars, and haunted the hollows of his eyes. It had transfixed him like an arrow from a hundred-pound bow. When Hazel put her hand on his arm he was shaking. She didn't tell Gorman that.

'OK,' said Gorman. 'Stay with him. Have him keep his appointment – if the doctors think he needs any medication, tell them I don't want his head filling with cotton wool. I'll see you in the foyer in twenty minutes.'

He was as good as his word. 'Do we know where those flowers came from?'

Hazel nodded, eyes dipped. 'I'm sorry, Chief, I think I've brought you here on a wild goose chase. China Roses is the florist's in Windham Lane. Everyone refers to it as Mrs Kiang's, but it's actually called China Roses.'

'Good.' He peered at her crestfallen expression. 'Not good?'

'You don't buy a lot of flowers, do you? Mrs Kiang is a tiny, ancient Chinese lady who can't lift her watering can if it's more than half full. I don't think she's the head of an international gang of people traffickers.'

They regarded one another in silence for a few moments. Then Gorman said, 'So where did Sperrin see those words before?'

It was confession time. Hazel had figured it out while she was waiting for her boss to arrive. 'I think that's kind of my fault. When ICU called to say he was waking up, I grabbed some flowers from Mrs Kiang on the way here. They were wrapped in cellophane, with the name of the shop printed on it, just like the ones in the kiosk. It must have been the first thing he saw when he opened his eyes. He mumbled something about roses. I thought nothing of it until he started talking about the girl, then we assumed Rose was her name. But I think he was just reading what it said on the wrapper. Somehow, in his head, the two things got confused – the events at Myrton, and the first thing he saw as he woke up.'

DCI Gorman looked deeply sceptical. 'Is that even possible?'

'We're talking about a brain injury, Chief,' said Hazel wryly. 'According to the experts, there are almost no effects *too* bizarre to be caused by a brain injury.'

'Hm.' Even for a man accustomed to setbacks, his grunt had a ring of finality. 'Do we know if this Mrs Kiang has a van?'

'I'm sure she has. Though I don't know how she reaches the pedals.'

'Go and look at it. Measure the tyres and take some photos – have Sergeant Wilson compare them with the ones he took in Myrton. Maybe we'll get lucky, and it'll be something really rare and distinctive.'

'We're due some luck,' said Hazel diplomatically. In the privacy of her own head, though, she was thinking: Ford Transit, bet you anything.

It was indeed a Transit, seven years old, standard factory issue except that the load bay had been fitted with an aluminium grid to keep the flowers from banging into one another. Apart from the China Roses logo discreetly emblazoned in silver on each side, there was nothing distinctive about the cream paint-job either, and the standard-issue tyres were neither brand new nor worn in significant and identifiable ways. The pedals, Hazel noted with a grin, had extensions fitted.

Tiny, ancient, and by now rather annoyed, Mrs Kiang watched Hazel measure and photograph the Transit, tapping the pavement impatiently with the pointed toe of one red shoe. 'You want to tell me again why Norbold Police are interested in my van?'

'I'm sorry to be a nuisance, Mrs Kiang, but someone reported a van rather like this as having been involved in a crime. We're trying to rule out all the ones it couldn't have been.' It wasn't gospel truth, but it was close enough and it reassured the florist that she wasn't being singled out for harassment.

What it didn't do was mollify her. 'It's a Transit,' Mrs Kiang pointed out irascibly. 'Everybody got one. Half everybody got a cream one. You going to measure them all?'

'If I'm told to,' said Hazel wearily. 'Does anyone else drive it?'

'My Bill, sometime. But flower markets start before dawn, and my husband lazy sod. No get up early enough.'

Hazel smiled. 'You're doing it again.'

The florist gave a puzzled frown. 'Doing what? Oh – Widow Twanky? I'm sorry, dear,' she continued in quite a different accent, 'it becomes a habit after a while. The things you have to do to sell flowers!'

'At least nobody makes you go round measuring people's tyres,' sighed Hazel.

FOURTEEN

Sergeant Wilson compared Hazel's measurements with his own, studying both sets of photographs through a magnifying glass. At length he said, 'You know what I'm going to say, don't you?'

'That it's a very common vehicle? That it's a standard tyre as regards make and size? That the tracks at Myrton weren't clear enough to make a definitive ID?'

Meadowvale's scenes of crime officer gave her an appreciative glance. 'You're getting the hang of this detecting lark, aren't you? Right on all points. Plus, only the nearside tyres went up on the verge, so I can't say how wide the vehicle was. But judging from the impressions of the nearside wheels, and for all the good it'll do you, it could have been a Transit. Without any evidence at all, I'd still have risked a small wager on it being a Transit. They're adaptable, reliable, and everywhere. Have you shown a picture of your van to the witness?'

'I'll take one home tonight. You know he's staying with me? He's an old family friend,' she added, then wondered why she felt the need to explain. 'I'm just not sure how much help it'll be even if he thinks he recognises it. His memories are all scrambled.' She told him about the cellophane wrapper on the flowers she took to the hospital.

'I can see how that would complicate matters,' nodded Sergeant Wilson lugubriously. 'Oh well – if our job was easy, anyone could do it.'

'Can you think of anything else I should be doing? You know – lines of inquiry I should be pursuing?'

'Oh no, you're asking entirely the wrong man about that,' said SOCO, back-pedalling furiously. 'I don't do detecting. I never did do detecting. I gather evidence, analyse it and collate it. Detecting is a whole other ball game.'

Hazel felt a surge of affection for the rotund sergeant – the title his by courtesy only now – a man who had been too slow to be a good beat officer and too amiable to be a good detective, but had found his milieu in the painstaking world of crime scene analysis.

She thought they were finished and was heading for the stairs – SOCO's lair was in the basement at Meadowvale – when he called after her, 'Ask Gabriel Ash. He's a rare hand at thinking outside the box.'

To Hazel's astonishment, it felt exactly as if he'd plunged a knife into her belly.

After she'd put the boys to bed, Frankie Kelly asked to see Ash in his study. He ushered her in; she closed the door behind them. He had a good idea what was coming. He asked her to sit but she remained on her feet. After an awkward moment he lowered himself onto the edge of his desk, which put their heads at approximately the same height.

She began without preamble. 'Mr Ash, the current situation is not tenable.' Perhaps because she was so small, or perhaps because she spoke perfect, classless English as only foreign nationals learn it, she could use words like 'tenable' without sounding pompous. She didn't sound angry either, just resolute. 'Your wife's presence here makes criminals of both you and me.'

'I know,' said Ash miserably. 'And I know it's not fair on you. Do you want to take a few days off? – an extra week's paid holiday, go and visit those friends of yours in the Lake District? Then you won't find yourself having to tell any lies, and by the time you get back the . . . situation . . . will have been resolved.'

Her manner softened at the offer. Though she was employed to take care of the Ash boys, sometimes she forgot that there were only two of them – that the third was forty-two years old, over six foot tall when he stood up straight, and not actually one of her charges at all. But her respect for him had deepened over the last two years to a genuine regard, and it wasn't only concern for her own position that had brought her here. 'I'm not comfortable about leaving you to deal with this alone.'

'It's my job to deal with it,' he said simply. 'No one else

can. I suppose,' he ventured, 'you think I should tell the police?'

'It's no part of *my* job to tell you what you should do,' said Frankie tartly. 'I imagine, if you thought the boys were in any danger, you'd have told them already.'

Ash nodded. 'It occurred to me that you might.'

She considered. 'I wouldn't lie if the police asked me a direct question. I don't think you'd expect me to. But this is your family, Mr Ash, and I don't want to create difficulties for you in order to salve my conscience. Nevertheless, if Mrs Ash stays here much longer, her presence will be noticed. You and I will be able to keep the secret for as long as necessary, but sooner or later one of the boys will make a mistake. Will say something to a friend, that the friend mentions to his parents, that the parents will feel obliged to report to the police.

'She's not a petty criminal, someone whose misdemeanours might be overlooked by a good neighbour. People know what she was involved in, what she did. There would be nothing malicious about someone feeling they had to report her presence here. And she would be in a lot of trouble, and you would be in a lot of trouble, but worse than that, those boys would know that their mother was going to prison because of something they said, a mistake they made. I don't believe you're any more comfortable with that prospect than I am.'

Despair was aging Ash in front of her. 'I don't know what to do. Of course the boys come first. But will they forgive me if I turn her away and they never see her again? Or the police catch up with her because I deny her our home as a refuge? I wish to God she'd never come here, but she did, and I don't know what to do to keep this from blowing up in our faces. But Frankie' – he looked directly at her – 'much as we all think of you as a member of this family, our problems are not your problems, and there's no reason for you to stand in the firing line beside us. Take yourself away for a winter break.' He managed a pale smile. 'Keswick must be charming at this time of year.'

'It is,' agreed Frankie. 'And that would probably keep me safe from any legal repercussions. It would do nothing to help you and the boys.'

'No,' he said. 'But then, what will?'

'Have you talked to Miss Best?'

A wave of guilt and discomfort passed across his face. 'How can I talk to Hazel? She's a police officer. If she knew – if she even suspected – that Cathy was here, her career would be on the line. I can't put that burden on her.'

'No, I suppose not. So what *are* you going to do?'

'What can I do? Apart from trying to keep Cathy out of sight until it suits her to leave, what else can I do?'

But some problems even Frankie Kelly had no answer for.

After she had left him alone, sick with worry, too dizzy to clamber off the endless roundabout of what he could do and what he should do and what he wanted to do and what consequences might follow from each, he felt a cool damp touch on the palm of his hanging hand. Patience was looking up at him with liquid caramel eyes.

This isn't as complicated as you're making it seem. You know what you should do.

He barked a little laugh that was half a sob. 'No, don't spare my feelings – tell me what you really think!'

I think you're putting everyone at risk in order to protect the one person in all this who doesn't deserve it.

'Maybe *you* should phone Dave Gorman and tell him where she is.'

Don't be silly, said Patience severely. You know he wouldn't hear me. Only you hear me.

'That's because you're a dog,' said Ash weakly. 'Just a dog. I only think you're talking because the PTSD never quite went away. What I'm really listening to is the voice of my own conscience.'

That's as good an explanation as any, agreed Patience. Though I'm not sure about the *JUST a dog* bit.

Ash gave a frayed smile and stroked her head, which – dog or conscience – she had always liked. She leaned into his hand. 'You're right,' he said. 'I know what I should do. But how can I do it? How can I send my sons' mother to prison?'

She tried to kill you.

'I haven't forgotten.'

Have you forgiven?

'No, not that either. But . . . I don't need vengeance. I have everything I need – my children, our home, my shop, my friends, you. The problem is, I'm not sure I can keep them all. I genuinely don't care what happens to Cathy now, but I do care passionately about my relationship with my sons. But if I help her for their sake, I'm going to lose Hazel and probably Frankie too. Or I could go to prison, and lose them all.'

Yes, you could. That should make the decision easier, not harder.

Ash searched through his pockets until he found his mobile phone. He offered it to her.

I'm just a dog, remember? said Patience. No opposable thumbs. If you want someone to make the call, it'll have to be you.

The study door opened again – no knock – and it was Cathy. 'Talking to yourself again, Gabriel? You do know that's not a good sign?'

Ten o'clock on Wednesday morning, and Hazel *did* knock on DCI Gorman's door before she went in to update him on her progress; or rather, the lack of it. He didn't seem surprised.

'This is the reality of CID,' he said resignedly, 'as distinct from the mythology. We have a clear-up rate, nationally, of a little under eight per cent – i.e., twelve crimes go unsolved for every one that results in a conviction. OK, we do better with major crimes than minor ones – complain that someone's half-inched the hedge-cutters out of your garden shed and it'll figure in the statistics even though we know, and you know, and the guy who nicked the hedge-cutters knows, that we haven't the manpower to chase him down. But we're still running at twelve-to-one against, and not many races are won at those kinds of odds.'

'This isn't petty theft,' said Hazel, quietly rebellious. 'It's murder, and it may be modern slavery. That girl crossed two continents in search of a better life, and someone shot her in the back and dumped her in a reservoir. If we can't pull out all the stops for her, who can we pull them out for?'

'We don't even know who she is, or where she came from. And I don't know how to set about finding out.'

'David says she came from Vietnam.'

'Which is a country,' Gorman pointed out, 'not a village. Go stand in the middle of Hanoi and shout, "Anybody here know a Rose?" and see how far it gets you.'

Hazel gave a demure smile. 'We could try that. Or we could try stable isotope analysis.'

Gorman stared as if she'd grown an extra head. 'What?'

'We did it before,' she reminded him. 'To prove that Gabriel's sons hadn't been held hostage in Africa at all but had in fact been living in Cambridge. It was David Sperrin who put me onto it: it's a technique they use in archaeology. They use teeth, but we used samples of the boys' hair. It all comes down to the ratio between – between – don't tell me, I'll have it in a minute – between strontium and oxygen in the drinking water. Or something like that.'

Now Gorman remembered. He'd had to sign the chit. Hazel had had to spell out some of the words for him, and she'd had to look them up in a dictionary. 'But what's that going to tell us that we don't already know? Is the drinking water different in different parts of Vietnam? Even if it is, how much will it narrow down the search?'

Now she thought about it, Hazel wasn't sure either. 'Maybe it won't,' she said, deflated.

'Maybe it's worth doing anyway,' said Gorman, more to encourage her than out of any real hope. 'The poor kid's not going to miss a bit of hair or even a tooth, is she? And it'll be another piece in the jigsaw. She's probably got family somewhere, and any time now they'll start wondering what's happened to her. If they get worried enough to report her missing, we might be able to make contact. If we can't find her killers, we should at least try to find her family, let them know that she won't be phoning home. I'll do the paperwork, you go back to the morgue and explain what we need.'

'Thanks,' said Hazel; and after a moment, 'It's not easy, is it?'

'What isn't?'

'Being a detective. Knowing you're the last best hope for a bunch of desperate people, and that you've only got one chance in twelve of giving them what they need.'

DCI Gorman gave a sombre smile. 'No, it isn't. But it is important. Sometimes, even when we're not successful, we find the answers to some questions. Sometimes, that's the best people can hope for.'

Hazel rather liked the morgue. Compared to the rest of the hospital, it was an oasis of calm: no drunks to be evicted, no children to be dodged, no one throwing up in the waste-paper basket. She had no problems with dead people. Sometimes, particularly if the police had got involved, their stories were sad ones, but their sufferings were over. They were at peace, a peace which permeated the whole department.

Her only reservation about the morgue was the people who worked there. It might not be an official career path for medicos whose bedside manner gave cause for concern, but pathology departments always ended up with more than their fair share of characters.

Dr Fitzgerald was a case in point. Like Sergeant Wilson, he hadn't really the figure for his working clothes, in his case a set of one-size-doesn't-fit-anyone theatre scrubs. His fondness for highly coloured waistcoats and bow-ties, often visible through his plastic apron, rendered the already memorable unforgettable. He referred to the cadavers as his clients, and kept them entertained by humming pieces more usually rendered by a full orchestra.

He studied Gorman's request, grasping the import without further explanation. 'Ah. Yes. You want me to do a bit of ad hoc dentistry on Rose Doe.'

'If we can figure out where she came from, we may be able to find her family. They deserve to know what happened to her.'

'Of course they do. She'd want them to.' Humming portentously – Hazel was no opera buff but she thought it was that football thing from *Turandot* – he went directly to the girl's cabinet and slid her out. 'You might not want to watch this bit.'

'If she can put up with it, I can,' muttered Hazel.

The chosen molar extracted, Dr Fitzgerald returned Rose to her cool-box and moved over to his bench. He glanced up as he worked. 'Any progress finding these bastards?'

'Not that you'd notice,' admitted Hazel. 'Our star witness is still suffering from amnesia.'

'Take the scunner down a back alley and kick him a few times,' advised the poster-boy for the caring professions.

'No, really,' said Hazel, smothering a grin. 'Head injury. Bits keep trickling back, but there's no consistency, and we're not sure which are proper memories and which are bad dreams.'

'Ah, well, that's a bit different,' admitted Walter Fitzgerald. 'Pity, really. It's surprising how many amnesias can be cured by a good kicking. And these bastards need finding.'

Hazel nodded. 'Yes, they do.'

'Did you see her knees?'

'Her knees?'

'It was in my report,' he said reproachfully. 'The marks on her knees.'

'What kind of marks?'

The pathologist gave a cumbrous shrug. 'Circular bruising round both knees. I'm guessing they used hobbles to restrain her.'

Nodding, he returned to the cabinets, slid Rose out again and slipped the sheet up from her feet. 'See? Not very thick – about a centimetre – but it caused both bruising and abrasion. Depending on the length of the chain, she'd have been able to walk but not to run.'

'She was able to run when our witness met her. That's why she was shot, because she was running away.'

'They'd taken the hobbles off, then, or else she'd found a way of getting them off.' He put the sheet back, smoothing it around the girl's feet. 'There you are, pet – sorry to disturb you.' He closed the cabinet, waved a hand towards the bench. 'I'll get these off to the lab. Get the results in a couple of days, maybe.'

Hazel was still puzzling over the circular bruises. 'What was she wearing?'

'When I got her? Not even a smile. Why?'

She didn't answer him, spent the drive back into town crystallising her ideas and then took them up with DCI Gorman.

'I've been wondering why they'd tie her knees instead of

her ankles. Maybe it's because hobbling her knees wouldn't be obvious if she was wearing a long skirt. Which might suggest that, at some point in her journey, she was in plain sight. If people realised she was being restrained they'd have done something about it.'

Dave Gorman nodded slowly. 'It could mean that, yes. So maybe she wasn't landed on a bit of east coast shingle at the dead of night, but came through a commercial port or airport like an ordinary traveller. Which would mean having some kind of papers. They wouldn't have to be top-quality ones to get her off, say, a container ship docked at Tilbury, under the guise of captain's stewardess or crew cook or something, but they'd have to pass at least a cursory inspection.'

'It also means she was no longer an illegal immigrant, she was already a prisoner.'

'Looks that way.' Gorman considered a moment. 'That's a good bit of thinking, Hazel. I read that PM report, saw Fitzgerald had noted bruising on her knees. I didn't spot the significance.'

If Hazel had been a cat she'd have purred. 'To be fair, Dr Fitzgerald drew my attention to it. I didn't have to wade through the whole report.'

'Still, good work.'

Emboldened by her success, she ventured another theory. 'She was found naked.'

'Yes.'

'Is that how she went into the dam?'

'Probably. It's a reservoir – well, it was: it isn't used any more – there isn't much current to pull at her clothes.'

'She wasn't naked when David saw her.'

'*That* he'd have remembered,' agreed the DCI.

'So they stripped her after she was shot and before they disposed of her body. Not a pleasant task: they must have had a good reason.'

'People's clothes can identify them,' said Gorman. 'Not just the contents of their pockets – the labels on their underwear as well. Can suggest at least the general locality they came from.'

'I doubt if the entire wardrobe of the average illegal

immigrant contains a single traceable item,' murmured Hazel.
'If the traffickers thought she was worth stripping, that may
mean her clothes *were* distinctive. Not a cheap mass-market
T-shirt but something that could be traced. To one manufacturer
or one city. Conceivably, to one shop.'

The DCI was listening carefully. 'How does that help?'

'Maybe it doesn't,' admitted Hazel. 'Except that it confirms
what we thought: she wasn't trying to escape from poverty.
She was from a successful family, people who could afford
expensive things. They didn't wave her off expecting never to
hear from her again. They thought she had a good job waiting.'

'So when they realise she's missing, they may have enough
clout to get their concerns listened to,' said Gorman. 'If we
can't find them, maybe they'll find us.'

'What are we going to tell them? That their daughter died
with a bullet in her back because the people who promised
her a good job in England made a slave of her before she ever
landed here?'

'No,' said Gorman gruffly. 'We're going to tell them that we
found the bastards, and they're going to pay. For what they did
to Rose, and God knows how many other girls just like her.'

'Not just like her. The others submitted to their fate and
never found a way of letting us know what was happening to
them. But Rose was brave enough to take them on. Her death
should count for something.'

'It will,' promised Gorman. 'I meant what I said. We will
find these bastards, and we'll find them in time to give Rose's
parents a little consolation when we have to break the news
to them.'

'How?'

'Right now I have absolutely no idea,' he said honestly.
'But we will. We must.' He peered at her. 'You're the one
with the bright ideas. How would you find them?'

Put on the spot like that, Hazel quailed and then rallied.
'The two biggest markets for girls trafficked into Europe are
as prostitutes and domestic servants. We should talk to people
involved in both trades.'

'If our girl was so insistent that she wasn't Chinese,'
suggested Gorman, 'maybe it's because there were other girls

in that van who *were*. Maybe the traffickers specialise in Chinese immigrants. Can we narrow the search down to people who employ Chinese girls specifically?'

'I'll get onto it,' said Hazel.

Gorman hid a smile. Her enthusiasm reminded him of him at the same stage in his career. 'You make a start on the domestic service side. I'll get Tom Presley to look into the prostitution scene.'

She blinked, disappointed. 'Why?'

'Because the people farming these girls out will believe that you're interested in employing a Chinese maid. And they might believe that he's looking for a Chinese prostitute. Other way round? – not so credible. Horses for courses, Hazel,' he said. 'Horses for courses.'

Perhaps he was right. But privately Hazel doubted if she fitted the profile of an employer of domestic servants either. She was the wrong age, the wrong social class, and a brief glance at her hands would have confirmed that she was accustomed to doing pretty much whatever needed doing herself.

On the other hand, she did know someone who could tell her first-hand about the employment of Asian women by English families. She glanced at her watch. Ash would be at the shop: there was no likelihood of bumping into him if she called on Frankie Kelly.

If he hadn't had to part with his car, or had shown more urgency about acquiring a new one, she would have been forewarned by its presence in his drive. As it was, the first she knew that Ash was at home was when he answered her knock at his door.

It was hard to say which of them was the more surprised. They gaped at one another for a moment, each for their different reasons discomfited. Hazel recovered first, and cleared her throat.

'Sorry, Gabriel, it wasn't actually you I was looking for. Is Frankie in?'

At least he could answer that honestly. 'I'm afraid not. She's visiting some friends in the Lake District for a few days. The boys have gone with her.'

Hazel went on regarding him speculatively for just a little longer than was polite. What she was thinking was: You risked your life to get them back. Now, because you've got a new little friend to play with, they're in the way. Well, damn you, Gabriel Ash.

What she said was, 'Isn't it a bit early for school to have broken up for Christmas?'

Her tone was carefully neutral – practice with her tutor Sergeant Mole had brought this fundamental police skill to a high pitch of perfection – but Ash heard the disapproval in it anyway. It brought a faint dark flush to his cheeks. 'Is it anything I can help with?'

'I'm sure you're busy,' said Hazel, holding his eye with her own. 'Plus, you're not a nanny from the Philippines.'

He tried a hint of gentle humour. 'I can't keep anything from you, can I?'

She didn't even smile. 'Oh, I wouldn't say that, Gabriel.'

If she had stood on his doorstep for half a minute longer he would have broken down, dragged her inside, made a full confession and thrown himself on her mercy, accepting whatever the consequences might be. But she didn't. She gave him a crisp little nod, more dismissal than farewell, and headed back to her car.

If she had known what she was doing to him – what he was doing to himself – she wouldn't have left him standing there in his own doorway, bereft as a priest who has lost God. But she didn't, and she did, and she even rather enjoyed doing.

FIFTEEN

Deprived of one source of background information, Hazel hunted around for another. Not for the facts and figures about human trafficking, which were a matter of record somewhere within the great interactive police estate and which could all be accessed by someone with a command of information technology. She would do that as well, probably from the comfort of her own sofa this evening.

What she wanted now was some insight into the immigrant's world. How it felt to be so far out on your national limb that you'd actually fallen off and landed in someone else's long grass. The stresses and vulnerabilities of living in a foreign country, and how those pressures reinforced the ties with fellow exiles. She'd hoped Frankie Kelly could give her a glimpse into a society within a society which knocking on doors and showing her warrant card would not.

In truth, she had no idea how a greater understanding of the social structure of Norbold's Asian community would help in the search for Rose Doe's killers. Perhaps it wouldn't help at all. The girl hadn't died here. She might have been coming here, but there was no real evidence that she was. Norbold was on a fairly direct route from Myrton to either Coventry or Birmingham, both large cosmopolitan cities. Norbold had a long-established Chinese community, and Hazel was on friendly terms with several of its members. But the information she wanted was fairly specific. She doubted, for instance, that Elizabeth Lim, the faintly patrician head of Norbold Quays High School, could give her much insight into the world of domestic service. Horses for courses, as DCI Gorman had said.

Frankie Kelly wasn't a domestic servant either; nor was she Chinese. But as a professional nanny working in the area for fifteen years she would probably have known several Asian girls employed in local households, as nannies themselves or in other capacities. Now Hazel wished she'd remained on Ash's doorstep long enough to ask for Frankie's phone-number. She'd been too startled to think quickly enough. But she could have quizzed the nanny as effectively on the phone as in person, and she was probably going to have to call Ash to get her number. The prospect annoyed her.

Before she did that, though, she thought she'd try another member of Norbold's Asian community she knew well enough to chat with. Admittedly, Mrs Kiang had been born and bred locally, and when not selling flowers spoke with as broad a Midlands accent as anyone on the terraces of Norbold Tanners Football Club. (The name derived from the town's once-strong, now virtually defunct leather industry. So did the club's slogan, 'Never Say Dye'.) Just how great a connection she felt to more recent arrivals from her ancestral homeland Hazel would only learn by asking her. It would mean buying some more flowers, but they would cheer her up in this dark spell, of the year and of the spirit.

Mrs Kiang was alone in the shop, using her quiet time to make up some bouquets. Hazel watched admiringly as her deft fingers selected the stems for height, colour and foliage, and wrapped around each the cellophane sleeve with its subtle silver logo.

'I call them Apology Bouquets,' explained the florist. 'Not too big, not too expensive, just right for men to pick up on their way home if they've forgotten their anniversary or not noticed their wife's new hairstyle. The big orders – weddings, funerals, milestone family celebrations – pay the mortgage. Apology Bouquets put food on the table every day.'

'I'm going to need a couple of them,' said Hazel. She explained her mission. 'It's probably a long shot. I want to talk to people in the local Chinese community who came here to work as housekeepers, nannies and so on. I hoped you could point me in the right direction.'

She saw suspicion in Mrs Kiang's gaze and hurried to reassure her. 'I'm not looking for illegal immigrants – really I'm not. We're trying to solve the murder of a girl we think was trafficked here. We're trying to make sure that what happened to her doesn't happen again – that however they get here, with or without the right paperwork, these girls are going to be safe in this country. They're not criminals, they're victims. I'm not asking you to betray any confidences. I'm just trying to help some abused and frightened girls who're a long way from home.'

The florist thought about that for some time, her fingers continuing to work on autopilot. Finally she gave a fractional nod. 'I can't tell you much. As you know, I was born here – I never was an immigrant. But you hear things. Things that happened to a friend of a friend; to someone's neighbour's niece. We can talk about them, if you want.'

A man in his mid-thirties came in. Apology Bouquet, thought Hazel, relishing her new knowledge, and so it proved. He picked a bunch out of the bucket without, so far as she could see, looking at anything but the price tag, paid for them and left. There were no other customers, so Mrs Kiang made tea in a kitchen even tinier than the one behind Ash's shop.

Hazel sniffed the scented steam rising from her cup and nodded appreciatively. 'Lapsang souchong?'

'Is it? It was on offer at Tesco,' said Mrs Kiang absently.

'The first thing you need to understand about these girls,' she went on after a minute's reflection, 'is that they're not refugees. They're not even economic migrants. They've fallen for a scam. They're mostly educated girls from decent families, who answer a newspaper advert – or these days, a post on-line – offering them the chance of a career in Europe. Foreign travel was so difficult in China for so long that now anyone who can afford it wants to see a bit of the world. If they can earn while they travel, so much the better. The advertisements say that English families – and French families, and German families, and Swedish families – are seeking au pairs and nannies and housekeepers, and offering good wages and excellent terms of employment including use of a car and holidays with the family. More travel, you see. Very attractive to Chinese girls.

'Maybe you think they're naive. But there's nothing suspicious about these adverts. They appear in respectable newspapers and they seem perfectly genuine. Real jobs with real European families will be advertised the exact same way.

The girls probably have school-friends who answered them and are having a wonderful time. They have no reason to doubt that these agencies will do what they say they'll do: vet the families, agree wages and conditions with them, arrange work permits and provide transport. All the girls have to do is pay an upfront fee as an earnest of good faith – the employers will pay most of their travel expenses – pack a bag, and meet at a given railway station at a given time. Everything else will be done for them.'

She sighed. 'Only of course, somewhere on the journey the story changes. Once they're safely out of China, where they speak the language and can turn to any state official for help, they find themselves being treated less and less like clients and more and more like product. The Cathay Pacific flights they were promised turn into a bunk on a flag-of-convenience freighter. The bag they packed doesn't contain enough for a month's sea voyage, but the traffickers sell them what they need, at a price. If they haven't got the money, there are other ways of paying. They end up owing more than they'd have earned even if the jobs had been proper ones, paying proper wages.

'When the freighter finally docks, they're landed in a country they don't even know the name of and herded onto lorries for the last dash across Europe. It may be days before they see the sky again. If they're lucky, somewhere along the road the Greek or Italian or French police may stop the lorry and repatriate them. They might get home hungry, penniless and ashamed, but they will at least get home. The unlucky ones will reach their destination.'

'I take it there are no eager families waiting for them to arrive,' murmured Hazel.

'Not for these girls, no,' said Mrs Kiang. 'Some of them will find themselves working in private houses, more as skivvies than servants – poverty wages, minimal time off, no foreign holidays, no car. Some of them will be directed to sweatshop labour in small factories on nameless industrial estates, living in houses that have been or should be condemned, paying everything they earn for the privilege. And some of them – the pretty ones, the ones with nice manners and soft hands – will be bought by pimps and brothels.'

'Can't they get away? Are they under constant guard? Don't they know we'd help them if we knew?'

'They are guarded,' said the florist, 'quite closely at first. That's when they still have the strength and spirit to want to escape. Later they're just too tired, too beaten down. And then, you see, they've been told that the police are looking for them. Not to help but to punish them. Miserable as their lives are, they're afraid of something worse. They no longer try to escape. They try to stay out of sight.'

'Mrs Kiang,' said Hazel, appalled, 'how do you know all this?'

The woman looked at her levelly. 'Detective Constable Best,' she said, 'how come you don't?'

There was a phone-call. Cathy took it into the kitchen, dismissing Ash with a smile, and closed the door between them.

He knew then, if he hadn't known before, that whatever had brought her here had nothing to do with affection, for himself or for old times, had nothing to do with the still unresolved situation between them. She wasn't in Norbold to seek any kind of forgiveness, or understanding. The decision he'd agonised over for two years, whether to end their marriage, was a matter of no consequence to her. She had other irons in the fire, was using him as a windbreak while she tended them. That was all he had ever been to her: a useful shelter from life's inconveniences. From having to be careful with money, from anxiety about the mortgage, from wearing last year's clothes when this year's were so much more becoming. She had used him, always, and she was using him still.

He opened the kitchen door, just had time to register her look of surprise, took the phone from her hand – the call still unfinished – dropped it onto the quarry-tile floor and crushed his heel down on it. He said quietly, 'I want you out of this house tonight.'

All the way home, Mrs Kiang's words haunted Hazel. She should have known. None of this was occult information: human trafficking was a criminal enterprise, and that made it

CID business. No doubt efforts were being made to eradicate it, and no doubt they were difficult and only intermittently successful. Was that why it wasn't top of Division's to-do list? Why it wasn't the subject of fierce debate at every table in the Meadowvale canteen? Or was the reason that the victims of this crime were not blue-eyed blondes but golden-skinned girls with black hair and dark eyes?

Hazel knew there had been occasions in the not-too-distant past when British police had been judged guilty of institutional racism. She believed – she hoped – no one would have applied the description to her. Of those she worked with, some were better officers, and better human beings, than others, and some probably shouldn't have been police officers at all because they didn't like people, any people, enough. The disrespect, overt or tacit, with which they treated members of the black and ethnic minorities was routinely evident in their dealings with the white community as well. At least those officers who harboured racist views now kept them largely to themselves instead of parading them for general approval. The best legal system in the world can't police what goes on in people's heads. Sometimes you have to settle for controlling outward manifestations, in the belief that weeds will die if you cut off their access to the sun.

But if some individuals still got it wrong, the law got it right. It made no distinction between citizens of different ethnicities. Nowhere did it say it was a lesser offence to victimise people whose appearance and antecedents differed from those of the law-makers. So why was this vile trade being tolerated by the authorities? Perhaps, Hazel thought, for the simplest of reasons: because their best efforts weren't good enough. Perhaps it was like asking why the National Health Service tolerated the common cold. The answer was, Because it defied every attempt to do anything else. One reason trafficking was so difficult to tackle was that all the parties to it wanted to keep it secret. The traffickers did, the girls' employers did, even the girls themselves did, told and believing that discovery would only make their situation worse.

Rose hadn't succumbed to the brainwashing. Rose had recognised the trap she'd stumbled into and known that her only hope lay in alerting the authorities in this cold, damp, distant land. She'd seen the least scruple of a chance in a wind-blown archaeologist peering at a standing stone in the middle of a field, and risked everything on the possibility that he would help her.

And she'd lost. Her courage and determination had won her not freedom but the coldest, dampest end imaginable, and she would never know if her sacrifice had been of value or not. If she'd died for nothing, or set in motion events that would finally confound her abusers.

Hazel found that she wanted, more than she'd wanted anything in a long time, that Rose Doe's death would not have been in vain.

Before she was a police officer, Hazel was a teacher. Her subject was information technology, so she knew her way around the shadowy corners of the worldwide web. After supper – David Sperrin had finally made a contribution to the catering arrangements: she got home to find he'd been to the chippy – she began to do a little research.

Her first thought was to go straight to the dark web, where surely anyone engaged in human trafficking would have their presence. But then it occurred to her that, in the area of domestic service at least, the potential employers didn't see themselves as criminals. They just thought they were being smart, getting their help cut-price and under the counter, and would have resented deeply any suggestion that they were effectively bidding for slaves. Such people clearly had money and property, might well be pillars of their communities, and would probably never find their way to the dark web.

Instead she concentrated her efforts on advertisements that anyone could see. There were more agencies in the domestic service sector than she would have expected in these egalitarian days. There were even a couple in the Norbold area, and she made a note of the contact details. But there was nothing to indicate any kind of hidden agenda – nothing calculated to attract clients looking for special arrangements. No one offered a tariff of girls from different parts of the world.

As the hour grew late and her focus began to slip, on a whim Hazel ran a search for those words that had so unsettled

Sperrin. She still thought the likeliest explanation was that the branding on the flowers she'd taken him had slid under his guard at a vulnerable moment. But just because Mrs Kiang called her shop China Roses didn't mean no one else used the name. And she was surprised again by the sheer range of enterprises which identified themselves that way, from a producer of hand-painted porcelain in Nottingham to the operator of narrowboat holidays on the Grand Union Canal.

Finally she found an advertisement that sent a tiny frisson of recognition up her spine. It wasn't offering staff to clean your house, walk your dog, do your shopping and serve the drinks at your cocktail parties. It was, she thought, offering Asian prostitutes.

It didn't, of course, say so in as many words. It was still in a place anyone could see it, and left an e-mail address anyone could respond to. But she didn't know what else would be meant by:

China Roses
Beautiful girls fresh from Asia
skilled in the ancient arts of the Mystic East.
Qualified masseuses and expert practitioners in many
physical therapies.
Discretion guaranteed.

She had not forgotten DCI Gorman's injunction to concentrate on the domestic side while Tom Presley explored the market for imported totty. Hazel justified herself on the grounds that she was sitting on her own sofa in her own house, on her own time, using her own computer to surf the internet for background information. She couldn't see how anyone could object to that, or how it could conceivably interfere with the detective sergeant's inquiries.

Also, the first point of contact was an e-mail address. Anyone can be anyone in an e-mail.

Hazel amused herself by adopting the mindset of a twenty-three-year-old under-manager in a call centre, a bit of money in his pockets for the first time, moved from his parents' house into a small flat on the fringes of trendy downtown Coventry, swapped his old banger for a hatchback with go-faster stripes, everything on the up except he'd suddenly realised that he had no friends. No girlfriend, and no male friends who could help him find one. So here he was, sitting on his white leather recliner, under his glitter-ball lampshade, trawling the internet in search of . . . Well, yes: an expert in many physical therapies.

She acquired an e-mail address for him – *HotRod* seemed a likely enough tag – and carefully crafted his response. *Mystic arts sounds cool. Could do with a massage. Me in Coventry – where you? Please send photo.*

She hesitated a moment, trying to work an *Innit?* in somewhere; then decided it was a cliché too far. If she wanted the recipient to believe in this call-centre under-manager as a potential client, she'd better not turn him into a caricature. The e-mail would do well enough as it was. She'd hit *Send* almost before she'd decided to.

SIXTEEN

'Well, that was stupid,' said Cathy calmly. 'You want me to go, so you destroy my access to someone who can take me somewhere else? You just don't think things through, do you, Gabriel?'

'I'll call you a taxi,' he said thickly.

'To go where? You know I can't take commercial flights. Anyone would think you wanted to see me arrested.'

'How did you get here?'

Incredulity made her laugh out loud. 'I'm not telling you that! So you can call your little friend in the bowler hat? Whatever do you take me for?'

'I don't think you want me to answer that.' Ash's voice was low.

For just a moment Cathy seemed to see herself in the mirror of his gaze and find the image not to her liking. But the moment passed and her old self-possession returned. 'Idiot boy, you'll have to help me now.'

'Help you do what?' He didn't want to know. He couldn't not ask.

'Evade the long arm of the law,' she replied theatrically, with a flourish of her hand. She had always had very eloquent hands, long and graceful. If you could ignore the blood on them.

'Tell me what you want me to do.'

She favoured him with a speculative half-smile while she considered. 'First, you can give me your phone while I try my SIM in it.' She bent and raked up the remains with her fingers. 'No, wait – no point.' When she extracted the little card from the plastic detritus it was cracked in half. 'So, Plan B.'

'Which is?'

She was still watching him with that half-smile, weighing him up, wondering how far she could push him. 'There's a place where I can get help. Organise transport, make contact with my friends. I need taking there.'

'I already said, I'll get you a taxi.'

She shook her head. The auburn hair danced on her shoulders. 'Taxi drivers talk. They have their licences to consider, and if someone produces a warrant card and asks where they took a fare, they'll remember and they'll tell. You wouldn't. Would you, Gabriel?'

It wasn't a rhetorical question: she waited for an answer. She wanted him to say it, to commit. She knew how hard he found it to break his word.

'I don't have a car,' he said, which was accurate if disingenuous. He was prevaricating, and both of them knew it.

'Well, do you know,' said Cathy easily, 'I don't think that's an insuperable problem. There are these places you can go to, and you show them your driving licence and give them some money, and they'll rent you a car for a day or two.'

'A day or two?' He stared at her.

'Actually, a few hours would be long enough. What do you think, Gabriel? Is it worth a bit of trouble to be rid of me?' She had her head on one side, amusement dancing in her eyes.

He gritted his teeth. 'What about the divorce?'

Cathy's smile broadened. 'Ah – so now we're getting down to the small print. That's a good sign. Do you have the papers?'

They were with his solicitor. Ash silently cursed himself for not having them at his fingertips. 'I can get them first thing tomorrow.'

'Tomorrow. Well, clearly I can't both leave your house tonight and sign your divorce petition tomorrow. Which matters most to you?'

The Ash family, mother and son, had been good clients of Lucas, Lucas & Boyne for many years. Ash knew where Jim Boyne lived, and would have thrown stones at his bedroom window and made him fetch the papers from his office in the small hours of the morning, but for one thing. It was so uncharacteristic a way for Gabriel Ash to behave that Boyne would know exactly what it meant: that his client was in immediate contact with his wife. Client privilege would prevent him from reporting his suspicions, but Ash was ashamed of the position in which he found himself and didn't want anyone knowing. He wanted to get Cathy away from Norbold without anyone knowing she'd ever been here. If it came to a straight choice, having his wife under his roof another night was marginally the more attractive option.

'Very well,' he said curtly. 'I'll hire a car in the morning, get the papers from the solicitor, and when you've signed them I'll take you wherever it is you need to go. And that is the last we'll see of one another. You do understand that? We're not doing this again. You stay out of my life. And you stay out of the boys' lives until they're old enough to make their own choices. Agreed?'

'If you like,' said Cathy; but she said it with a lilt of ambivalence that entirely failed to reassure.

It made no difference. Either Ash did as she asked or he didn't. If he didn't, he was stuck with her until either she chose to leave or he gave her up to the police. And if he did, he'd have to devise a credible explanation for how he got the divorce papers signed. Some cock-and-bull story about a friend bumping into Cathy in . . . in . . . somewhere Britain had no extradition treaty with . . . God, it would sound so feeble! And Ash had no talent for lying. He'd have to trust to the fact that Dave Gorman knew he had contacts in national security, and probably wouldn't ask too many searching questions.

'So where are we going?' he asked.

'I'll tell you tomorrow,' said Cathy.

'Is there anything to drink in the house?'

'Hm?' Hazel looked up vaguely from her screen. 'Oh – yes. There should be something in the fridge.'

Sperrin regarded her bitterly. 'There's a couple of bottles of *shandy* in the fridge.' If he'd found a flask of virgin's blood with an eyeball bobbing in it, he could hardly have sounded more disgusted. 'I'm looking for something to *drink*.'

'I'm sure you're not supposed to drink alcohol after a head injury,' she said primly; and then, relenting, 'Oh all right, I'll nip round to the off-licence. What do you want – beer?'

'They say brandy's medicinal,' suggested Sperrin hopefully.

'They do say that, don't they?' nodded Hazel. 'And when it's you going to the off-licence, you can buy as much brandy as you can afford. Since it's me, you can have beer. *One* bottle of beer. And if it makes your brain leak out of your ear during the night, don't wake me to complain about it.'

She left her laptop on the coffee table, pulled on a coat, pocketed her purse and went out. The off-licence was just round the corner: she didn't take the car because it would be as quick to walk.

In the event, it wasn't the walk which took the time, or buying the beer, it was listening to the licensee's complaints about supermarkets stealing his trade. She kept saying, 'Joe, it isn't a police matter, it's the council that grants liquor licences,' but he was not a man to be cut off in mid-tirade and he went on reiterating his grievance until she was reduced to backing out of the off-licence door with the bag containing her purchases held between them like a shield.

So what should have taken five minutes actually took nearly twenty. She expected Sperrin to be waiting at the front door with the bottle-opener, was surprised and slightly annoyed to find he'd given up altogether and gone to bed. She took one of the beers herself and returned to her laptop; and only the possibility that she might be called out in the middle of the night stopped her from drinking Sperrin's share as well.

While she'd been out, her e-mail had been answered. Hazel almost didn't notice, because the new HotRod account had unaccountably marked it as read; but as soon as she opened it she felt a thrill of anticipation. It was an invitation to do business, and a phone-number.

Hazel Best had been a police officer for four years and if she'd ever expected the job to be easy, she didn't any longer. She knew that the number would belong to a pay-as-you-go account with no name attached to it, the phone cheap enough to be dumped the moment it attracted the wrong kind of attention. But until then it could be traced by the GPS signal it exchanged with its service provider, so that its location could be determined even if its ownership could not.

She toyed with the idea of calling Gorman at home. There would be procedural hoops to jump through, and a better chance of finding the phone while it was still in the hands of the advertisers if he started immediately. On the downside, it would mean explaining to him why she'd ignored his instruction to leave this aspect of the inquiry to DS Presley.

On the whole, she decided the matter would wait until morning. She made a mug of chocolate and took it up to bed, murmuring 'Good night' at Sperrin's bedroom door, softly in case he was already asleep. Perhaps he was, because there was no reply.

She slept well and woke early, meaning to be at work by eight. Gorman was habitually at his desk by then, and she wanted to see him before the cares of the day fell on his head like an avalanche. She hoped he'd be impressed by what she'd done. But she knew she'd owe Tom Presley an apology.

So she wasn't surprised that David Sperrin failed to show his face at the breakfast table. In fact, the breakfast table was no more than a pot of strong coffee and a stack of toast, eaten on her knee in the living room while she checked the laptop for any more e-mails. There were none, not for her and not for Rod.

She might have gone straight out then, and not expected to see Sperrin until lunchtime or later. She actually had her car keys in her hand when that sixth sense for something amiss, which good police officers develop and the best police officers are born with, jogged her elbow and pointed out the little anomalies that had added up all unnoticed. Sperrin turning in while she was out buying his beer; neither sight nor sound of him since; the e-mail on her open laptop that claimed to have been read already . . .

She took the stairs two at a time, only to confirm what she already knew. David Sperrin wasn't still asleep in her guest room. He hadn't *been* asleep in her guest room. The bed hadn't been slept in since – exasperated by his efforts to do it with one good hand – she'd made it for him the previous morning. He'd read the e-mail from China Roses, understood immediately why she was in communication with an on-line pimp, and gone out while she was listening to Joe Green's diatribe against the supermarkets that were stealing his trade. And he hadn't been back since.

Meadowvale was three minutes away. She thought it would

be as quick to explain to DCI Gorman in person as to phone him. She took the laptop to show him the results of HotRod's enquiries.

He heard her out in silence, wearing the expression he had honed for his dealings with Hazel: a mixture of irritation, mild incredulity and secret amusement. He loved her enthusiasm for the job; but he'd always known that one day she'd do something that would get them both fired.

'So what you're saying is,' he summarised when she stopped to draw breath, 'you want me to whistle up the Seventh Cavalry because your friend, who's wandered off before, has wandered off again.'

'It's a bit more than that,' complained Hazel, wondering how she might convey her sense of deep unease. 'When he went AWOL from the hospital, he was still concussed, he was in a state of shock because of what had happened, almost the only memory he had of the event was of someone dying in his arms and he thought he might have killed her. There is no sense in which he was in his right mind.'

'And he is now?'

'Well – yes.' She knew Gorman had noted her hesitation and tried to explain it. 'I mean, the guy's an archaeologist. He thinks it matters what happened in some bog thousands of years ago. Plus, he inherited all his family's brains and none of its charm. So maybe he views the world from a slightly different perspective to you and me, or most people. That isn't grounds enough to break out the station straitjacket. Maybe he's a bit eccentric. He's not crazy.'

'He is unpredictable. Maybe he just decided to go home and forgot to mention it.'

'At ten o'clock at night? When he'd just sent me out to buy beer? That's not eccentric, that's stupid! And the one thing David Sperrin is not is stupid.'

Dave Gorman sniffed and considered the situation. 'You think he saw that e-mail?'

She nodded. 'I thought it was odd at the time, that it was marked as read when I hadn't opened it. I just thought it was a server error. This morning, when I realised he'd gone out instead of going to bed, it all fell into place.'

'All right, let's suppose that is what happened.' Hazel could tell from his measured tone that she had failed to infect the DCI with her sense of alarm. 'How would he react? Where do you imagine he went?'

'I don't know where he is,' she exclaimed, 'that's why I'm so worried!' She saw Gorman raise one bushy eyebrow at her and made an effort to be calm. 'Sorry. I was gone maybe twenty minutes. The e-mail is timed at 21.52, just after I went out. Before I got back there was time for David to read it, phone the number, get his coat on and head out to whatever address he was given.'

'Have you phoned the number?'

She shook her head. 'I tried David's number but it went straight to voice-mail. I wasn't sure if it was a good idea to try the China Roses number or not. I wanted to talk to you first.'

'So maybe you have learned something these last few months,' said Gorman with a trace of a smile. 'I'll get a trace organised, then we'll call and see if anybody answers. There's a good chance they won't. Whether or not there's any connection to human trafficking, there's enough money in prostitution for the pimps to treat their phones as disposable. They're only the weak link in the chain if they hold onto them.'

'We've still got the Land Rover,' Hazel reminded him. 'If the China Roses brothel was more than half a mile away, David probably took a taxi. I'll phone round the cab firms, shall I?'

Gorman nodded. 'He won't have been given an address, just a rendezvous. Someone would meet him with a car. But finding his cabbie might put us in the right general area. Give us some idea if we should be looking for him in Norbold, or Coventry, or somewhere else.' There was a pause while he debated how much he should say. 'Hazel, I still have my doubts about this. I think you've built an awful lot of theory on not very much foundation. The likeliest outcome is that it'll prove to be just a brothel, nothing more, and the name's a coincidence.

'But I have to tell you, if Sperrin's playing at amateur detectives, and it turns out China Roses is *not* just another brothel, he could be in trouble. We'll try triangulating his phone as well, see if that'll give us his location. In the meantime, wherever he's gone, whoever he's with, he's out there on his own.'

'If these are the same people, and if they realise who he is, they'll kill him.'

The DCI nodded sombrely. 'Probably the best we can hope for right now is that I'm right and you're wrong. There's every chance, you know. I'm a detective chief inspector: it says so on my door. Hold onto that thought. If the China Roses On-Line Brothel has as much to do with the people who shot our girl as the China Roses Narrowboat Company does, then your friend will have spent an interesting night and will show up any time now with a lighter wallet and a faintly embarrassed smile on his face.'

SEVENTEEN

Ash phoned the car-hire office as soon as it opened. They offered to pick him up, but he didn't want anyone to see Cathy, or hear her, or have any reason to guess at her presence in his house. He thought he was probably being neurotic – she had as good a reason to stay out of sight as he had to hide her – but the idea of someone coming to Highfield Road made him deeply anxious. He said he'd walk into town to collect the car.

Oh good, said Patience, who'd been eavesdropping. Can I come?

Ash shook his head regretfully. 'If I turn up at a car-hire place with a dog in tow, I think I'm going to be walking home again.'

That's species-ist, said Patience, narrow-eyed, peering down her long nose at him.

He was crossing the park when his phone rang. For the rest of his life he would regret answering it. He knew it was Hazel – not many people had the number – and if he hadn't answered she'd have assumed he'd left it on his hall table again. But the insistent drilling was hard to ignore, and he fumbled through his pockets until he found the thing, and had pressed Receive before he'd wondered if he should.

'Gabriel – thank God.' The cool reserve with which they'd parted on his doorstep the day before had entirely gone. Apprehension laced her voice. 'I thought you weren't going to answer – that you'd left the phone on the hall table again.'

'Not this time,' he said carefully. 'Are you all right? You sound . . . worried. Where are you?'

'I *am* worried,' she answered tersely. 'Gabriel, I need your help. I'm sorry to trouble you when' – how to put it? – 'you have other things on your mind, but I really need to see you. I'm at Railway Street. Can you come right away?'

'Hazel, I can't,' he demurred. 'I'm just' – how to put *this*?

– 'in the middle of something. I'm going to be out of town for the rest of the day.'

There was an uncomfortable silence. Hazel had never made a habit of begging; but then, she'd never had to. She *had* made a habit of being there, whenever Ash needed her, whatever he needed her for, when it was convenient and also when it most assuredly was not. He had no right to refuse her now, regardless of what she wanted, and they both knew it.

'This is really important,' she said eventually. 'I think David's in danger. He's gone off on his own, following up a lead that might go nowhere but might take him to the people who murdered Rose Doe. And Dave Gorman's doing what he can, but everything takes time and before he can trace the brothel's phone it's going to be in the bottom of a waste bin somewhere.'

She became aware she wasn't making much sense and tried again. 'He's been missing since last night. David. I found some kind of on-line brothel called China Roses. He got their number while my back was turned, and I think he went out straight away, and he hasn't been back since and I haven't heard from him and he isn't answering his phone. I looked for the website again but it's vanished.'

Between the rose garden and the lake Ash stood frozen, a monument to indecision. He knew what he should do. He knew what he wanted to do. He didn't think he could do it. 'If Dave's dealing with it, I don't know what more you and I could do . . .'

As if she'd been there beside him, he heard Patience's voice in his head: You could be there with her. For all the times that she was there for you.

'I thought maybe . . . Oh, I don't know what I thought,' exclaimed Hazel, and it was impossible to know if her impatience was for herself or Ash. 'You're the smart one – I thought you'd come up with an idea.'

'Sorry,' mumbled Ash.

'If I can't think of anything better, I'm just going to drive round looking for him. Looking for China Roses. Trawling the red light districts. Here – well, that won't take very long – and Coventry, and if there's still no sign of David I'll go on to Birmingham. I've OK'd it with the chief. I think he'd have OK'd anything that would get me out of the office for a bit. Will you come with me?'

It cost him blood to say it, but say it he did. 'Hazel, I really am sorry but I can't. I have to be somewhere else. It's not something I can put off.'

From the quality of her silence, he thought he'd managed to surprise her. That she'd believed that when push came to shove he'd do as she asked rather than refuse her. He knew she'd counted on him. She had every right to; he had no right to let her down.

And because he knew he was behaving badly, and his conscience was pricking him in consequence, he did what guilty people do: he tried to justify himself by putting the other party in the wrong. 'Anyway, you're never going to spot him by driving round blindly. You have a number for these people? Then wait till Dave traces the phone. As soon as he has a location, he'll be straight in there and hauling David out, whether he wants to come or not.'

'But I need to be *doing* something!'

'I'm not sure there's anything you can usefully do, or I could help with. David will be fine. The brothel you found has probably nothing to do with what happened to him, it's just a coincidence that they're using a name that seems to mean something to him. It's not as if he's been able to tell us why. China Roses? – it could mean anything. This brothel, the flower shop in Windham Lane, heaven knows how many other businesses, or something quite different. If he hasn't found what he's looking for, he'll turn up again any time now.'

'That's what Dave Gorman said,' growled Hazel. 'I didn't think he was right, and I don't think you are. What if it isn't a coincidence? What if David's found his way to the people who killed Rose?'

But Ash had no answer. 'I'm sorry,' he said a third time. 'I can't help. And I don't think you can either. Hazel, I have to go. I'll call you when I get back. With luck he'll have turned up by then. But if he hasn't, we'll go out and look for him. All right?'

'Not really, no,' she said quietly, ending the call.

Ash stood another minute beside the lake, oblivious to its winter charms, feeling sick to his soul. He felt like someone who'd been entrusted with a treasure, something rare and beautiful and fragile, and he'd dropped it. No, not even dropped it because, however careless and unfortunate, that would have been an accident. He'd done something worse: he'd made the conscious choice to let it fall. He'd chosen the needs of a woman who'd almost destroyed him over those of the one who'd dragged him back from the abyss. He couldn't imagine how he would ever explain that to Hazel. He didn't understand it himself.

He pulled himself together and walked on through the park to the car-hire depot; and the girl behind the desk wondered if the big bear-like man with the slight habitual stoop and the polite, diffident manner knew there were tears on his cheeks.

Whether DCI Gorman wanted her in the office or not, Hazel returned to Meadowvale. She had nowhere else to go.

There was a brief bustle of activity while the necessary formalities were met, then DS Presley joined DCI Gorman and Melvin Green the computer geek in Gorman's office, and closed the door. The office fell quiet. Knowing this was personal, no one wanted to bother Hazel.

After ten minutes Dave Gorman emerged. He went out to the corridor to kick some coffee out of the vending machine, returning with two unpleasant cardboard mugs. He pulled a spare chair up to Hazel's desk. 'Get that inside you while I tell you what's happening. We're running a trace on the phone number in the e-mail, and another on Sperrin's phone. That's the one I'm pinning my hopes on. If Sperrin has it with him, we'll be able to triangulate his location. If he's still in Norbold we'll go and pick him up, you and me. If he isn't, I'll have the closest unit do the honours. Try not to worry. There's no reason to suppose he's made any more progress at finding these people than we have.'

'Then why hasn't he come home?' she demanded fretfully.

Gorman shrugged. 'Pride? He doesn't want to admit that he's drawn a blank? You know the guy better than any of us – you tell me.'

'I don't think he drew a blank,' said Hazel in a small voice. 'And that's my fault. For doing what you've told me, time and again, not to do – trying to sing the solo when my place is in the chorus.'

Gorman gave a wry grin. He *had* told her that. He hadn't thought she was listening.

'And as if that wasn't enough,' she continued, determined to drink the cup of guilt to the dregs, 'I was *stupid* enough to let him see what I was doing. To go out and leave him alone with the laptop. Of course he read the e-mail when it came in. Of course he acted on it. I knew how much this meant to him. He blamed himself for not saving Rose. If I'd been thinking with more than half a brain I could have kept him safe. And I didn't.'

'You couldn't guess he'd have an attack of the vigilantes.'

She refused to be comforted. 'Yes, I could. It's typical of the man. I've known him, on and off, since I was a child. He was always an arrogant sod who knew he was smarter than the people around him and thought that meant that most people were stupid. Who was he going to ask for help? You? Me? When he's so much smarter than the pair of us put together? He'd think he was quite capable of doing what we couldn't and finding out if the people behind that ad were the same ones he'd seen at Myrton.'

'But what then?' asked Gorman, puzzled. 'How did he think the situation was going to end well? He's not exactly fighting fit.'

'It wouldn't make any difference if he was: he's outnumbered, and they have guns, and we know they're willing to use them. I don't know what he had in mind. Maybe he meant to call us in as soon as he was sure, only something – someone – stopped him. Or maybe he didn't know himself what he was going to do.'

'Clever men don't walk into the enemy's camp without some sort of a plan,' Gorman pointed out.

'He was so angry, I don't think he was thinking straight.' Hazel struggled to put into words what she was only now coming to understand herself. 'In his head, it was history repeating itself. His brother's death, and Rose's death. He was too young to deal with the first so he put it out of his mind entirely, but that meant he never got the chance to make his peace with it. To feel the remorse, and recognise how little of it was appropriate, and forgive himself.

'So when a desperate girl ran to him for help, and now he was a grown man, and in spite of that the result was the same – Jamie died, and Rose died too – I think the guilt overwhelmed him. Every fragment of memory that he got back, every bit he was able to add to the picture, only made matters worse. Faced with the chance to confront these people, he was never going to wait until I got home and took over. He didn't want us – the police – to get justice for Rose: he wanted to avenge her himself. It was the only way he could make his peace with history.'

Gorman still thought they could be dealing with a black comedy rather than a tragedy. 'I know you think Sperrin's in danger. But we don't know that yet. This could all still be a coincidence. In which case, when he went to meet his China Rose for the night, he'd find a hooker and her pimp, and nothing else. No connection at all to people trafficking.'

'Then he'd have come home,' Hazel said simply. 'If he could have called us, he'd have called; if he could have left, he'd have left. Someone stopped him.'

Gorman watched her, his square, frankly ugly face creased with concern. He knew she was hurting. He didn't know how to comfort her. 'Gabriel should be here.'

'Gabriel's busy.'

Two words, unremarkable in themselves, which in that context were enough to send the DCI's thick eyebrows racing up towards his low-slung hairline. A few comments he might have made he thought better of and didn't say out loud. She was his friend as well as his colleague: he didn't need to make what was already a bad day worse.

The door of his office banged open and Tom Presley was at his elbow. 'No luck with the China Roses number, but we've got a location for Sperrin's phone. Just this side of Coventry.'

Gorman was already calling Coventry police. 'Give me the map reference.' He explained the situation in as few words as he could, passed on the location. 'We'll be with you as soon as we can.'

As the three of them hurried down to his car, he said to Presley, 'Moving or stationary?'

Presley gave him a significant look. 'Stationary.'

They might have thought they were being discreet, but Hazel knew exactly what they were thinking. A moving target meant the phone was still being carried. 'He could have dropped it,' she said. 'Or maybe they've locked him up somewhere.'

'Yes, that's probably the answer,' said Tom Presley without inflection.

The first thing Ash did with his newly hired car was drive to his solicitor's office.

Jim Boyne had been the family's solicitor when Ash's mother was alive. He knew more about Ash's background – where he'd worked, who for, why he stopped – than Ash actually realised; and he knew when to ask questions and when to hand over a sealed envelope without comment.

Ash wanted confirmation of one point. 'I get this signed, and the divorce will go through? No sitting on our hands for five years in case she turns up to defend it?'

Boyne nodded soberly. 'That would be my expectation. The Proposed Arrangements for Children form is the important one. If she'll sign that, the rest is not much more than a formality.'

'And I have sole custody?'

'That's what you asked for, that's what I drew up. In the circumstances, with your wife' – he searched for a tactful term – 'unlikely to return to this country of her own volition, it seems the only practical arrangement. Er . . .'

Ash raised one eyebrow in a gesture which acknowledged the other man's curiosity without encouraging it.

A lifetime of not asking questions he didn't want to know the answers to was no help to Jim Boyne now. Professional curiosity was just too strong. 'The county court was unable to locate your wife to serve this petition on her. How did you?'

Deadpan, Ash said, 'I got lucky, Mr Boyne.'

What the solicitor thought of that was plain in his face even if he didn't voice it. He debated with himself a moment longer. 'Mr Ash, you're not going to do anything . . . rash . . . are you?' He meant, illegal.

Ash fixed him with a deep, dark eye. 'Mr Boyne, have you ever known me to do anything rash?'

The solicitor heaved a mental sigh of relief. He could honestly say that he had not. What he didn't know, including what he knew he didn't know and a few things that he didn't know if he knew or not, was neither here nor there.

The sat-nav took them almost all the way into Coventry, but then drew them aside into an urban desert of depots and small industrial units, a blasted heath of concrete yards and steel sheds and almost no people. Gorman was driving, Presley acting as navigator. Hazel had the back seat to herself. Anxiety crowding her on every side made it feel cramped.

They saw the police cars before the sat-nav told them they'd arrived. They were drawn up in front of a steel shed indistinguishable from a dozen others, with no sign on the gate and no name over the door. There were no external windows. Both gate and door had been secured by padlocks, which someone had sheared with bolt-cutters.

Closest to the door, half masked by the police vehicles, was an ambulance.

Gorman and his sergeant got out of the car. But as Hazel went to join them, Gorman shook his head. 'You stay here.'

Objections rose as far as her tongue – references to equal opportunities, assurances that she could deal professionally with whatever they found – but no further. She subsided onto the seat without a word. If it was good news, it could wait; if it was bad news, it would always come too soon. She watched the two men walk quickly across the wind-scoured concrete and disappear into the shed.

She thought: This isn't a brothel. It isn't even a cheap brothel. By the time he got here, he knew what he was dealing with, and so did they. Everyone's cards were face-up. By the time he got here, getting laid was no longer an option.

She thought: The first thing they would do, the very first thing, would be to take his phone off him. But if this was a place that was important to them, they wouldn't just have put it on a desk and forgotten about it – they'd know as well as we do we could trace it. They'd have destroyed it, and then taken the pieces away to be sure.

She thought: Maybe he got rid of it before they searched him. Maybe he dropped it behind a radiator in a split-second when no one was looking. That would explain the signal not moving. Of course, it meant that neither Sperrin nor his captors might still be here. Even so, knowing they'd used this shed had to be worth something. Coventry's answer to Sergeant Wilson might turn up some forensics to work on . . .

Dave Gorman was coming back towards the car. His head was down, the gritty wind whipping at his thick hair. He never wore hats, Hazel thought inconsequentially; he never even brought out a scarf until February.

He opened the driver's door and got in. After a moment he half turned in his seat, looking at Hazel over his left shoulder.

She said, 'He's dead, isn't he?'

'Yes,' said Gorman.

EIGHTEEN

Sperrin hadn't dropped his phone behind a radiator. He'd posted it through a crack in an old fifty-gallon oil drum standing empty just inside the door. It had been an act of desperation. He'd known he would never get the chance to call for help, had accepted that the phone's only utility now was to pinpoint the place where his quest, and his story, had come to an end.

The officers from Coventry who'd responded to Gorman's summons had found the phone first. But it hadn't taken them much longer to find the body. No very serious attempt had been made to hide it, only a few cardboard boxes stamped with the name of a well-known purveyor of tinned goods had been tumbled over it as a shield from casual eyes. David Sperrin had been dead long enough for rigor mortis to set in, not long enough for it to wear off.

DCI Gorman had someone stay with Hazel while he returned to the shed. He found DS Presley keeping vigil over the body while the local FME finished her initial assessment.

'Shot?' asked Gorman, only to confirm the evidence of his own eyes.

'One bullet, back of the head. Not a fight – an execution.'

'Any other injuries?'

The doctor nodded. 'A lot. Mostly about a week old.'

'Those I know about,' said Gorman. 'I'm interested in the last twelve hours or so.'

'Let me get him back to my place and have a proper look. I'll call you. Or you can come, if you like.'

Gorman thought quickly. 'Tom, you stay with him. Call me as soon as you have any information. I'm going to take Hazel home.' He turned to the senior investigating officer from Coventry. 'We'll need to work this together. He was part of an ongoing investigation in Norbold. He was my only witness to a murder.'

The DI nodded. 'We'll co-operate any way we can.'

For most of the drive back to Norbold, Hazel was silent, sunk in grief and reflection. Once she looked up and said, 'I need to call his brother.'

Gorman shook his head. 'I'll deal with it. Someone will go out from his nearest station. He shouldn't have to hear that over the phone.'

'But I'm his friend . . .'

'And when you've got your breath back, go over there and be with him. Tell him what happened, tell him what we know and what we're doing about it. But he shouldn't have to wait to learn that his brother is dead.'

'I told Pete I'd look after him. I told him not to hurry back, because I'd be looking after him.' Her voice was empty.

Gorman sighed. 'You did your best, Hazel. We can't save everybody. Especially, we can't always save people from themselves. Sperrin wanted this confrontation. He must have reckoned the chance to bring these people down was worth any price he had to pay.'

She turned her head slowly. 'He knew he was going to die?'

'Oh yes. When he used his phone as X marks the spot, he knew it was the only message he was going to be able to send us.'

Silence descended for a little longer. Then Hazel said, 'But they won't go back there, now, will they? Whatever they were using the shed for – as a staging post, somewhere to keep the girls until their new employers' – she couldn't bring herself to say *owners* – 'had paid for them, somewhere to keep their vehicles out of sight – they won't go back. They wouldn't have left David there if they meant to.'

'No,' agreed Gorman. 'There's nothing special about the shed. It's just four walls and a roof. It was supposed to be empty, waiting for a new tenant. One of the neighbours, stock-taking late at night, saw a van on the forecourt a couple of weeks ago, but he assumed it was just someone checking the security.'

'A light-coloured Transit van, was it?'

Gorman nodded.

'If they never go back, how are we going to find them?'

'I don't know,' said DCI Gorman honestly.

'Then it was all for nothing. David threw his life away for nothing.'

'He didn't throw it away,' Gorman said quietly. 'He gave it away. Hazel, he knew what he was doing – the risk it could blow up in his face, what would happen if it did. He thought it was worth it. It wasn't just Rose he wanted justice for. He knew as well as we do there'll be others, probably a lot of others – past, present and future. Breaking this pipeline is the only way to find them and rescue them. Your friend wanted that more than he wanted to come home safe. He was a brave man, Hazel: don't ever forget that. I told him not to get involved . . .'

'So did I,' said Hazel mournfully.

'It was good advice. He should have walked away and left it to us to sort the mess out; or not. That's what most people would have done. Sperrin wasn't prepared to. I don't know if he really believed he could pull this off – get the information that would let us progress the investigation, and get away safely with it – or if he was past caring. Whatever his motives, whatever unresolved conflicts in his life led to that decision, he staked everything he had and played the hand he was dealt the best way he could.'

'And lost.'

'Yes. But if he thought the prize was worth the gamble, are we entitled to say he was wrong? When we find his killers – and I did say *when* – a lot of people will owe David Sperrin a debt of gratitude. A lot of frightened, lonely, abused girls will be going home instead of wasting their youth in misery.'

'Somehow, it isn't much comfort,' mumbled Hazel.

'No. I don't suppose it is.'

No one had ever mistaken the CID offices upstairs at Meadowvale Police Station for Scotland Yard, and no one ever would. Here, teams of forty officers worked one case only in DCI Gorman's dreams. In the throes of a major investigation, he could ill afford to lose even the most junior member of his squad. In spite of which he took DC Emma Friend off duties for the afternoon and had her drive Hazel out to Byrfield, ninety miles away.

Hazel protested that it was unnecessary, she was perfectly capable of driving herself. Gorman didn't bother to argue with her. He tossed his car keys over her head to Friend. 'Dent it and you're dead.'

The local police had been and gone by the time they reached the big honey-coloured stone house, half-screened by its avenue of sycamores on the edge of Burford village. The 28th earl had been watching for them: he came down his front steps as Hazel ran up them and they met at the halfway point in a confusion of hugs and tears. Recognising the moment as one the friends should share undisturbed, the Countess Tracy waited quietly at the top of the steps and DC Friend waited at the bottom.

After a long minute, Pete Byrfield recollected his duty as host and managed a tremulous smile. 'Come inside, both of you. You must be tired after your drive.'

Friend hesitated. 'Maybe I'll just nip into the village. I could pick you up later, Hazel.'

Hazel shook her head. Her eyes were puffy with the tears that hadn't come until she had someone to cry with. 'I'll stay here tonight. Have a cup of tea with us, then head back when you're ready.'

But it wasn't a very cheerful party, and Friend made her excuses as soon as she decently could. 'Call when you want a lift back to Norbold. One of us will come for you.'

Byrfield said, 'I'll bring her back. I'll need to . . .' He couldn't think of a way of ending the sentence. But then, he didn't have to.

When they were alone – Tracy had diplomatically withdrawn to count calves or something – Byrfield came and sat by Hazel on the long sofa in front of the drawing-room fire; and though it was a very long sofa, they were close enough for her to put her head on his shoulder and for him to put his arm around her.

'I couldn't believe it,' he mumbled, still deeply shocked. 'When the policemen came and said . . . said David was dead. I thought they'd got it wrong. I started saying No, he's fine, he was in the hospital but he's staying with a friend now, he's *fine* . . . But they were right, and I was wrong.'

'He should have been safe with me,' whispered Hazel. 'I promised you I'd look after him. Oh Pete, how are you ever going to forgive me?'

She told him everything: all the details that the Cambridge officers hadn't had. Including how Sperrin had found the people who killed him. She expected Byrfield to push her away then; to get up and poke the fire, perhaps, to take the sting out of it because he was a kind and decent man, but anyway to put space between them. But he didn't. He continued to hold her close, murmuring into the top of her head.

'David and I knew one another most of our lives, long before we knew we were . . . related.' It wasn't the perfect word, but there probably wasn't one. 'In all those years I never knew him do anything he didn't want to do, or not do anything that he did. You couldn't have stopped him, Hazel. After what happened at Myrton, he was bent on destroying them if he got the chance, whatever the cost might be. Nothing less would have satisfied him.'

'Then we've let him down too,' she moaned. 'We're no closer to knowing who they are or how to find them now than we were a week ago.'

'Has your boss closed the file on this?'

Hazel pulled back far enough to stare at him. 'Of course not!'

'Then it's too soon to say that. I've met your DCI, I know he's not going to give up. Maybe it will take time to get justice for David. Maybe it'll take more time than we think we can bear. But I believe it will happen. I want you to believe that too.'

Two-thirds of the way there, Ash realised where they were going. Grantham. Cathy had had a partner, in life and in crime, there once. She wasn't going to find him there today – she'd left him dead on a houseboat on Ullswater – but she must have had other contacts in the area. She was calling the directions from memory.

Ash saw a lay-by ahead and pulled in. 'Time for you to keep your half of the bargain.' He took Mr Boyne's envelope off the back seat.

'The divorce papers?'

'Yes.' He passed her his pen.

After a moment she opened the envelope and ran her eye down the forms. 'Sole physical custody?'

'It means you can't take the boys anywhere without my consent. Which will not be forthcoming.'

'In essence, you're asking me to give up being their mother.'

'Cathy, you gave up being their mother a long time ago. All I'm really asking now is that you give up being my wife.'

A brief flicker of displeasure crossed her face but didn't dwell there. She took the pen and signed and dated the form. She handed it back. 'Satisfied?'

It wasn't the right word. He didn't know what the right word was. 'This address . . .'

'. . . Isn't where I'm living, so you needn't bother Interpol with it. You're not the only one with a tame lawyer, Gabriel. Anything sent to this address will find me, sooner or later.'

He nodded, ambivalently. There was nothing more to be said. He said it anyway. 'What is it you're involved in, Cathy? What brought you here? What was so important it was worth risking your freedom?'

'I told you,' she said off-handedly. 'I wanted to see my sons. And my husband.'

'You told me a business deal had gone bad. What kind of business?'

'Mine,' she said. 'And none of yours.'

He knew he wasn't going to get anything from her that was both honest and informative. He didn't know why it mattered to him. 'Are you in any danger?'

She laughed aloud. 'Gabriel! I didn't know you still cared.'

'Neither did I,' Ash said quietly.

Looking at his face, at his grave expression that had amused her once and had come to irritate her unbearably, she felt herself unaccountably moved to answer. 'No, I'm not in any danger. I'll be out of the country by tonight. I probably shouldn't have come. I was never going to resolve the situation: it was rather arrogant of me, thinking I could. I'll have to leave it to the people on the ground. If they make an awful mess of it, as they very well might, at least I'll be out of range when the shit hits the fan.'

Ash started the car again, and drove on towards Grantham.

Ten miles short of the town she directed him into the countryside and finally down a concrete lane that ended in a field. Ash stared about him. 'Are you sure?'

Cathy smiled and nodded. 'Very flat country around here,' she observed, looking at the distant horizon under its vast white winter sky. 'Almost nowhere you *couldn't* land a light aircraft.'

And that was it; almost. Cathy got out. Ash turned the car. Cathy leaned down to the window. For a surreal moment he thought she was going to kiss him. But she said, 'Tell the boys I'll always love them. In my fashion.'

After a moment Ash nodded. 'I can tell them that.'

He drove back the way they'd come; and he didn't wave, and he didn't watch her in the mirror until she was out of sight.

'Are you sure you want to do this?'

Hazel nodded. 'Pete wants to see his brother. I want to take him.'

'You'll warn him?' Gorman said gruffly. 'What happens with head shots.'

The hand that had been clutched around her heart for twenty-four hours fisted tighter for a moment. 'I'll warn him.'

In fact the Coventry FME had done a good job of making David Sperrin presentable for his visitors. Hazel could guess at the damage beneath the carefully arranged sheet; she didn't think Pete Byrfield did.

He said pensively, 'He looks . . .'

Peaceful? Well, perhaps, thought Hazel, in that Sperrin's own personal war with the world had come to an end. To her he just looked lumpen, now the animating spark that drove him had been extinguished. The savage mocking grin, the wicked humour, the intellectual arrogance, which were impossible to admire and yet hard not to like, had vanished as if they'd never been. Now he looked like any other dead man: shorter than most, probably more dirt under his fingernails, but nothing special. The David Sperrin who had been uniquely, irreplaceably special to his family and friends was entirely gone.

Byrfield may have been thinking along the same lines. He finished, with a hint of impatience: '. . . So *stupid* lying there! I want to kick him.'

Hazel let out a bray that was half a chuckle, half a sob. 'Be fair: we have him at a disadvantage.'

'All he had to do was leave well enough alone,' gritted Byrfield, 'and everything would have been fine. And he couldn't do it.'

'Of course he couldn't,' said Hazel. 'David – leave well enough alone? Of course he couldn't. And for the record, everything wouldn't have been fine if he had.'

The 28th earl dragged his gaze away from his brother's face and glanced at her. 'No, I suppose not. I'm sorry. Right now, this is the only tragedy I can deal with. Maybe later I'll understand what he did. If it turns out to have done any good.'

'We have to make sure it does.'

Hazel found the FME, who'd backed away to give them some space, standing at her elbow. 'You got my report?' she murmured.

'I haven't seen it. I'm sure my chief has.'

'I wondered if you had any ideas about the abrasions.'

'Abrasions?'

'Above his right knee.' The doctor glanced at Byrfield and, getting a nod, lifted the sheet to show them.

'That looks recent,' said Hazel.

'It is. It was still bleeding when he died.'

'So he didn't do it jumping on the train.' She frowned, peered closer. 'It almost looks like writing.'

'That was my first thought,' agreed the FME. 'It isn't, though. Whatever way you look at it, you can't make letters out of it.'

'What about Chinese characters?'

Her companions stared at Hazel with various degrees of incomprehension. 'What?'

'The people who killed him were trafficking girls from the Far East.'

'You think they did this to him?' The FME sounded unconvinced.

'You don't?'

'I don't know what it was meant to achieve. It didn't contribute to his death. It would have felt unpleasant, but if I wanted to get information out of someone I wouldn't faff around scratching his knee with a nail-file.'

'That's what caused it?'

The doctor shrugged. 'Possibly. Something like that. Maybe a nail; maybe a ring-pull from a drinks can. Not a blade as such, the wounds aren't deep enough.'

They all peered closer at the scratches above David Sperrin's right knee. 'I suppose it could be a Chinese character,' said the FME doubtfully.

'There was a picture in your report?' She nodded. 'We'll get an expert to have a look at it.' Hazel looked at Byrfield. 'Shall we head back or do you want to stay a bit longer?'

For a moment he laid his hand flat on the sheet above his brother's chest. Then he turned away. 'No, I'm done here.'

Mary Han was not only an accredited interpreter of Mandarin and Cantonese Chinese for the courts, she was a teacher of Chinese brush painting. If anyone was going to make sense of the marks on Sperrin's leg, she was.

She studied the photographs at length, turning them first one way, then the other. She had brought a book which she consulted, reading from the back forwards. Finally she shook her head. 'I'm sorry, Detective Chief Inspector Gorman. I cannot identify these markings as a Chinese character, in whole or in part. I can make no suggestion as to what they might represent.'

'Could they be somebody's name?' asked DS Presley.

Ms Han looked surprised. 'A chop? I don't think so.'

After Hazel had seen her out she returned to Gorman's office, where he and Presley were still poring over the pictures. Gorman straightened up with an exasperated grunt. 'Could they be somebody's name?' he mimicked bitterly. 'What, you think Chinese murderers go round signing their work?'

'You never know your luck,' said Presley, unabashed.

'Assuming our expert's right,' said Gorman, 'which we have to, it isn't Chinese writing at all. And it isn't English writing. So what is it?'

'It's too deliberate for him to have got it in a scuffle,' said the sergeant. 'It isn't significant enough to count as torture. It's almost like a doodle – the sort of thing you'd do in your notebook if you were talking on the phone.'

'You think someone doodled on Sperrin's leg with a nail-file because he was talking on the phone?' If Gorman had sounded any more incredulous, his voice would have broken again.

'Wait a minute.' And though Hazel's voice was low and quite hesitant, the men stopped bickering to look at her. 'You're assuming this is something that was done to him.'

'Well, yes,' said Presley, rolling his eyes. 'It's not a birthmark, is it?'

But Gorman waved him to silence. 'Go on, Hazel. What are you thinking?'

'What if he did it to himself?'

There was this to be said for Hazel's intuitions: sometimes she was right. Gorman frowned, but that was because he was thinking. 'What if he did? The same question applies – why? Why would he scratch meaningless patterns into his own leg? What was he hoping to achieve?'

'If they *were* meaningless, nothing. So unless he was so bored in the last few minutes of his life that he was reduced to drawing doodles in his own blood, they meant something to him. And he believed they would mean something to us.'

The more she thought about it, the more sense it seemed to make. 'It's like the phone. He knew he couldn't use it to tell us what was happening, but he could use it to tell us where. He knew that, there or somewhere close, then or soon, he was going to die. They'd tried to kill him before, they couldn't afford to leave him alive now.

'But he knew we'd find his body. Nearly all bodies turn up eventually: it's like they want to be found. So he put his phone where no one was going to find it until we ran a trace on it, and he left us a message the only way he could – scratched on his own skin.'

Now Gorman was seeing the same picture Hazel was. 'Under his clothes, where they'd only have seen it if they'd stripped him, and they had no reason to do that. How did he do it without being seen?'

He sent for the bag of Sperrin's clothes from the evidence locker. Coventry had made an inventory and then sent them on. Gorman studied the right leg of the jeans, inside and out. There were traces of blood from the scratches, no more – it hadn't soaked through to the outside – and a small hole in the dense weave of the denim.

'He could have made the hole with a nail or something he found lying around in the shed,' said the DCI. 'But could he have made all those scratches through one small hole?'

'One way to find out,' said Hazel decisively. She tore a sheet off the pad by Gorman's phone and – turning her back modestly on her colleagues – unfastened her waistband and worked the piece of paper down the leg of her trousers until it lay just above her right knee. With a sigh of regret – she'd liked those trousers – she used the DCI's letter-opener to poke a small hole in the twill. Through it she inserted the tip of a biro.

It was more fiddly than she'd expected. The constraints imposed by the fabric made it hard to manipulate the pen. If this was what Sperrin had done, it explained the rather random design he'd come up with, that looked a little like a Chinese character and a little like a bunch of flowers. Hazel followed the marks as best she could and then, again turning her back, extracted the sheet of paper.

They studied it together. They compared the small hole in Hazel's trousers with the one in Sperrin's jeans. They compared the piece of paper with the photograph.

'That's a pretty good match,' admitted Gorman. 'All he needed was a nail about ten centimetres long, not an unlikely thing to find lying around on the floor of a shed, a couple of minutes where no one was watching him too closely, and the use of his right hand. Then he could have done exactly what you just did. He could even have done it with his hands tied, if they were tied in front of him.'

'We still don't know why.' Hazel's voice was querulous with distress. 'What was he trying to tell us?'

'We'll figure it out,' Gorman assured her. 'But not tonight. It's time you went home. Is Byrfield staying with you tonight?'

She nodded. 'I didn't want him driving home alone in the dark, not today. We'll all be a bit calmer in the morning.'

'And calmer still by Monday,' said Gorman pointedly. 'Take the weekend off, Hazel, get your head in some sort of order. By Monday we'll have a better idea where we're going with this.'

Hazel blew her nose. 'So you're going to have a quiet weekend too, are you, Chief?'

'Don't be silly,' said DCI Gorman severely.

NINETEEN

Hazel couldn't remember the last time she was drunk. But she got drunk that evening. She and the 28th earl between them disposed of two bottles of wine, a half-bottle of vodka, and some brandy which they agreed didn't count because it was medicinal.

Halfway through the vodka, Byrfield asked where Ash was. Hazel gave an over-elaborate shrug. 'I don't know. Or care.'

Byrfield stared at her, or at least at the median point between the two of her. He shut one eye to resolve the problem. 'Since when?'

She pulled a handkerchief from her trouser pocket. By the time she recognised the lace edging as the hem of her shirt, she'd blown her nose on it. 'Since I asked him to help me look for David, and he said he was too busy.'

Mention of his brother's name sent Byrfield hunting for his own handkerchief. When he pulled it out, bits of straw and coarse calf mix fell onto Hazel's living-room carpet. 'He must have been *very* busy,' he said judiciously.

'He wasn't busy at all,' she snarled. 'He's got himself a girlfriend. Can't bear to drag himself away from her.'

'Gabriel?' Byrfield considered. '*Gabriel? Are you sure?*'

'I've seen them together.'

'Really? What's she like?' He seemed to be struggling to get his head round the idea of Ash with a girlfriend. Which was a measure of how much he'd drunk, because when he'd proposed to Hazel – twelve months ago now, before he and Tracy rediscovered one another at an agricultural college reunion – he'd known perfectly well why she refused him.

'Oh, I didn't see her close up. Just a shape at the bedroom window.'

There was a silence while he absorbed that. 'And that's why he wouldn't help you look for David?'

'I guess.'

Byrfield gave a morose sniff. 'The bastard.'

'The bastard,' agreed Hazel. With not much more than air in the vodka bottle, she fetched the brandy. They'd called at the off-licence on the way back to Railway Street. The knowledge that if she'd kept a well-stocked drinks cabinet David Sperrin would still be alive twisted her heart.

'Would it have made a difference?' Byrfield asked when she came back.

'Well, no,' she admitted. 'According to the FME – forensic medical examiner,' she explained, carefully, for the farmer's benefit – 'it was all over by then. He died during the night sometime. Still. Still.' She tried to take the top off the brandy bottle by screwing it the wrong way. 'Still. He could have helped. I've helped him often enough.'

'You have.'

'Times when *I* could have stayed home getting some nooky, I didn't. I went out and helped him.'

'You did,' said Byrfield. He upended the vodka bottle over his glass and tapped its bottom a few times, to be sure. 'Nooky?'

'You know. Fun and games. Afternoon delight. Having it off. Getting your end away. Getting laid.'

'Oh – sex.' Byrfield bent an almost paternal eye on her. 'Hazel, nobody's called it nooky for ten years.'

'Which is about how long it is since I got any,' said Hazel sadly.

'Celibate by choice, I'm sure,' said Byrfield with a boozy attempt at gallantry.

'Oh yes. Just, not my choice.'

Maybe Byrfield wasn't quite as drunk as he seemed, because he was watching her with compassion. 'Have you told him how you feel?'

'Gabriel? Good God, no. He'd run a mile.'

'Maybe he thinks you would.'

She cast him a slightly unhinged smile. 'Maybe I would, too. I don't know. Anyway, it's adacem – academ – it's beside the point now. He's made other arrangements.'

'Maybe he has,' conceded Byrfield. 'And maybe he was just . . . you know . . . scratching an itch. He might just have fallen in with someone who was amiable and handy. You don't know. You're not going to know until you talk to him.'

She stared mightily. 'And say *what*?'

The 28th earl shrugged. 'What you said to me. That you know about her. That you saw them together. That you felt hurt he wouldn't help when you needed him to.' Something occurred to him. 'Does he know that David's dead?'

Hazel considered. 'He might not. Coventry issued a brief press release, but with no identifying details there was no reason Gabriel would have noticed it, or thought of David if he had.'

'Don't you think we should tell him?'

Hazel *did* think they should. She didn't want to. She knew that, if she called him, he'd be shocked and terribly upset, and she'd end up forgiving him, and she wasn't ready to do that. She didn't blame Ash for David Sperrin's death. He'd been dead hours before she phoned Ash, and on the road to death hours before that. Hazel might have saved him if she'd thought to check that he'd gone to his bed when he should have, but nothing Ash could have done would have made any difference; except to her. An angry, small-minded part of her wanted him to stew in the knowledge that he'd let her down, and it mattered.

She prevaricated. 'It's Friday night – they've probably gone out for the evening. Dancing.' Even drunk, she knew this wasn't very likely. 'Maybe I'll call him in the morning.' But she didn't, and Byrfield noticed that she didn't, say that she would.

His mind wandered on to the arrangements he had to make, decisions he had to reach. 'I'll bury him at Burford, of course. But Hazel, whatever am I going to put on his grave-stone? He was no one's cherished husband, no one's devoted dad, and I can't put *Beloved son* when his father never acknow-ledged him and his mother disliked him for most of his life.'

'I suppose someone's told Diana?' ventured Hazel.

Pete nodded. 'I should have gone, but I couldn't bring myself to. The policemen who came to Byrfield went down to the village to see her afterwards. I've no idea how she reacted. Unconventionally, I imagine. But you have to feel sorry for the woman. To have both her sons shot dead, thirty years apart.'

Hazel hadn't had much sympathy for Diana Sperrin since

she realised she'd rejected a five-year-old boy for playing with a gun he should never have had access to. 'The way she behaved towards David, from when he was a small child, was nothing less than emotional abuse. A less robust individual might never have recovered from it. I'm not going to waste my pity on her.

'And the answer to your question,' she added, 'is *Beloved brother.* His name, the years he was born and died, and *Beloved brother and true friend.*'

Byrfield smiled slowly. 'Yes. That'll do.'

Perhaps they were beginning to sober up. Hazel put the remains of the brandy, which was looking increasingly medicinal, in the kitchen cupboard, returned with a pot of coffee and mugs. Also on the tray was the design she'd drawn through a hole in her trouser leg. 'I think I may have drunk too much. I can't remember if I showed you this.'

Byrfield looked at it and frowned. 'I may have drunk too much too. I can't remember if you showed it me or not. It looks vaguely familiar. What is it?'

She explained how she'd come to do it, and why. 'Those scratches on his knee? I think he made them himself.'

'Why in heaven's name would he do such a thing?'

'That's certainly the right question,' said Hazel, pouring the coffee. 'To send us a message, but what message? What does it look like to you?'

Byrfield tried looking at it with his head on one side. 'A Chinese character?'

'Could David write Chinese?'

'Not that I know of.'

'He was an archaeologist.'

'His field was Iron Age Britain, not the Ming Dynasty.'

Hazel thought some more. 'Maybe he was copying it. Something he could see that he thought would lead us to the traffickers.'

'You should show it to someone who reads Chinese. They might be able to identify it.'

'We did that. She said it made no sense.'

'Ah.' Byrfield tried again, this time with his head tilted the other way. 'It looks a bit like a bunch of flowers.'

Hazel sighed, obscurely disappointed.

'Well, it does,' said Byrfield defensively. 'There's the vase, there are the stems, and the little circles are the flowers.' He shrugged.

'Roses again?' said Hazel, giving way to exasperation. 'It was the first thing he said after he came out of the coma. We thought it was her name – the girl who died. But it was the name of the brothel that was going to be her new employer. The argument that David witnessed before she was shot – the men were telling her she was going to be a China Rose. She shouted back that she wasn't Chinese, she was from Vietnam. Then she saw David, and she took her chance and ran.'

Byrfield was following, more or less. 'That sounds . . . feasible.'

'What makes no sense,' frowned Hazel, 'is that he'd draw a bunch of flowers on his knee if all he had to say to us was China Roses. That wasn't new information. He knew I knew about the brothel, so why spend his last few minutes hurting himself to say the same thing again? It has to be something new – something we weren't going to know unless he found a way of telling us.'

'Could he have found out who was behind the trafficking?' hazarded Byrfield. 'Rose is a reasonably common surname; so is Flowers. And we once had a vet called Bunch.'

'I suppose it's possible,' Hazel said doubtfully. 'If they were stupid enough to use one another's names where their victims could hear.'

'That would be pretty stupid, wouldn't it?' admitted Byrfield. 'Though if David knew they were going to kill him, I imagine they did too. It might have made them careless.'

'Anyone who's ever seen a cop show on television knows that the one thing you must never, ever do is make a full confession to someone on the basis that you're about to kill him. If you do, he *always* gets away.'

'Well – almost always,' said Pete Byrfield with infinite sadness.

Ash was on his way to bed – though probably not to sleep – when his phone rang. It was on the hall table: he had almost reached it when the ringing stopped. He lifted it anyway and gave it a puzzled look. He was fairly sure there was a way of returning the call, but he hadn't been paying attention when Hazel explained it. He was still pondering when the landline rang in the study.

'Gabriel. Have you talked to Hazel?'

'Dave?' Ash was aware of an odd, terse note in Gorman's voice. He hoped to God no one had told him about Cathy. 'I talked to her yesterday morning. Why?' A quiver of anxiety ran up his spine. 'Is she all right?'

If anything, Gorman's manner grew shorter, more clipped. 'Before you talk to her again, you need to know something. David Sperrin's dead.'

'What?' His office chair was pushed into the well of his desk, close enough to touch. Ash was too shocked to pull it out and sit down. 'When? I thought he was getting better.'

'He *was* getting better,' agreed Gorman grimly. 'Until someone put a bullet in his head.'

Ash's groping hand found the edge of the big Victorian desk and he lowered himself onto it carefully, as if unsure it would take his weight. 'Hazel said . . .' He hesitated, trying to remember what it was that Hazel had said. 'He'd got hold of a number that might have had something to do with the traffickers but just might have been a brothel?'

'I think we can assume it wasn't just a brothel, Gabriel,' said Gorman.

'I . . . I suppose you're sure . . .?' Ash heard himself clutching at the flimsiest of straws and winced.

'Pretty sure. Live people bend more in the middle.'

Ash took a moment to get his emotions under control. Then he said, 'Where did you find him?'

'Empty workshop on an industrial estate outside Coventry. But actually, I didn't phone to update you on my investigation. I didn't want you calling Hazel before you knew what had happened. She's had a rough enough time without you blundering in.'

'How's she taking it?'

'How do you think? Her friend's been murdered. She's blaming herself for letting him see her laptop, and for not realising he was missing until nine hours later. If you can make time in your busy schedule, she could probably do with some company.'

'Dave . . .' Ash swallowed. 'Do you know when he died?'

DCI Gorman barked a mirthless little laugh. 'What you mean is, was he still alive when she asked you to help look for him and you said no. And the answer, you'll be glad to hear, is no. Wednesday night sometime. Nothing you could have done would have been any help to Sperrin. Only to Hazel, Gabriel. Only to Hazel.'

It was far too late to go visiting, but this wouldn't wait. Ash had already returned the rental car or he'd have driven to Railway Street. Instead he grabbed his coat and scarf, intending to walk through the dark winter streets.

Patience said, I'm coming with you.

It wasn't a question, a suggestion, or even a proposal so much as a statement of fact. Ash nodded.

He'd expected to see Hazel's sapphire hot-hatch parked in front of her little house. He was taken aback by the big 4x4 with the *Byrfield Estate* badge on the door. Perhaps he should have guessed that Pete Byrfield would be there, but he hadn't.

In fact it was Byrfield who answered his knock. 'Keep the noise down, Gabriel. I've finally got Hazel to go to bed.'

'Pete. I've just heard. I'm so sorry.'

'Thank you.' There was an unaccustomed formality in both his words and his manner that suggested he knew of Ash's fall from grace.

'May I come in?'

'Do you know, Gabriel, I really don't think you should. Hazel's exhausted. I don't want to disturb her if she's managed to get to sleep.'

It was reasonable enough. But there was a coolness in Byrfield's tone that wasn't there last time they spoke.

Ash could have insisted, and Byrfield would probably have yielded rather than make a scene on the doorstep. But Ash didn't feel to be in any position to insist. It wasn't his house, and though Hazel was his friend, she'd been Pete Byrfield's friend for longer. If she'd made him her gatekeeper, Ash wasn't going to force an entry.

'All right,' he said unhappily. 'Then, will you give her a message? In the morning, if she's asleep now.'

'I'm not asleep.'

Both men looked up the stairs, Byrfield turning where he stood in the doorway, Ash looking past him. Hazel in her pyjamas was halfway down. Ash had never seen her look so pale. But she was calm, and if she'd been crying it hadn't been recently. There were few signs of the alcohol she'd drunk.

Ash had come here to speak to her; and when he'd been denied, he'd been ready to leave a message. Now they were face to face he had no idea what to say. Any apology he could make was going to be offensively inadequate; any attempt to explain could only make things worse. Hazel showed no indication of wanting a shoulder to cry on and, if she had, Ash was fairly sure she wouldn't have chosen his. Perhaps it had been a mistake to come.

Finally he mumbled, 'I just heard.'

'Yes?' Her voice was clear, uninflected, non-committal.

'Dave Gorman called.'

'Shall I leave you alone?' asked Pete Byrfield, standing back from the door.

Ash flicked him a grateful half-smile, but Hazel said, 'There's no need. Gabriel won't be staying long. Will you?' Her glance scythed across his face like a whip.

Ash's eyes dropped to his shoes. 'If that's what you want.'

'What I want,' she echoed, trying the words for size. 'When did what I want start to matter?'

He tried again. There didn't seem to be anything else he could do. 'I know I let you down. It wasn't from choice.'

'You were otherwise engaged,' said Hazel, measuring each word and clipping it off precisely.

Ash nodded miserably. 'But please don't imagine—'

'Imagine?' This time the echo bounced back from cliffs of flint. 'Gabriel, I don't need to imagine anything! I saw her. I saw you together.'

Shock, horror and guilt crashed through Ash's expression like an avalanche. He'd come here expecting an emotional confrontation and to have the moral shit kicked out of him. This he had not expected. Completely wrong-footed, he floundered to make any kind of intelligent response.

Hazel thought he was groping for a lie. He'd never been any good at lying: it didn't surprise her that, caught out in an infidelity that had less to do with sex than with honour, this was the best he could do. 'Please don't bother to deny it,' she said wearily, 'that would demean us both. Go home, Gabriel. There's nothing useful you can do here. I need to sleep. There are things I have to do tomorrow.' She turned and went back upstairs. The sound of her bedroom door closing was like a full stop.

'I'm sorry, Gabriel,' murmured Pete Byrfield, 'I did try to warn you. Give the dust time to settle. Talk to her again in a few days.'

Ash was turning into Highfield Road before the irony struck him, that a man whose brother had just been murdered felt sorry for *him*.

TWENTY

Dave Gorman looked up at the knock on his door, called, 'Come in,' then looked up again, startled, as the door opened. 'I wasn't expecting to see you today.'

Hazel shrugged. 'I gave Pete his breakfast, saw him off, stared at the wall for a bit, tried to think of anything productive I could be doing anywhere but here, failed, so here I am. Use me.'

'All right,' he said after a moment. 'This isn't the only case we have to deal with. I need someone with advanced IT skills to—'

She didn't let him finish. 'This is the case I want to work. Don't worry, Chief, I'm not going to go girly on you. I lost a friend. He wasn't an especially close friend, but he was a friend and I want to know who killed him. I want to help find who killed him.'

Gorman leaned back in his chair, considering her. 'It's not a good idea. You must be – what's the expression? – emotionally compromised.'

'Not to the point that I can't do my job. Maybe I was yesterday. Yesterday I thought it was my fault. Around three o'clock this morning, though, I realised his brother was right. You too. David would have sold his soul for the chance to take these people down. If he hadn't got it by reading my e-mails, he'd have found another way. Maybe I should have been more careful with the laptop. But in the long run, it wouldn't have made any difference. He was set on a path that didn't go anywhere good.'

'What about Gabriel?'

'What *about* Gabriel?' A hard edge barred her tone.

'Hazel, it doesn't take a mind-reader to see that you're angry with him. I'm not saying you haven't every right. But I can't risk you losing your temper at the wrong time, in the wrong place or with the wrong person. Can you promise that you won't?'

'I can do better than that,' said Hazel tersely. 'I can promise you I won't lose my temper at the right time, in the right place and with the right person. I'm not angry any more, just . . . disappointed. He came round last night. He said you called him.'

'What did he say?'

'Nothing that made things any better. But then, I didn't give him much of a chance to. Also about three o'clock this morning, I began to think maybe that was a bit unfair. If he's in a relationship with someone, his first duty isn't to me.'

'But it wasn't her – whoever she is – who put her life and career on the line to keep him out of the kind of hospital where the doors lock on the outside!'

Hazel managed a little smile at that. 'I know. But he's already repaid that favour. He's pulled me out of some holes too. Some big, black holes. In all honesty, I'm not sure he owes me anything any more.'

'I didn't realise we were supposed to keep count,' said Gorman hotly. He seemed more indignant on Hazel's behalf than Hazel was. 'Keeping a tally of favours done and received, and settling up at the end. I thought the definition of friendship was that you *didn't* keep count.'

'I suppose friendships are like everything else,' Hazel said sadly. 'They grow, they flourish, then they wither and die. Nothing is for ever. We're fooling ourselves if we think it is. Anyway.' She made an effort to move on. 'It wouldn't have changed anything, you know. David was dead before I missed him. Nothing Gabriel did or didn't do – nothing I did or didn't do – would have saved him.'

'No,' agreed Gorman. 'But we wouldn't be having this conversation if Gabriel had stepped up to the plate. Maybe he couldn't have been much use to Sperrin, but he could have been some use to *you.*'

'I'll get over it,' promised Hazel, and Gorman believed her. 'In the meantime, what can I do?'

Gorman cleared his throat. 'As I was saying, I need someone to—'

'No, Chief,' she interrupted him quietly. 'What can I do that needs doing? That'll help get justice for David, and Rose, and God knows how many other victims we don't even know about.

It's Saturday morning and I'm supposed to be off duty: there's only one reason I'm here. Only one case I'm working on.'

The file was open on the desk in front of him. The murder wall was at the far end of the big CID room adjoining his office, visible through the glass wall unless he closed the blinds. There were places to go and people to see, but the one thing DCI Gorman knew for sure was that he didn't want Hazel seeing them. Not yet. She thought she was fit to work, but he needed to be sure before she left Meadowvale.

He took out the autopsy photographs. Not all of them: the ones that showed the scratches etched into Sperrin's right leg. 'We need to figure out what he was trying to tell us when he did this. He thought it would make sense to us. He thought that, when we found his body, these marks would tell us who his killers were or how to find them. That took a cool head. He knew what he was doing. They're sketchy because of the conditions he was working under, but he believed we could figure it out. So figure it out.'

'I spent half of yesterday trying to figure it out,' complained Hazel. 'If it isn't a Chinese character, and it isn't a bunch of flowers, I don't know what it is.'

'He didn't stick a nail in his leg to leave us a message that couldn't be deciphered.'

Hazel reminded herself that being a detective was something she'd wanted very much, and that apparently insoluble puzzles came with the territory. She took the photographs. It wasn't the first time she'd seen them. Still there was something disturbing about a photograph of a dead man's leg, when you'd known that man most of your life.

'I'll give it another shot,' she said.

Sometimes life gives you lemons, and sometimes it gives you lemonade. And sometimes you don't know which was which until later.

This time Constable Budgen had actually finished his shift and was on his way home when the accident occurred more or less in front of him. He could have pulled his hat down over his eyes and walked crab-wise, and if he'd claimed to have seen nothing he would probably have been believed. But

though no one had ever accused Wayne Budgen of ruthless
ambition, he did take his job seriously and he tried to do it
well. He sighed, put his breakfast on the mental back-burner,
and went to sort out the snarl-up. Saturday morning in Norbold
wasn't like Saturday morning on Oxford Street, but a modest
gridlock had been achieved and tempers were already fraying.

The facts were easy enough to establish. An eight-year-old
girl walking to gym class with her mother, her younger brother
and their dog had let the lead slip from her fingers, and had
chased the animal into the traffic before her horrified mother
could grab her. The big white 4x4 she ran in front of managed
to stop but the delivery van travelling behind it didn't, and it
shunted the car into the child. The little girl ended up sitting
in the road, clutching her leg and screaming. The dog ended
up back on the pavement, looking innocent.

Budgen thought the damage amounted to no more than cuts
and bruises, but he called for an ambulance in case the child's
leg was broken. She was making too much noise to have sustained
any other injuries. He then checked that no one in the 4x4 was
hurt – the driver, a woman in her mid-thirties, said she was fine,
and so were the three children on the back seat – and finally the
delivery van, where the driver was mopping his bloody nose
with a handkerchief that was none too clean before he started.

'No warning, nuffink – she just stopped! Stopped dead. Of
course I hit her: anyone would have. Have you seen my
bumper? What's my boss going to say?'

'If she hadn't stopped dead, that little girl would probably
be on her way to the morgue,' said Budgen mildly. 'Your boss
is going to say that his bumper is a small price to pay. And
you should have been wearing your seat-belt.'

'I want her prosecuted,' insisted the driver. 'Her in front.
Stopping dead like that! I fink she's broken my nose.'

'You may not want to go that route,' suggested Constable
Budgen. 'The law requires you to keep enough distance
between you and the vehicle in front that you can stop in an
emergency. She managed to stop when the child ran out. You
should have been able to stop too.'

'Look,' said the delivery driver, demonstrating. 'It shouldn't
wiggle like that. It never used to wiggle like that.'

Budgen took down the relevant details, and cleared a path for the ambulance, and went to wave the 4x4 on. Afterwards, he never quite knew what stopped him. He had no issues with the driver: she'd done well in difficult circumstances. But there was something not quite right. The way she looked at him. The way the eldest child didn't. In fact, now he came to look again, she wasn't actually a child at all . . .

He asked the driver to lower the back window. She hesitated. Budgen looked at her until she did. He leaned down and spoke to the young woman in the centre seat. 'Are you all right, miss?'

There was a long pause before she looked up, looked straight at him. 'No, sir,' she murmured; then, louder, 'No, I am not all right. I am an illegal alien, and I wish to be sent home.'

Her name was Soo Yen, she was from Shanghai, and she'd been in the country for four months. She'd been promised a work permit and a job as a nanny. Her family had found the equivalent of £5,000 to pay for these and her travel expenses. Her family were not wealthy, but they had some savings, and they'd borrowed from relatives and friends. They thought they were buying her a start in life. She was nineteen.

The travel arrangements were rudimentary, the journey long and arduous, and the work permit was never forthcoming. But she thought, at first, she'd got the job she'd been promised. There was a nice house in Whitley Vale, a pretty village a few miles from Norbold, and there were two children to take care of. But the work was more for a skivvy than a nanny, and the wages – what was left of them after various unspecified dockings – went to the people who brought her here. She was told she would be paid directly when the shortfall in her travel expenses had been covered. She did not believe there had been a shortfall.

When she asked about the work permit, her employers expressed astonishment that she thought she qualified for one. They explained that she was an illegal immigrant, and if detected she would be sent to a detention centre which she would probably never leave.

The children had televisions in their bedrooms. Soo Yen was not allowed to watch television. But just occasionally, when the family were all busy elsewhere and she was cleaning upstairs, she would turn one on very quietly and try to make sense of the world she found herself in. And gradually it became clear to her that it was not as she had been told. She came to believe that people sent to immigrant detention centres did not all leave in zip-up bags. Sometimes they left on aeroplanes.

Still, it was a gamble. Her life in Whitley Vale was wearisome but not intolerable, and she was afraid of making her situation worse. For four months she did what she was told, and didn't make trouble, and stayed out of the way when there were callers to the house, and only went outside when one of the couple employing her was there to supervise; and quite possibly she would never have got up the desperate courage necessary to entrust herself to the British authorities. Except that a little girl on her way to gym class let slip her dog's lead, and a British policeman heard – over the child's screams – a silent cry for help.

'If she's been here for four months, she didn't travel with Rose.' Hazel swallowed her disappointment.

'No,' agreed DCI Gorman. 'But she may have come the same way, been brought in by the same people. Surely to God we haven't got multiple gangs of human traffickers working the area?'

'Was she able to tell you anything about them?'

'I haven't spoken to her yet,' said Gorman. 'I let Emma Friend do the first interview. I thought it might be less intimidating for her. I think she was half-expecting to be sent to some kind of a gulag.'

'Where did you put her up?'

The DCI looked embarrassed. 'Mark Lassiter's mum runs a nice little boarding house. We took a room there for her. Well, it was that or a cell downstairs. And I don't think she poses much of a danger to anyone.'

'What about the couple she was working for?'

'Them I would happily put in a cell,' growled Gorman. 'Only his legal representative, who wanted me to know he was a personal friend of a permanent secretary at the Home Office, wouldn't let me. Insisted it was far from clear that his clients had committed an offence – that they were the victims of the traffickers' lies as much as the girl was. All they'd done was offer work to a foreign national on the basis of documents which appeared to be legitimate. They're not experts in spotting forgeries: he owns a hardware emporium and she organises the flower-arranging rota for the local church. What are they supposed to know about human trafficking?'

'You believed them?'

'Of course I didn't believe them,' snorted the DCI. 'They got exactly what they paid for: cheap labour that couldn't give notice and take a better job somewhere else. But what I know and what I can prove aren't always the same thing.'

'Well, if their brief's a personal friend of a permanent secretary at the Home Office . . .' said Hazel slyly.

'That will make me try harder,' admitted Gorman, 'but it's still going to be uphill work. Anyway, it's the traffickers we want most. I'm going over to Lassiter's mum's place now, see if Soo Yen can help with that.'

'Can I come?'

He shook his head. 'The girl will need a familiar face, and that's Emma. You exercise your brain cells on those marks. Sperrin left us a message. Figure out what it was.' He stood up, opened the glass door and glanced around the big CID room. 'Anyone know where Friend is?'

DC Lassiter looked up from his desk. 'What for?'

Gorman glared at him. 'Because I want to know, you cheeky beggar.'

Lassiter flushed, and enunciated clearly, 'Watford. She's in Watford, Chief. The seminar on ATM raids. You sent her.'

'That's not till Monday.'

'It is Monday, Chief.'

'Is it?' Gorman did some calculations that involved touching his fingertips to his thumbs, then nodded. 'I knew that.' Over his shoulder he said, 'You'd better come after all, Hazel. I don't want the girl thinking I'm going to rough her up.'

Lassiter kept his eyes studiously on his work, and Hazel considered the strip-lighting on the ceiling. The only member of CID who thought people found the DCI intimidating was Gorman himself.

TWENTY-ONE

Mrs Lassiter showed them to her sitting room and called Soo Yen downstairs. 'I'll be in the kitchen if any of you want anything.' She left the door ajar.

Sitting opposite her, Hazel could see why Wayne Budgen had initially mistaken her for a child. She was no bigger than an adolescent, and had a habit of sitting with her knees together and her elbows tucked in, as if acutely aware of how much space she was allowed to occupy. Her eyes were lowered under the sweep of dark fringe.

Gorman began. 'Detective Constable Friend couldn't be here today. This is Detective Constable Hazel Best, and I'm Detective Chief Inspector Gorman.' The girl made a tiny nod of acknowledgement. 'I'm told you speak really good English. But if you'd prefer to have an interpreter, I'll arrange for one.'

Soo Yen raised her gaze briefly from his toe-caps to his face. 'Thank you. That will not be necessary.'

'How should we address you?' asked Hazel.

'My name is Soo Yen. Miss Soo is appropriate.'

'You gave your details to DC Friend during your first interview,' said Gorman, 'and we're trying to contact your parents. It may take a day or two. Don't think we've forgotten.'

'Thank you,' said Soo Yen again.

'I know you've had a difficult time, and you want to get home as soon as possible. We'll do all we can to facilitate that. Er – to make it happen.'

'I understand *facilitate*,' murmured the girl.

Gorman gave a wry smile. 'You speak better English than most of the kids at the local comprehensive. But while we're getting it organised, any information you can give us about how you came to England and what happened to you here would be enormously useful to us. We think the people who brought you here were responsible for other shipments' – he winced, but couldn't think of a better word – 'including one two weeks ago which resulted in two murders. We need to stop them. Can you help us?'

'I can try,' nodded Soo Yen, quietly eager.

Emma Friend had written up her account of how she was recruited in Shanghai and transported to England. Gorman had studied it carefully, and given Hazel a synopsis on the way over. He let Soo Yen tell the story again, to get her comfortable with talking to them, before he started asking questions.

'The last leg of the journey was in the back of a lorry, on a cross-Channel ferry,' he prompted when the story began to flag. In an aside to Hazel he said, 'I'm not sure how they managed to trick the surveillance at the docks. Remind me to ask when we find them.

'Then the lorry drove for an hour or so before it stopped, and you were transferred to a smaller van.' Soo Yen nodded again. 'Where did this happen? A lay-by, a motorway service station?'

The girl shook her head. 'A country road. No buildings, no people. Some sheep.'

'I don't suppose you can tell us where. Even approximately?'

'No, sir. I am sorry.'

'The smaller van. Do you know what kind it was?'

But she didn't. 'A white one?' she offered apologetically.

'Could you see out?'

She shook her head again. 'It was . . . enclosed? No windows. Only a small view ahead, past the driver.'

'What did you see?'

'Sometimes fields. Sometimes many cars and lorries. We were on the . . . motorway?' She checked with him that it was the right word; Gorman nodded. 'On the motorway for perhaps another hour, then off again. More fields. The van stopped at a place surrounded by fields. A house and some long sheds. Two members of our party disembarked.'

'Two girls?' asked Hazel.

'No, two young men. They had applied for a job driving tractors on a farm. Perhaps that is what they got.'

'We'll try to trace them, check that they're all right,' said

Gorman. It was in his face that it would be easier said than done.

'My information is not very helpful,' said Soo Yen sadly. 'I am sorry.'

'Stop saying that,' said Gorman gruffly. 'You have nothing to apologise for. You've been badly treated, and *I'm* sorry you haven't had a better experience of my country. It isn't perfect, but most of the people here don't think it's all right to treat visitors as slave labour.'

'Were you ever tied up?' asked Hazel quietly. 'Your wrists, your ankles? Your knees?'

'No,' said the girl, surprised. 'We believed we were being taken to where we had paid to go. There was no need to compel us. The journey had been uncomfortable, but it was nearly over. We were excited to be arriving. It was only later that I realised that I at least had been misled.'

'The man driving the smaller van,' said Gorman. 'Was he alone?'

'No, he had an assistant. A younger man.'

'Can you describe them?'

She tried, but really all she could remember was that they weren't Chinese. The younger one was shorter and thinner than the older one. They spoke with a strange accent that made it hard for her to understand them. She lowered her voice. 'Like Mrs Lassiter.'

Hazel hid a grin. 'A Birmingham accent. What we call Brummie.'

'Brummie,' echoed the girl carefully.

'What did they say to you?' asked Gorman.

'Very little. Get out here, take your bag, knock on that door. They talked more between themselves.'

'Can you remember what they were talking about?'

Soo Yen gave it some thought. The journey was now a distant memory, she'd been tired, the strangely accented conversation of the two men in the front of the van had not interested her much at the time. 'She who must be obeyed,' she said finally.

Hazel burst out laughing. Gorman stared at her without understanding.

She tried to explain. 'It's Rider Haggard, isn't it? *She?* And then John Mortimer uses it in *Rumpole*, as Horace's nickname for Mrs Rumpole . . .' She saw that she wasn't getting through to him. English literature had never been his strong suit. 'It's a nickname men use for the significant women in their lives – wives, bosses. Women who tell them what to do.' She turned to Soo Yen. 'Did it sound as if they were talking about the wife of one of them? Or about a woman they both worked for?'

The girl knew it was important. She tried to remember exactly what had been said. But it was four months ago, and it hadn't seemed remotely important at the time. She was a long time answering, not because she was reluctant but because she was trying to get it right. 'I think – I *think* – both of them used that name. The young man and the older man. She could not have been the wife of both, could she?'

'No, she couldn't,' agreed Gorman. 'What did they say about her?'

'They made jokes. They pretended to be frightened of her. But I think perhaps they really *were* frightened of her, a little.'

They tried to coax more information from her, about the journey and the men and the woman who made them nervous, but after a while DCI Gorman was satisfied there was no more information to be had. Soo Yen had told them everything she could remember.

'Please,' she said then, 'when shall I be able to go home?'

'Just as soon as I can arrange it,' Gorman promised.

It was a short drive back to Meadowvale. Too short: Gorman turned aside, driving along the park railings and on towards the canal. He parked beside the little humpback bridge and sat staring at the water.

Hazel said nothing to disturb him. She knew exactly what they were doing here. The DCI was Thinking – the capital letter was intrinsic – and before long he would want to bounce his Thoughts off her. The towpath was quieter than the police station, with fewer interruptions, when there was serious Thinking to be done.

At length Gorman looked round at his newest DC as if

mildly surprised to see her there. Then he sniffed and said darkly, 'I blame the feminist movement. You never used to find women running international crime gangs.'

Hazel grinned. 'They should never have given us the vote. That was the first mistake.'

Gorman gave a chuckle. 'OK. We don't want to read too much into this. Firstly, because we might be wrong – these two guys might have had a mistress in common. Unlikely, in view of the age difference, but not impossible. And secondly, She Who Must Be Obeyed probably isn't running anything. If she's giving orders to the two muppets driving the van – the guys who're most likely to take the fall if something goes wrong – she's probably only a couple of rungs up the ladder.'

'How long do you suppose the ladder is?'

'Long enough to keep the guys in charge well above the shit,' growled Gorman. 'That's how these things work: little fish reporting to slightly bigger fish until you come to the shark at the top of the tree.' He paused there, aware that his metaphor had become somewhat mixed. 'So nobody can give the whole game away if he ends up talking to us.'

'Which makes She Who Must Be Obeyed some kind of middle management,' suggested Hazel. She wasn't sure if he actually wanted her input as well as a receptive ear, but if he didn't he'd shut her up soon enough.

Gorman nodded slowly. 'Less disposable than the drivers, but disposable enough if push came to shove.'

'How do we find her?'

Gorman didn't know either. 'At least we've an idea now what that van was doing at Myrton.'

Hazel blinked. 'We have?'

'It was making a delivery. Rose or one of her fellow-travellers was being delivered to their new employers.'

Understanding kindled in Hazel's eyes. 'That's farming country. I doubt there's anything *but* farms for ten miles in any direction.'

Gorman shrugged. 'Cheap labour would be a godsend to lots of farms. Picking fruit, mucking out the chickens, milking the pigs.' Dave Gorman was a city boy at heart: he'd hardly seen a green space bigger than a rugby pitch until he came to

Norbold. 'Those two lads who travelled with Soo Yen – that's the kind of job they went to. Someone travelling with Rose must have been heading for the same thing.'

Hazel had pulled the road map out of his glove compartment. 'The drivers are using the big lorry and the motorways to cover distance, then switching to the van so they can make deliveries up narrow country roads. Since it was the van that David saw at Myrton, maybe they'd made a delivery not long before, or they were just about to. If we visit farms on the road between Myrton and the motorway, we might find the right one.'

'Maybe,' said Gorman doubtfully. 'I guess we'll have to try. The difficulty will be recognising it when we find it.'

Hazel, who had done much of her growing up around farms, had a better idea what they were looking for than Gorman had. 'It's the wrong season for fruit picking, so a big vegetable producer would be favourite. They've always used overseas labour. Picking veg is hard work for not much money: lots of home-grown workers would rather be on the dole. Agricultural workers from Europe – eastern Europe in particular – come for the picking season, live on site, work long hours and go home with money in their pockets. It works for both parties.'

'Then why the need for slave labour?'

'Because someone always gets greedy,' sighed Hazel. 'The margins aren't enormous at the farm gate.' No, she'd lost him again. She tried to make it simpler. 'There isn't that much profit on a carrot once you've paid for the seed and the fertiliser, and the stoical Romanian to pick it. The price the housewife pays in the supermarket is a lot more than what the supermarket pays the farmer. The seed and the fertiliser always go up in price, so the only way to boost the producer's income is for him to pay less for his labour.'

'Is it skilled work?'

'Not particularly. I mean, people who do it for a living are a lot better at it than casual labour, but anyone can master the basics pretty quickly. I've done it myself, to make money for college. It's murder on the back but it's not difficult.'

'So a couple of illegal immigrants could be put to work without much training, without anyone asking too many questions, and without much risk of the neighbours reporting suspicious activity,' ruminated Gorman. 'They'd just look like part of the regular overseas crew.'

'The regulars would know they weren't, though. They're the ones we need to talk to. We need to find a vegetable operation gearing up for the Christmas market somewhere on that road, and talk to the overseas pickers. They'll know if there have been any ringers in their ranks.'

'Will they talk to us?'

Hazel saw her chance and took it. 'They might not talk to you, Chief. But I bet they'll talk to a fellow yokel like me.'

When she got home that evening, there was a visitor waiting on Hazel's doorstep. She felt an unexpected surge of anger under her breastbone. 'All right, where is he?'

Patience regarded her with calm, toffee-coloured eyes. The end of her scimitar tail waved.

'Gabriel?' He didn't have a key to her house, and though he knew where she kept the spare, she doubted he'd have let himself in and left his dog sitting on the pavement. She glanced at her watch. Quarter to seven: with the boys away, he was probably still in the shop, bringing his accounts up to date. Some days he needed the fingers of both hands. It was a short walk from Railway Street to Rambles With Books. Hazel pointed a commanding finger towards the street corner. 'Go on, off you go.'

Patience stayed where she was, sitting on Hazel's doorstep, watching her expectantly.

Hazel breathed heavily. 'He'll be worried when he misses you.'

There was nothing remotely aggressive about the lurcher's posture; at the same time, it was obvious she wasn't going to do as she was bid. 'Oh, for pity's sake . . .!' Hazel shrugged her coat up around her ears and dug her hands deep into the pockets. 'Come on then, I'll take you back.'

Apparently that was the desired response: immediately Patience came to her feet and fell into step beside her.

She'd been right about the accounts. Though the shop was closed, there was a light on and she could see Ash bent over the long table, pen in hand. She'd tried to convert him to the convenience of digital bookkeeping, in vain. With a quiet obstinacy to match his dog's, he'd explained that he liked doing it the old-fashioned way. He kept a fountain pen for the purpose.

The door was locked. She rapped on the glass and when he looked up, startled, pointed down at the dog. Then she turned back the way she'd come.

Ash threw aside his books, and even his fountain pen, and hurried to the door. 'Hazel. Please don't go.'

To keep walking would have been both childish and churlish. She stopped and after a moment looked back. 'Patience found her way to my place. I thought I'd better bring her back.'

'I hadn't missed her. She must have gone out the back way.'

'You need to make it secure.'

'I thought I had.' He was standing in the street in the icy blast of a winter's evening in his shirtsleeves. His head was down and his shoulders hunched, and there was a look of helpless misery on his face that had nothing to do with the weather.

She almost said, 'Whatever,' and kept walking. But they had meant too much to each other once for it to end like that. Whether or not she was still angry with him, whether or not he deserved her anger, their shared history meant that the least they owed each other now was a civil parting. Perhaps that was why she'd come. Perhaps – a fanciful thought – that was why Patience had fetched her.

Hazel's tone softened. 'Go back inside, Gabriel. You'll catch your death of cold.'

'Will you come in? Just for a minute?'

She went on watching him; still she didn't leave. 'There's no point.'

'I want to . . .' What? Explain? How could he possibly? Apologise? No apology he could offer could begin to set things right between them. 'I want to say how bitterly I regret leaving you to deal with David's death alone.'

'I wasn't alone,' said Hazel; and it came out rather more sharply than she meant it to. 'Dave Gorman had my back. Pete's been a star too.'

'I could tell.' Ash's teeth were beginning to chatter. 'That doesn't make what I did all right.'

Almost against her better judgement, Hazel found herself taking pity on him. She ushered him back into the shop and closed the door, shutting out the dark street. But she didn't sit down. She had no intention of staying.

'Isn't it time you went home? Your time isn't your own any more, you know,' she added, a shade maliciously.

The needle went home: she saw him flinch. 'Actually, it is.'

Hazel's eyes saucered. 'She's gone?'

'Yes.'

'For good?'

'Absolutely,' said Ash.

'Well – that's a bit sudden!'

Ash shook his head despairingly. 'It wasn't what you think, Hazel. She was never going to stay any longer than it took to sort a few things out. I'm sorry I wasn't honest with you. I thought, the more you knew, the more difficult your position would be. If that was stupid, I really am sorry. I couldn't find a way of doing everything that needed to be done. It won't be much comfort, but I was feeling a complete bastard even before I heard about David.'

He wasn't a man who swore easily or very effectively. He didn't get enough practice. On those rare occasions that the Queen's English failed him, he always sounded like a nine-year-old afraid of being overheard by his mum.

Hazel gave a weary sigh. 'You don't need to. It was all over before I even missed him. There was nothing either of us could have done.'

There was a lengthy pause. Neither of them made any move towards the door. Patience settled herself under the long table, curled round like a bagel with her chin resting on her tail.

Eventually Ash said, 'How did you know? About . . .?'

'Your visitor?' Hazel's smile was brittle. 'I saw the pair of you, at your bedroom window.'

'She stayed for three nights. I slept in the study.'

Oddly enough, she believed him. She still didn't understand. 'If you didn't want to share, why didn't you put her in the guest room?'

Ash looked at his shoes. 'The boys broke the bed, playing at paratroopers. I haven't got round to buying a new one.'

'And these things you needed to sort out . . .' She saw his hunted expression as he glanced up. 'Don't worry, I'm not going to ask for the gory details. I'm going to make a wild guess, and you can tell me if I'm right or wrong. That thing you were busy doing – was it something to do with the boys? With keeping them safe?' That would explain his actions as nothing else could.

Ash considered for a moment. The answer he gave then was overly simplistic but it was the truth. 'Yes. Yes, it was.'

Hazel let out a long breath. 'Then you did the right thing. They have to be your priority. They always will be. Is everything all right now?'

'At home? Yes, I think so. Frankie and the boys will be back in a few days. But it's not all right. We've both lost a friend. And I've been afraid I lost something even more precious.'

'Oh Gabriel,' sighed Hazel, finally sinking onto one of the chairs drawn up at the table, 'why do we always make such a mess of something everyone else finds easy? Even teenagers; even people with half a brain. I'm not stupid, and you're positively smart, and still we can't figure out what we want from one another.

'Shall I tell you something? When I saw you together and I thought you were . . . well, a couple . . . a bit of me was relieved. Relieved that you'd taken it out of my hands, that you'd made a decision so I didn't have to wrestle with it any more. Didn't have to decide what I wanted and how much I was prepared to pay for it. I was sorry, I don't mind telling you I felt hurt, but there was a part of me that figured it was probably for the best.'

She was only telling him what he already knew: that he'd managed to trash any future they might have had. He was bereft but also resigned. At least he consoled himself with the tentative hope that the anger she had borne him had begun to mellow.

'I let you down,' he said in a low voice. 'Regardless of what we could or couldn't have accomplished, you came to me for help and I let you down. I'm not going to ask you to forgive me. In view of what's happened, that wouldn't just be unrealistic, it would be impertinent. There must have been a way I could have protected the boys without hurting you, and I'm more sorry than I can say that I couldn't find it.'

She believed that too. It was etched in every line of his face, the awkward, unhappy set of every muscle in his body. He was a terrible liar, like Guy insisting he hadn't raided the cake tin when there were crumbs all over his jumper, but even if he'd been much better at fibbing he couldn't have been that good. He looked broken. He looked more like the man she'd first met than he had in two years.

Hazel put her hand on the table. After a moment she extended it towards him.

Ash made no move to take it.

'Gabriel – you have to meet me halfway.'

He stared at her hand, then at her face. 'I wasn't sure you'd want me touching you,' he murmured.

The smile came more easily than she'd expected. 'That ship sailed long ago.'

It crept into his face that he knew what she was saying, but still didn't quite dare to believe it. 'We can get past this?' It was much more a question than a statement.

'Stranger things have happened. Actually, stranger things have happened to *us*.'

She drove Ash and Patience home to Highfield Road. The big stone house was empty, the curtains drawn back, no lights showing. Diffidently, he asked if she would come in; almost without hesitation she agreed.

The house felt cold. Ash apologised, hurried to put the central heating on. He went to take her coat, then worried that she might want to keep it until the heat came through. As if they were strangers, and he wanted to be polite.

As Patience walked between them into the kitchen, Hazel could have sworn she saw the dog wink.

Ash made coffee. An hour later, when Hazel still hadn't left, he put a stew to reheat in the oven and set the table.

After supper they talked about David Sperrin.

Hazel described the scratches Sperrin had spent the last

minutes of his life carving into his flesh, through a pin-hole in his jeans that no one would notice until his body was stripped. She was not wholly dissatisfied to see Ash turn pale.

'It's hard to imagine that kind of single-mindedness,' he murmured. 'That much strength of purpose.'

'He was very angry,' Hazel remembered. 'He was consumed by a kind of furious grief that he hadn't been able to save that girl. That fate had put him in a place where he, and she, thought he might have done, and then he couldn't. There was a bit of him, I think, that almost wished he'd died trying. That put a higher value on his self-respect than on his life.'

'It's something that people sometimes say. I don't think many of them follow through.'

'David always wrote his own rules. He didn't have much of a family life – well, you know that. Apart from Pete and his sisters in recent years, I never heard that anyone held him in much affection, or that he felt anything much for anyone else. That's usually a recipe for emotional meltdown. But if people are sufficiently strong-minded, sometimes they turn social isolation to their advantage. Instead of peering wistfully through windows at other people's lives, they turn their backs on the chocolate-box version of happiness – the trophy spouse, the two-point-four children, the flash car and split-level executive home – and fashion a world that fits them better. I think that's what David did. I don't think he gave a damn for what anyone else thought of him: the only opinion he cared about was his own. It was his tragedy that what happened at Myrton left him feeling like a failure.'

'And yet, what more could he possibly have done?'

'Well – *this*,' said Hazel. She brought the file she'd been taking home in from the car and spread its contents on Ash's kitchen table. 'He found the people who killed the girl we're calling Rose. And he left us a message to tell us who they are. And – God forgive me – I can't read it.'

Ash turned the image towards him. 'Could it be a Chinese character?'

'We thought of that. Dave Gorman got in an expert. It didn't mean anything to her.'

'It looks a bit like a vase . . .'

'. . . Of flowers,' finished Hazel. 'Yes, everybody says that. Well, the brothel I found called itself China Roses. But I already knew that, and David knew I knew, so what would be the point?'

'What else could it be, then?'

She shrugged, at once helpless and angry. 'I don't know! I didn't know when I first saw it, and now I've been staring at it for three days and I *still* don't know!'

Ash indicated the photograph. 'What about this mark here? Just under his knee.'

Hazel got up and walked behind him, to see where he was looking. She hadn't noticed anything other than the scratches; and indeed, the mark was so faint it might have been an artifact of the photography, except that clarity is of paramount importance in autopsy photographs.

'A bruise?' she hazarded.

Ash nodded. 'Probably. Maybe it's a hangover from his encounter with the train.'

But it didn't altogether look like an old bruise, the yellow and purple staining surviving at the edges after the centre of the lesion has dispersed. Hazel dug in the file for her copy of the FME's report. 'No, the doctor reckons it was a newly acquired contusion that never had time to develop. Possibly from a blow, possibly from something he bumped into.'

'I don't imagine he just stood quietly while they decided what to do with him,' said Ash.

'No, I don't suppose he did.' Hazel frowned, reached for the photograph and studied it more closely. 'I've seen something like this before. Rose had marks like this on her legs. More prominent but in exactly the same place, just under the kneecap.'

'Which doesn't really sound like the result of a scuffle,' ventured Ash.

'We wondered if she'd been hobbled, to restrict her movements. We wondered – well, all right, *I* wondered – if it meant she'd been brought through a public area, an airport or ferry terminal, where someone would have noticed if she'd been handcuffed. But I don't think David went through an airport between here and Coventry. And I think someone *would* have noticed if he'd been wearing a skirt long enough to cover his knees!'

'Then perhaps it was something he bumped into,' said Ash. 'Something they both bumped into. Perhaps in the place where they were kept there was some kind of structure that made it hard *not* to bang your knee on it.'

'What kind of a structure?'

He tried to picture it. 'If the shed where they found David was some kind of a transit point, where migrants were held for onward transport, there was probably somewhere they could be locked up. Storerooms, or' – he swallowed – 'cages. Perhaps there wasn't much leg-room. Or perhaps there was a window they could see out of only by kneeling on the windowsill.'

Hazel shook her head. 'There were no windows. Dave Gorman said there was nothing inside, just an empty space. I suppose there could have been cages, if they dismantled them and took them away when they left. It was big enough, and high enough, to drive vehicles inside, so no one would see what they were doing.'

Ash frowned. 'Vehicles plural?'

'We found a girl who travelled in an earlier shipment. She said they used both a lorry and a van. The lorry for long distances, the van for making deliveries. That's what David saw at Myrton.'

She related other things Soo Yen had remembered about her journey from Shanghai. It didn't take long: for all that the girl had done her best to help, she hadn't had much useful information to pass on. Of course, it had been in the traffickers' interests to keep their charges in the dark.

'One thing she said,' Hazel finished. 'One of the traffickers seems to be a woman. Soo Yen never saw her, but she heard the drivers talking. It sounded as if the woman was the one who gave them their orders – told them where to go, who to collect, where to take them.' She grinned. 'They called her She Who Must Be Obeyed.'

It had got late while they were talking. Hazel gathered her file together and shrugged her shoulders back into her coat.

'I'm going home. I'll call you tomorrow.' She let herself out at the front door, and never noticed that Ash didn't answer her, that he didn't move, that all the colour had once again drained from his face.

TWENTY-TWO

Gabriel Ash had never been a good sleeper, even when his life was at its calmest. He'd always been able to find things to think about, often to worry about, in the quiet reaches of the night. He'd tried going to bed early and going to bed late, reading something uninvolving, and cocoa. On the whole he preferred the insomnia. Like most poor sleepers, he usually got *some* sleep, and often rather more than he thought he had. He found he could function reasonably well even after a run of bad nights, as long as he didn't fall into the trap of worrying about it.

Tonight was different. He had neither the time nor the emotional energy to spare for worrying about insomnia when his head was filled, *filled*, with the desperate conviction that he now knew what had brought Cathy to England when every scintilla of self-preservation she possessed should have been telling her to stay away.

He didn't even go to bed until three in the morning, by which time his body was chilled through and he could hardly drag himself up the stairs. He lay in a cold cocoon of bedding, and a cold sweat of fear, with no prospect of sleep, aware of every one of the night's seconds dragging by, until a little after six.

He didn't dress. He pulled a sweater on over his pyjamas, made a pot of coffee and took it back upstairs.

Patience looked up from the end of his bed. In theory she had a basket in the corner. In practice, she slept curled up beside him, pressed into the small of his back. So if he had a bad night, she had one too.

She said, So what are you going to do?

'I'm not sure I should do anything,' he countered warily.

Yeah, right, she yawned, you're really good at doing nothing. At dodging the difficult decisions. It's why your life is so devoid of incident and interest.

'So what do you *want* me to do?' he demanded. 'Tell Dave Gorman that not only have I been harbouring a wanted criminal, not only did I help her get out of the country, but there's a good chance she's a prime suspect in his current investigation? Which will mean, of course, Hazel knowing that my wife may have been responsible for the murder of her friend.'

Is that what you think?

'I can't prove it,' he said evasively. 'Not to a jury's satisfaction; perhaps not even to mine. It's not much more than a notion, really, based on the timing of Cathy's arrival, the manner of her departure, and what I know about who and what she's become.'

But is it what you *think*?

'God help me,' whispered Ash. 'Yes. Yes, it is.'

The lurcher's caramel-coloured eyes were compassionate. Then what choice do you have? she asked. People have died. One of them was a friend of ours. If you have any information about the people responsible, you have no right to keep it to yourself.

'If you can call it information. It's only a theory. A hypothesis. I don't know how much help it would be.'

Exactly. You don't know. You need to share it with someone who does.

'Hazel already knows that Cathy was here.'

Has Hazel any reason to think there's a connection between her and the traffickers?

'Well, no . . .'

No. But you have.

'I can't talk about this to Hazel!' The mere idea filled him with dread.

Hazel will find out. If Cathy is involved, sooner or later Hazel's going to know. It would be better coming from you now than from someone else later.

'What if I'm wrong? It could easily be a coincidence. Things Cathy said that I'm reading too much into. I need more information before I do anything that can't be undone.'

What kind of information?

'The police may have evidence that puts Cathy out of the frame completely. Dear God, I hope they have.'

If you start asking questions, Hazel will want to know why.'
'I shan't ask Hazel.'

Detective Chief Inspector Gorman had never had any difficulty sleeping. He fell asleep every night as soon as his head
hit the pillow, or the back of his armchair, or sometimes
the wooden screen dividing the snug from the rest of The
Poacher's Arms. The Poacher wasn't Norbold's official
coppers' pub, but it had the massive advantage of being
within spitting distance of Gorman's flat. When they woke
him up at closing time, he could be home and asleep again
in two minutes.

He was woken by his phone a little before seven. The fact
that his alarm would have roused him within minutes anyway
did nothing to salve his sense of injustice.

He didn't need to look at the caller display. 'What do you
want, Gabriel?'

'I didn't wake you, did I, Dave?'

The polite response on these occasions is to deny it, however
sleepily. 'Yes,' growled Gorman.

'I couldn't sleep.'

'What do you want me to do – sing you a lullaby?'

'No, I mean, that's why I'm calling so early. I've been awake
all night. I nearly called you an hour ago.'

'And I'm supposed to feel grateful that you didn't?'

There was a pause. 'Shall I call back later?'

Gorman relented. 'No, I'm awake now. What's the problem?'

'Something Hazel told me. She said you're looking for a
woman in connection with the people smuggling.'

'That's right. Someone overheard the lorry drivers talking
about her. Why?'

'Did they give any kind of a description? Anything you
could identify her from?'

'Nothing. Why?'

If ever there was a time to learn how to lie, it was now. 'I
– er – um – thought . . .' What? How could he explain his
suspicions without confessing everything? A psychic dream?
An alien visitation? At least that would have the merit of some
truth. Gorman wouldn't believe he'd overhead something in

the pub, and it wasn't the sort of information you stumbled across in a second-hand bookshop.

'Come on, Gabriel, spit it out. You've been thinking again, haven't you?' Gorman said darkly. 'I'm sure I've warned you about that.'

'Well – in a way. It's probably nothing. I thought it was in the middle of the night, but now it's morning I think perhaps . . . You know how it is. You can think you've cracked cold fusion in the middle of the night.'

Gorman had almost no idea what he was talking about. 'It's *still* the middle of the night as far as I'm concerned,' he grumbled. 'I'd like to think you had some reason for waking me, other than to discuss your fantasies. If you've had a bright idea about who this woman might be, for God's sake tell me before one of us dies of old age.'

'I'm probably wrong . . .'

'Every chance,' agreed Gorman. 'And when you get round to giving me a name, maybe I'll be able to tell you. Gabriel – *spit it out! Now!*'

'Oh God,' Ash moaned, defeated. 'Dave – is there any chance it could have been Cathy?'

Now Gorman was wide awake. '*Your* Cathy? Your wife? Why the blue blinding blazes would you think that?'

'I've seen her, Dave. Here, in Norbold.'

Even now, the old question over Ash's sanity made it easy to dismiss what he said, even for someone who knew him as well as Gorman did. The temptation to play amateur psychologist was too strong. 'Gabriel, you imagined it. Wherever Cathy is now, she'll be giving Norbold a wide berth. A berth as wide as a continent, if she's any sense. If you caught a glimpse of someone in a crowd, or passing in a car, and thought you recognised her, well, that's understandable. She meant a lot to you at one time. You're bound to think about her still, to wonder where she is, what she's doing . . .'

Ash spelled it out as clearly as he could. 'She stayed in my house for three days.'

People talk about cutting silence with a knife. *This* silence would have required a chainsaw. It was thick and gnarly, and dripped with import like resin from an old pine. Ash didn't dare break it, and Gorman wasn't ready to.

Finally the DCI said, 'Why am I hearing this now?' There was iron in his tone.

Ash knew he was in trouble. He didn't expect Gorman to protect him from the consequences of his actions because they were friends. He clung to the faint hope that he might get a fool's pardon. 'You said it: she's my wife. I couldn't turn her in.'

'You could. You should have done.'

'I know.' Though Gorman couldn't see him hang his head, he could hear it.

'Where is she now?'

'I don't know. I left her in a field in Cambridgeshire.'

'*Why?*'

So Ash gave him a digest of everything that had passed between them. The divorce papers that guaranteed their mother would have no part in his sons' upbringing. The business deal that had gone wrong, that explained her covert return to England. His certainty that only a genuine crisis would have induced her to take the risk. The timing: how she'd arrived soon after the episode at Myrton, and left immediately after the murder of David Sperrin.

'I didn't put any of it together,' he assured Gorman abjectly, 'until Hazel told me about the other girl, and the lorry drivers, and She Who Must Be Obeyed. Then it all made a kind of sense. At least, I think it does. That's why I needed to talk to you as soon as was reasonable – or slightly sooner,' he amended apologetically. 'I was desperate for you to tell me you'd identified this woman, that she was a fifteen-stone Birmingham granny and you already had her in custody.'

'Hazel told you that?'

'She was here last night. We were talking about David, trying to work out what had happened.'

DCI Gorman had benefited from these brainstorming sessions of theirs too often in the past to object to one now. Ash deliberately concealing a wanted criminal in his house for three days was a trespass of a whole different order. 'You're telling me Hazel knew about Cathy?'

'Only that she'd been here,' Ash said hurriedly. 'Not that . . . not what I suspect. That was the reason I wanted to catch you at home. I didn't want her there while we talked.'

'No.' DCI Gorman sounded remote, non-committal. As if he had a lot to think about. 'And you really can't say where Cathy might be now?'

'I think she was meeting a plane. A light aircraft, something that could land in a field. I imagine by now she's back where she came from – wherever she's been living.'

'I see.'

'You think it was her too, don't you?' Ash said miserably.

'Gabriel, I have no idea. And thanks to you, I don't know how we'd find her if it was. I have to go to work now. But this isn't finished. You understand that?'

'I am sorry, Dave.'

'You do keep saying that, don't you?'

Gorman left the blind up, so he could see from his office into the big CID room. He wanted to speak to Hazel the moment she arrived.

So he was startled when she arrived at his other door, the one connecting directly with the upstairs corridor, flinging it open and surging in like a tightly focused tornado. Her eyes were on fire and her cheek flushed with haste. But some lingering sense of what was appropriate made her rap on the door with her knuckles in passing.

'Come in, why don't you?' said Gorman levelly.

Either she didn't hear him or she didn't recognise it as a rebuke. 'I know what it means. The bruise on David's leg. And the scratches.'

'Bruise?'

'The same as those on Rose's knees. Less noticeable, because he wasn't in the van as long, but it's recorded in the autopsy report.'

'Van?'

'The van that left its wheel-tracks on the verge at Myrton. The one they used to make deliveries up country lanes where the lorry wouldn't fit, and would draw too much attention if it did. Chief, I know where it is!'

This wasn't what he'd intended to talk to her about. But it was both more important and more urgent than Hazel Best's future as a police officer. That conversation would have to wait. 'Take me. No, explain. No – take me, and explain on the way.'

Mrs Kiang looked up with a certain resignation as Hazel entered her shop. It turned to suspicion when she saw the detective constable had brought her boss. 'You want flowers?' she asked, more in hope than expectation.

'Not this time, Mrs Kiang. We want to talk to your William. Where is he?'

The florist spread tiny hands in a helpless shrug. 'Out on the lorry. I don't know where he's driving today.'

'Folkestone? Dover? Hull?'

'Could be. He was away overnight, I know that. Should be back tomorrow. What you want him for?'

Hazel ignored the question. 'You said, sometimes he borrows your van. How often?'

'A couple times a month, maybe. That lorry's too big for some jobs. Why? What's this about?'

'Did he have it six days ago?'

Mrs Kiang thought back. 'About then. He had business in Coventry, it wasn't worth getting the lorry out. Wednesday night, I think it was.'

'What time did he get back?'

'I don't know, I was asleep.'

'Is the van out the back, Mrs Kiang?'

The florist was becoming a little flustered and a lot annoyed by all the questions. More and more her accent was veering into the Brummie patois. 'Why do you want to know? If William's got himself some speeding tickets, talk to him about it, not me. I am not my husband's keeper!'

Gorman stepped in, his gruff voice commanding attention. 'The van, Mrs Kiang. I want you to show me, now.'

She threw up her hands in a gesture of compliance. 'If I must.' She locked the front door before taking them through the back of the shop, past racks of flowers steeping in tall zinc buckets, to the yard behind. To the cream Transit van with *China Roses* inscribed on its side in twining silver letters.

'It's just a van,' complained Mrs Kiang.

It wasn't locked. Hazel went to the back and threw open the load-bay doors. She looked at DCI Gorman. 'Do you want to try it or shall I?'

Gorman considered. She was younger than him, fitter and more flexible. Also, it was her idea. 'You.'

Hazel climbed up into the back. It was as she remembered, fitted out for the careful transport of flowers, with benches running the length of the bay on either side and, screwed to them, a grid of aluminium bars that the tall zinc buckets would slot into. Hazel manoeuvred herself onto one of the benches. The only place to put her legs was through the grid.

She looked at Gorman. 'See?'

'I see it.'

Her knee was resting just above the bar. Over a long journey, mounting weariness would make her lean on it more and more, leaving a distinctive mark. On a short journey, say from Norbold to Coventry, the bruise would be less pronounced.

'See what?' demanded Mrs Kiang, bewildered and irate.

But right now Hazel had no interest in updating the florist on her husband's extramural activities. She was talking to Gorman, the words coming fast and sure. 'He tried to tell us he'd seen this van. I thought he was confused: that he was remembering the China Roses name from the cellophane wrap on the flowers I took him. But he was right all along. And when he knew it for sure, he figured out a way of telling us.

'Everyone who looked at those scratches on his knee said they looked like a bunch of flowers. But I wouldn't have it, would I? I couldn't see why he'd keep saying the same thing – china roses, china bloody roses! But he wasn't. He was telling us what he could see – right then, immediately before he died. Flowers. He was surrounded by flowers.'

TWENTY-THREE

The lorry owned by William King travelled from Holland on the Harwich ferry, docking a little before seven the following morning. News of his coming preceded him: by five a.m., Harwich Police were talking to Meadowvale's senior detective.

'Do you want us to stop him or let him through?'

'What I'd really like,' said Gorman, stifling a yawn, 'is for you to let him through and follow him until I can take over. I don't just want him: I want every skinflint farmer and every snooty cow who's too posh to do her own ironing, who buy these kids' dreams for pennies. Without end-users there'd be no trade. There's as much blood on their hands as there is on Bill King's. I want to see where he goes, who he's doing business with.'

'It's a gamble,' the voice on the phone reminded him. 'Things do go wrong. Even in a big rig, he could give us the slip. If we take him on the dock, we can control the situation.'

'Your dock, your call. If it was mine, I'd let him run. We know who he is, we know where he is – and the lorry's the size of a bloody great whale. How can we lose it? The worst we're going to do is mislay it for a bit. We're always going to find it again.'

'If that's what you want,' said the voice at the other end dubiously. 'Where will you meet us?'

'He'll come through Colchester, yes?' Gorman had his finger on the road-map: it said all you needed to know about his life that he kept one beside his bed. 'Then where?' It turned out there were three feasible alternatives: north via Cambridge, south to pick up the M1 by way of the M25, or west to the M40. They wouldn't know which route King would take until he took it.

'We'll follow him through Colchester to see if he turns north,' proposed Harwich. 'If he heads south, he's probably heading for the M1. Hard to see why he'd go on round the Magic Roundabout to the M40.'

Gorman agreed, though he knew they could be wrong. It depended on where King had contracted to take his passengers. Assuming he had passengers on this trip. 'Can you stick with him as far as the M25 if you have to? We'll take over as soon as we can.'

'Yeah, I guess so,' said Harwich obligingly. 'You'll owe us.'

'We will,' admitted Gorman. 'Call me after Colchester. If he is going north-about, we'll meet you around Cambridge somewhere.'

He did some calculations, allowing leeway for things to go wrong in, and concluded that he needed to have his team on the road by seven thirty. He began phoning round the members of his department. By six forty-five the CID offices upstairs at Meadowvale were buzzing with activity.

The briefing didn't take long. Everyone in the room already knew what they were there for. 'We've plenty of time, so I don't want anyone driving into a ditch or having a fender-bender. We should take over from Harwich a bit after nine if he goes via Cambridge, a bit later if he heads south. We won't know which until we're on our way.'

He jerked his thumb at Hazel. 'You: with me. Everyone else: find cars. Unmarked. Your own, somebody else's, I don't care. I want wheels on the ground. I don't want this guy making us so we rotate: nobody sits in his mirror for too long. Every time he makes a drop-off, somebody goes in after he leaves. Arrest first, ask questions afterwards. There shouldn't be too much aggro, they'll be too surprised, but make sure you've got enough bodies to discourage arguments. I'll ask Miss for some spare plods' – he meant uniformed officers – 'but for God's sake make sure they take their hats off!'

Hazel claimed Wayne Budgen for the back seat of Gorman's car. She owed him an outing. Whether he entirely appreciated the favour was something else.

In the end five cars left Norbold and headed down the M1, dawn growing palely in their nearside windows as they went. Early commuters were already supplementing the heavy haulage which dominated the motorways at night, but there were no delays, and no one drove into a ditch or got involved in an accident, and Gorman's team had been an hour on the road when Harwich called to say the lorry had turned south after Colchester.

By the time Harwich reported King turning up the M1, Gorman already knew. He was waiting on the hard shoulder with his bonnet up, looking like a casualty, and could see the lorry coming. He had all the information necessary to identify it: the make, the colour, the registration number. Also, it had the words *William King of Norbold* emblazoned on the front and both sides in red metre-high letters. Gorman let it pass, then – engine miraculously cured – he took up the tail from a discreet distance. Hazel thanked Harwich for their help and wished them a safe journey home.

Songs have been written about the world's great highways. Very few of them are about the M1. For much of its length it is singularly charmless – which is perhaps just as well, because the last thing any motorist surrounded by thundering juggernauts ought to be doing is admiring the scenery. But the miles passed quickly, county boundaries coming and going as the road scythed across them. Gorman let himself be overtaken by DC Lassiter, then DS Presley took up the tail. King showed no sign of having spotted them, and no inclination to leave the motorway. Signs for Luton were superseded by those for Milton Keynes, for Northampton.

'Is he going straight home?' wondered Hazel. 'Hellfire, Chief, you don't suppose there's nothing in that truck except what ought to be there? What if he's clean this time? What if there's nothing to find?'

'We'll find something,' said Gorman bleakly. 'I'll have Forensics swab the inside with cotton buds if I have to. He's been carrying illegal immigrants in it, and even if they're not in it today, I don't believe they left no evidence behind.'

'You'll arrest him anyway?'

'Damn right I will. This is our one chance to take him by surprise: once he talks to his wife it'll be gone. Emma's with her right now, but I can't keep her incommunicado for ever. If we can't catch him in the act, I'll pull him in on suspicion and do it the hard way.'

Hazel stared at him, appalled. 'I'm pretty sure we're not supposed to thump the suspects any more.'

Gorman breathed heavily at her. 'I *mean*, by interviewing the shit out of him.'

The pursuit continued, the hounds changing places at random intervals, the fox apparently unaware of the hunt. They were only one junction short of the Norbold turn-off, and Hazel was becoming increasingly convinced that William King was simply heading home after a routine, entirely legal, trip to Europe, when the lorry's indicators came on. She heard Gorman's breath hiss in his teeth.

'So maybe he's only got one delivery to make,' he said, thinking fast. 'I'll take the lead. Tell everyone.' And while Hazel was on the phone he added, 'Have Lassiter stay on the motorway in case we lose him. Everyone else to follow me. Wherever King stops now, we'll take him, and just hope he does have passengers. Catching suspects red-handed makes the Crown Prosecution Service so much happier.' He cast Hazel a grim smile. 'This doesn't look much like vegetable-growing country to me.'

It wasn't. It was light industrial outskirts – the outskirts of where Hazel couldn't work out even by reference to the map in Gorman's glove-box – a linear estate on blighted land convenient to the motorway. Thousands of people came here to work every day. Their cars rafted on acres of cracked tarmac, but of the people there was no sign. Presumably they were all inside the steel and concrete sheds, translucent panels in the roofs supplying second-hand daylight, making whatever it was all those small businesses made: garden furniture and kitchen cupboards and house number-plates and dog beds and throwaway plastic cutlery.

The lorry swept off the motorway and seemed to leave the estate behind. But then the road curved back on itself, and King turned in. A sign popular with the local birdlife said *Danforth Industrial Estate*.

Gorman drove straight on. The high-sided vehicle remained visible across the asphalt desert, intermittently eclipsed by the commercial units but always emerging on the other side. Until it didn't.

Tom Presley, who'd been keeping his distance, followed it into the estate, pulling up on the first corner with an uninterrupted view down the service road. 'He's gone into the last-but-one unit and he's driving round the back,' he reported. 'I can move closer without him seeing me. If you turn in at the far end, we'll have him trapped between us.'

'I see him,' said Gorman, as the lorry reappeared between the shed and the road, clearly visible through the perimeter fence. 'I'm turning in now. Move up, but stay in your car till I give the word.'

The unit was in the business of manufacturing clothing, a fact which it advertised openly and indeed proudly on a board over the door: *Prestige Costumiers*. Hazel supposed the words *Cheap Tat Sweatshop* would have needed a bigger board.

Gorman drove down one side of the unit, Presley down the other, each pulling up at an angle to block both exits. Hazel went to open her door but the DCI pulled her back. 'You stay in the car. Call Lassiter – tell him we've got the lorry bottled up and to get back here ASAP. If it goes pear-shaped, we'll need all the bodies we can muster. And if someone takes off on foot,' he added, fixing her with a stern eye, 'you can follow – but do *not* try to apprehend him on your own.'

He waved away her protests impatiently. He let Presley know he was moving in, and six substantial police officers converged on the lorry. By now other cars were blocking the exits from the industrial estate.

William King had been inside the unit, presumably concluding business; he emerged together with a smaller man in a suit, the unit's owner or manager. One of them must have made a joke because they were both laughing. They stopped abruptly when they saw they had company.

Gorman identified himself, although he guessed from King's expression that he knew exactly who, or at least what, he was. 'I have reason to believe you have illegal immigrants on board this vehicle, and I intend to search it. You can save us all some time by getting them to come out now.'

William King was a big, florid-faced man in his mid-fifties. The fact that he was running to fat, straining the seams of the well-worn sweatshirt under his sheepskin coat, slightly disguised the *other* fact that under the fat was a bulk of solid muscle. But he was designed for fighting, not for running, and certainly not for running across broken ground with a pack of younger, fitter men on his heels. After a moment in which it looked like he was going to resist, he threw up his hands in resignation.

'Ryan, we're buggered,' he called wearily. 'Get them out.'

Ryan was his mate, a younger, shorter, thinner man with ginger hair and a seriously apprehensive expression. Presley walked him to the back of the lorry, and when he'd lowered the tail-gate climbed in after him.

The lorry was packed with wooden shipping crates labelled in a dozen languages and at least three scripts: shoes from Italy and mattresses from Croatia and bookcases from Indonesia and sports equipment from China and garden furniture from Greece. There seemed to be no room for people, or any way to reach them, even if a corner had been found. Ryan, throwing a hunted look back over his shoulder, tugged at a board in one of the shoulder-high crates. It was half empty, and on the far side another loose board pulled out to reveal a dark space at the front end of the load-bay, carefully insulated to mask telltale heat signatures. Presley shone his torch, and six young women were blinking fearfully in the sudden light.

'They're here, Chief,' he shouted.

Even experienced police officers make mistakes. Hearing movement inside the lorry, and mentally downgrading the threat in view of King's age, bulk and resigned co-operation, DCI Gorman craned to see what his trawl had netted. So, unfortunately, did the four officers behind him, each apparently believing that handcuffing Bill King was the job of one of the others.

Bill King might have been getting older, and might have been getting fat, but he'd been supplementing his income imaginatively for a long time now, and he hadn't stayed ahead of both the police and HM Customs & Revenue by being stupid. He identified the instant in which all the policemen whose function it was to curtail his liberty were distracted, and he acted without hesitation. One big hand grabbed the front of Gorman's coat and yanked, and he met Gorman's startled face with his forehead in that gesture of greeting commonly known as a Norbold smacker. While Gorman was still falling, King had used Wayne Budgen as a weapon to hit two other officers, and the tangle of limbs and bodies between him and the last man standing gave him all the time he needed to reach into the pocket of his sheepskin coat and come up with a gun.

It wasn't a big gun. Actually, in his digger-bucket hand it looked a bit wimpy. But you don't need to be a weapons expert to know that guns small enough to hide in a woman's handbag are still big enough to kill. There was every likelihood that this one had already killed twice, and that it was nestled wimpily in Bill King's hand at the time. Everyone except King froze.

King was backing towards the car blocking his exit. He knew better than to attempt a getaway in his lorry, a vehicle that would have been visible from space. 'Keys in the ignition, are they, Chief?' he asked conversationally.

Gorman had his hand to his face, blood dripping between his fingers. The bleak scene of steel units and cracked tarmac and scrubby wasteland was lit for him by a coruscation of tiny stars, but his mind was coming up to speed. He was thinking: Don't try it. Please, Hazel, don't even try it. Get out of the car and back away. We'll get him later. You know what he's capable of . . .

But that was the point. She *did* know what he was capable of. She was grieving for her friend, she was anxious for any member of the public who got in his way, but most of all she was angry: filled to the gills with a fury she had never suspected herself capable of. In all probability, the girl they called Rose had died for standing up to this man. David Sperrin had died pursuing him. Now Hazel had seen King decimate a team of Meadowvale's finest. Getting out of Gorman's car and backing away might have been much the most sensible thing she could do, but she was damned if she was going to do it.

She started the car, floored the accelerator and banged out the clutch in the space of three hot seconds, and she drove straight at the man with the gun.

Bill King had a momentary dilemma. He had enough bullets

for everyone but he couldn't fire in diametrically opposite directions. The six policemen had more or less disentangled themselves, and four or five of them were probably capable of posing a threat by now. But the car was closer, and faster, it represented his best chance of escape, and only the woman behind the wheel stood between him and freedom. He fired the gun at the windscreen. He didn't want to risk hitting anything important.

Braking now would be fatal. Hazel threw herself sidelong across the front seats, kicked down hard on the accelerator and hoped to break William King into a million pieces before he could get off a second shot. But from down here on the upholstery she could no longer see out: she just hoped her colleagues would have the wit to keep out of the way if she missed King and headed for the lorry instead.

She didn't miss him. There was a satisfyingly solid impact, a gratifying yell, and a metallic rattle that she desperately hoped was the gun bouncing off the bonnet of Gorman's car and disappearing from the equation. She eased back on the throttle, but the car was still travelling when the offside wing hit the side of the shed with a scream of tortured metal. Momentum rolled her off the seats and down among the pedals: if King was still on his feet, and particularly if he was still armed, there was nothing she could do to protect herself now. All she could do was hamper his escape, if escape was still foremost in his mind. She pulled the keys from the ignition and hurled them through the window into the scrubby grass that began where the cracked tarmac ended.

For an indeterminate amount of time, which was probably around ten seconds but felt much longer, she didn't move. No one came to kill her; no one came to help. If Gorman had seen what she'd done to his car, horror must have rendered him speechless.

Finally the passenger door opened and Tom Presley was reaching strong hands to pull her from her refuge. She gasped, 'Is he . . .?'

'Dead? No,' said Presley judiciously. 'Rendered incapable of presenting any further threat? – oh yeah.'

William King was not only still alive, he was still conscious.

Both his legs were broken where the car had hit him, and he was sitting on the ground with his back against the shed, eyes shut, rocking gently and moaning.

Gorman stumbled up, still nursing his nose. 'Are you all right?'

'I'm fine,' said Hazel; and if it wasn't entirely true, it was true enough for now.

'Good.' He glanced at the car without comment. Then he turned to King. 'William King,' he said sonorously. 'You are under arrest on suspicion of the murder . . .'

Please, thought Hazel silently, *please* don't call her China Rose, don't immortalise it on a charge sheet. She hated it, you *know* she hated it – it's one of the few things we know about her . . .

'. . . Of a female, name currently unknown, at Myrton in Bedfordshire on the eighteenth of November,' continued Gorman, blithely unaware both of the silent prayer and the relief that it had been answered. 'And of the murder of David Sperrin in Coventry, West Midlands, on the night of the twenty-seventh/twenty-eighth November; and the attempted murder of various members of Meadowvale Police in the arse-end of nowhere on whatever the hell today's date is. You do not have to say anything. You have the right to lie there and whimper while I organise an ambulance. One of the old-fashioned ones, that bounces as it goes over the potholes.'

Most of those involved spent the rest of the day in and around Norbold Infirmary. William King woke from surgery to the cheery countenances of his police guard. Dave Gorman got his nose pushed back into a fair approximation of its former shape. Wayne Budgen and a couple of the others had cuts and abrasions they wouldn't normally have bothered about, except that they needed a record of them for the book they were going to throw at King. Of course, a man facing two murder charges isn't unduly worried about bruises on a policeman's elbow.

And Gorman was in no particular hurry to begin the process of charging him. He knew what King's response would be, the only one his brief could possibly recommend: the classic no-comment interview. He had nothing to gain by co-operating, could only make things worse for himself.

The same did not apply to his wingman. Ryan Purbright was younger, he hadn't been doing this as long, he'd never entirely understood the risks that came with the handsome pay-out, and the prospect of years behind bars terrified him. When Gorman – conducting the interview himself though he should probably have been at home with a bottle of co-codamol – gave him the least glimpse of an opportunity, he almost wet himself in his haste to put clear blue water between his role in these events and that of his boss. He was eager to tell all he knew.

And he knew everything. He'd been there when Rose Doe died.

He'd been driving the van. Bill King had brought the lorry in from Europe, and Purbright had met him halfway up the motorway. When they had deliveries to make out in the sticks, the van was a lot handier, if Bill's missus wasn't using it.

Bill was napping in the seat beside him when they delivered their last load of cheap labour to the vegetable packer near Myrton. Purbright had been there three times before and knew the way. Bill woke up long enough to complete the business, and they drove off leaving two young men and a sturdy girl, each with a rucksack of their belongings, standing puzzled and apprehensive in the middle of the yard.

After that there had been some trouble. One of the girls in the back was complaining that the terms of the contract were not being met. She said the sturdy girl had believed she was coming to agricultural college in England. She was a farmer's daughter: she hadn't crossed half the world in order to pick cabbages. There were plenty of cabbages to pick at home.

'She spoke English, then,' said Gorman.

Yes, said Purbright, she spoke great English – you'd hardly have known she was foreign.

'What was her name?'

But Purbright didn't know. He'd never known any of their names; never wanted to know anything about them.

King was getting more and more irritated, and finally he told Purbright to pull the van over while he sorted this out.

He went round the back of the van and opened the door, and lifted the girl out bodily, her legs bumping over the grille that at other times supported his wife's flower buckets.

He read her the Riot Act. She was a long way from home now, there was nobody here to help her – if she gave him any more trouble he'd leave her here, in the middle of nowhere. Then either she'd starve or the police would find her, and it was a toss-up which would be worst.

She refused to be intimidated. She was an educated woman, she said; she knew better than to believe his threats. 'In spite of what it says on your van' – she shook an angry finger at it – 'I am *not* a China Rose. I am a Vietnamese citizen, and I can walk into an embassy in any of the world's great cities and they will look after me.'

'Here?' King looked around him. Apart from a finger of rock in an adjacent field, and the sound of a tractor ploughing half a mile away, there was nothing and nobody. 'Have you any idea how far you are from the nearest Vietnamese embassy? Or which way it is? Of course you haven't. You're in my country now, and nobody here gives a toss about what you want. So get back in the van, and shut your mouth, and do what you're told. You came here for a job, and we've a job lined up for you. We'll be there in another hour or so.'

And what kind of a job was she to expect, she wondered. If the agricultural college turned out to be a cabbage farm, what could she expect who'd been promised employment as a nanny in the household of a prominent businessman?

At which Bill King gave a world-weary sigh. Did she not understand yet? This was how the world worked. All right, it wasn't what she'd hoped for – how many people's lives were? You couldn't change the world: the best you could do was change your expectations. She was young and pretty: the men would be good to her. She just had to do what she was told and keep her mouth shut, and when she'd made enough money to go home she could tell her family anything she wanted. She could tell them she'd been a nanny if that's what they wanted to hear.

At that point Purbright became aware that someone was standing in the field, beside the big stone, watching them. 'I told Bill, and he went to chuck the girl back in the van. But she got away from him, started running towards the gate, shouting for help. The guy hurdled that gate like an Olympic bloody athlete, and the girl pretty well ran into his arms.'

Only then did Purbright realise that King had a gun. Gorman pressed him on that: he insisted it was the truth. He'd never seen a gun before that day, in the big man's possession, in the lorry or in the van. Maybe he always carried it but kept it out of sight, maybe he'd only just acquired it: Purbright didn't know.

He also didn't know if the shot he fired was aimed at the girl or the man. It could have been either, they were so close by then. It might even have been a warning shot that went astray. But it took the girl in the back and hurled her into the man's arms.

For two or three stunned seconds nothing more happened. Then the girl slid to the ground, King raised the gun again, and the man took to his heels, heading down the road. 'Bill told me to run him down. He belted after him on foot. He's not fast, Bill, but he was pretty determined – if he'd caught the guy, I wouldn't have given much for his chances.

'I got past him and blocked the road with the van. With Bill coming up like a herd of buffalo, I reckoned he'd nowhere left to go. And damn me, that's exactly where he went. Over the bridge, onto the railway line, just as a train was coming.

'I didn't want to look but Bill made me. There was nothing to see. I didn't suppose there would be, not after a train had gone over him. No one could survive that. But you can't call it murder. We didn't push him.'

TWENTY-FOUR

I t was the early hours of Thursday morning before DCI Gorman got back to his office. All Meadowvale was quiet: even chucking-out time hadn't produced more than a token amount of disorder, and the CID offices upstairs should have been empty.

Hazel had waited for him. He found her asleep at her desk, fair head cradled on her arms.

'Oi, Rip Van Winkle,' he said, nudging her. 'Go home. We'll talk tomorrow. Well – later today.'

She knuckled the sleep out of her eyes. 'I'm all right. I wanted to know what you found out.'

So he told her. Her eyes filled at one point, but it may have been weariness.

When he'd said everything he intended to for now, Hazel said sadly, 'So David died for nothing.'

Gorman frowned, then winced as his nose objected. 'How do you figure that?'

'Because he couldn't remember what happened, he was always afraid he hadn't done right by that girl. That he'd been too scared to help her. Everything he did afterwards was to make amends. To prove – to himself, or maybe to her – that he wasn't a coward. And there was no need. He did everything that anyone could have done.'

'He certainly impressed the hell out of Ryan Purbright.'

'Did you get what you needed from him? Tell me they're not going to get off on a technicality.'

'They're not going to get off on a technicality,' promised Gorman. 'We haven't got everything yet, but we've got enough. Purbright gives us King. King's a tougher nut, but it's hard to keep saying nothing when you're looking at a life sentence. I think he'll talk in the end. Maybe he'll give us enough to cap the pipeline once and for all.

'And the other thing you'll be glad to hear is, we've had a

response from Hanoi. They've looked at the results from the' – he couldn't remember the name of the test – 'tooth thingy and reckon Rose probably came from the Da Nang area. They've asked Da Nang police to make inquiries. In a few days we should have her name to put on the charge sheet. And be able to tell her parents why she hasn't phoned home.'

Both of which were important. Hazel wished she could feel happier about them. 'What about the others – those who travelled with Soo Yen and those who travelled with Rose? Will you be able to find them?'

Gorman nodded. 'With any luck. Purbright helped deliver most of them: he's making out a list of where. Plus, when we go through King's stuff, there'll be documents we can use. Ledgers. He must have kept a record of where he'd taken the kids because he was drawing their wages.'

'What about the woman?' asked Hazel. 'She Who Must Be Obeyed. Did Purbright tell you who she is?'

'Ah yes,' said Dave Gorman softly. 'She Who Must Be Obeyed. I know who she is now, I know where she is, and as soon as I've had a bit of shut-eye I'm going to arrest her.'

Weary as she was, Hazel felt her heart beat high at the prospect. 'Not now? Won't she make a run for it when she hears we've got King?'

'If she hears. If we do this right, the first she'll know that she's in trouble will be when we tell her. But even if she figures it out, I don't think running will be her strategy of choice. I think she'll sit tight and brazen it out – invite us to prove she was involved. Even when she realises Purbright's made a statement, she'll think it's his word against hers. And he's nobody's idea of a star witness.'

'She doesn't know about Soo Yen?'

'No.' Something resembling a smile spread across Gorman's tired and battered face. 'She doesn't.'

'Still,' said Hazel uneasily, 'it's a gamble. You could be wrong. She might think dropping everything and running before we knock on her door is her least worst option.'

'I could be wrong,' agreed Gorman with a yawn. 'It wouldn't be the first time. Which is why I'm having her watched. If she makes a move, we'll pull her in.'

All Hazel's instincts were to get the loose ends tied up, all those involved into custody, and figure out later who did what and how to prove it. But she deferred to Gorman's greater experience. 'And if she doesn't?'

'I've always felt six o'clock is the correct time for a dawn raid.' He looked at his watch, screwing his eyes to focus. 'Four hours from now I'll have had a bit of sleep, and a change of clothes, and coffee, and won't feel as if I've got bricks in my head. Or not as many bricks. Whereas she either won't know what's coming, or will have spent all night worrying and be feeling like a zombie.'

He picked up his coat and headed for the door. But then he paused. 'You can come, if you like. On the dawn raid. Before you clear your desk.'

She stared at him, uncomprehending. 'Chief, I'm sorry about your car, but people were about to start *dying* . . .'

He eyed her quizzically. 'You think this is about my car? You think I'm angry because you scratched my paintwork? Is that the only reason you can think of why I might be angry with you?'

'I can't think of *any* reason why you might be angry with me,' Hazel insisted vehemently.

'OK,' said Dave Gorman. 'Then that's something else we can talk about in the morning.'

At ten to six, Hazel – coming up the back stairs at Meadowvale – met Gorman coming down them. She turned and followed him back to the car park.

She knew – none better – that his own car was out of commission, assumed he'd borrowed one. Checked out one of the area cars, perhaps, or persuaded Sergeant Murchison to lend him his. But Gorman walked past them all, heading for the street.

'Are we taking my car then, Chief?'

The DCI gave her a smile, or a leer, or possibly a scowl: it was hard to be sure for the bruises that had spread, deepened and acquired a personality of their own overnight. 'I thought we'd walk.'

So William King's associate, the woman he and Purbright

had half-jokingly referred to as She Who Must Be Obeyed, was here in Norbold. Not just in Norbold but in downtown Norbold: Dave Gorman never walked anywhere that wheels could take him.

They turned two street corners in quick succession. Hazel began to speculate about where he was taking her.

'Just the two of us, Chief? Will that be enough? Only you probably shouldn't get involved in any more scraps for a while. Give the nose a chance to heal.'

He looked her up and down. 'You're pretty fit. If any scrapping's called for, you can do it.'

As they walked the empty streets, and Gorman made no reference to his comment of the previous night, Hazel began to wonder if it had been some kind of a joke. Not a very funny one, at least not to her, but could he have been having a laugh at her expense? Was he waiting for the perfect moment to hit her with the punchline? She'd always thought of him as having an uncomplicated sense of humour, the slipping-on-banana-skins, falling-down-manholes variety beloved of schoolboys of all ages; but perhaps he was growing subtle with age. In any event, she wasn't going to raise the subject if he didn't.

They turned another corner, and Hazel stopped dead. 'You are *kidding* me!'

Gorman shook his head. 'Nope.'

'Mrs Kiang? She Who Must Be Obeyed?'

'You said it. It's a nickname men use for their wives. Bill King's wife is Mrs Kiang.'

'But she's tiny! And ancient!'

'Size isn't everything. And I don't think she's as old as you think. King's fifty-three. I doubt he married a woman old enough to be his mother.'

'You think Mrs Kiang was the brains behind the operation, and her husband was the brawn? But . . . but . . .' She was trying to think of some reason that made it impossible. And actually, there wasn't one. The fact that Hazel had been buying flowers from her at intervals for three years didn't mean she couldn't have a profitable sideline in human trafficking.

'But it was Mrs Kiang who gave me all the background. Who told me how the girls were tricked and exploited.'

'Well, she'd know, wouldn't she?'

'Bill King put his wife in the frame?'

'No. Ryan Purbright did.'

'He could have lied.'

'Of course he could. But what would it gain him? It wouldn't earn him any Brownie points with us if we couldn't make it stick, and it would make an enemy of Bill King. The only thing that would make Purbright grass on the Kings is the belief that we could put both of them away where they couldn't hurt him.'

As she recovered enough from the shock to think about it, Hazel saw how it could make sense. King had the HGV and legitimate reason to drive it all over Europe. Perhaps his wife had contacts in the Far East. She was an intelligent woman: if she could run one successful business, she could run another. And the van – the van that David Sperrin had seen, the van that had left its mark on his flesh and on Rose Doe's – was hers. Had she found a way to make money without getting up in the middle of the night to attend flower markets?

She wasn't attending one this morning. Of course, her van was at Meadowvale, being combed for evidence. Perhaps she'd thought she'd enjoy an unaccustomed lie-in.

There was a car parked across the road from China Roses. Emma Friend raised a hand and an interrogative eyebrow as they passed. Gorman shook his head. 'I'll shout if we need you.'

Hazel rang the bell beside the shop door. When no one came, Gorman raised his voice at the upstairs windows. 'Mrs Kiang, it's the police. Will you come down and open up, please.'

Finally there was movement inside, and Mrs Kiang opened the door in a flowered kimono. Hazel did a quick reassessment. She was still tiny, but she wasn't ancient. She might have been her husband's age. Like the Widow Twanky accent, she had deliberately cultivated a persona no one would associate with vicious criminality.

It occurred to Hazel, just a little too late, that the woman could have been armed. Her husband had carried a gun: if his wife was also his partner, it was possible she would have one too. She kept a close eye on Mrs Kiang's hands. When she went to fold them into her sleeves Hazel said sharply, 'Please keep your hands where I can see them, Mrs Kiang.'

In the end Mrs Kiang behaved with more style than either Bill King or Ryan Purbright. She knew that the game was up, wouldn't stoop to tears, or lies, or anything as undignified as a wrestling match with a couple of police officers. 'You think I've got a gun?' she sneered. 'Didn't you search my whole house yesterday? Did you find a gun?'

'No, we didn't,' admitted Gorman. 'But Bill had one.'

'Where is he? Why isn't he answering his phone?'

Gorman scowled. 'How would you know? I've got your phone.'

The woman rolled her eyes in disgust. 'You've got *one* of my phones. Is Bill all right?'

'He's in hospital with two broken legs. He'll mend. But he won't be coming home when he has. We caught him in the act, Mrs Kiang. He had six illegals in the back of his lorry, and he tried to shoot his way out when we went to arrest him. Between them' – it was the smallest of white lies – 'him and his partner put you squarely in the frame.'

'Not my Bill,' said Mrs Kiang stoutly. It was the only point in the course of her arrest that she showed any emotion. 'There's nothing you could offer him would make him sell me out. That Ryan, he'd spill his guts if someone spoke harshly to him. He always was as wet as a Wigan weekend. I told Bill, you want to get rid of him – he's weak, he'll let you down. But he was easy to pay. Damned amateurs! You know what it is? You can't get the staff any more.'

Hazel, who'd known her for years, had to ask her first name before they could arrest her. It was Iris.

Sergeant Murchison sent the area car to collect her. DC Friend went home for some overdue sleep. Gorman declined the offer of a lift back to Meadowvale, indicating that he and Hazel would walk. And talk.

'What I said yesterday – no, earlier this morning,' he began.

'I've been hoping it was a joke,' Hazel said, watching him warily.

'It wasn't. Hazel, if I can't trust you, I can't use you. People have gone out on a limb for you, more than once. I have; Superintendent Maybourne has. We did it because we thought you were worth taking a gamble on. I always knew you could blow your last chance. I never expected you to short-change us.'

Hazel stopped dead, staring at him incredulously. 'How in God's name do you think I've done that?'

'You knew that Cathy Ash was in Norbold, and you didn't tell me. You put Gabriel's interests ahead of your duty as a police officer. That's not something I can tolerate.'

'*Cathy?*' exclaimed Hazel. 'She's here?'

'She was here for three days, and she was gone before I heard about it. And I don't care how much loyalty you owe to Gabriel Ash, you owe us more. You should have told me. You know we have a warrant out for her. You had no right to keep that information to yourself.'

'But . . . I didn't know!' insisted Hazel desperately. 'What makes you think I knew? Cathy was here? Are you sure? Why?'

Gorman was frowning again. He'd thought he knew what had happened: that, caught between a rock and a hard place, she'd followed her heart and not her head. That the history she had with Ash had ultimately counted for more than the commitment she owed to her job and her colleagues. It would have been understandable, but it would have ended her career.

The vehemence of her denial took him by surprise. He would have found it quite hard not to believe her, except that he had his information from an impeccable source.

'Who told you this?' demanded Hazel, caution thrown to the wind. Gorman might be her boss, but he wouldn't be much longer if she couldn't convince him of his error. 'I have a right to know. It's a malicious lie, and I want to know who told you.'

'Gabriel did,' said Dave Gorman.

They divided the list between them. Between the addresses supplied by Ryan Purbright, and those which figured in the notebook found in the cab of William King's lorry, there were

more victims to be located, and more co-conspirators to be
questioned, than anyone at Meadowvale would have believed.
Only now did they begin to comprehend the extent of the trade
which had taken place almost under their noses, unseen and
unsuspected.

In truth, there was no overwhelming need for haste. Migrants
who had spent months in indentured servitude would probably
have been happy enough to wait another day for their release.
But the whole of Meadowvale, not just CID, wanted to find
them as quickly as possible, inform them of their change of
circumstance, and start the wheels in motion that would get
them first to safety and then back home.

Sergeant Murchison returned to the boutique hotel in
Whitley Vale where he had taken Mrs Murchison for their
anniversary dinner, and came away with two frightened Korean
girls who did the cleaning and the laundry and ate what the
paying guests left.

DC Lassiter visited a millinery workshop. Among the candy-
floss clouds of tulle and reels of trimmings were six women,
aged between nineteen and sixty-two. Three of them claimed
not to know that the other three were receiving no wages, only
a box of groceries once a week, and were sleeping in the
stockroom.

DS Presley found two fifteen-year-old boys washing cars
within spitting distance of one of Norbold's main thoroughfares.
They were there from seven in the morning until nine at
night. They got fifteen minutes for lunch, and shared a
hamburger, the cost of which was deducted from their wages.
So was board and lodging – they occupied an unheated shed
behind the car wash – and the cost of protective clothing. Their
waterproof jackets had ceased to be waterproof months before,
and they had two rubber gloves between them. As best they
could figure it, they owed their employer a little over £200.

DCI Gorman pulled rank and paid Perfumed Nights a
visit himself. The bordello occupied a three-storey red-brick
house twenty minutes up the Coventry road, convenient for
both town and city and only five minutes from the motorway.
He thought about taking Hazel but decided against. The
temptation to take out her fury on the proprietors might have

proved too strong. Instead he took DC Friend, up and running again after two hours' sleep and a shower.

Perfumed Nights wasn't the only name the brothel went by. When Gorman took possession of the books, he also found entries under Eastern Promise, Russian Dolls, Birds of Paradise – and China Roses.

Somewhat disappointingly, the desk was manned by a plump middle-aged woman from Kidderminster called Celine Cassidy, who recognised Gorman for what he was before he had a chance to show his warrant card. 'Our turn, is it?' she said sourly. 'What, no real crime going on this week?'

'Actually, yes,' he said. 'Right here. Somebody called you three nights ago. Late – around eleven.'

'That's possible,' allowed Mrs Cassidy.

'A man called David Sperrin.'

'Sperrin? Sperrin . . .' She appeared to be thinking but then shook her head. 'I don't remember anyone of that name. A lot of John Smiths. Could he have given us a false name? People do, you know.'

'Maybe,' allowed Gorman. 'You'll remember him, though. He's the one who ended up dead.'

That got Mrs Cassidy's attention. She gave him a hard stare. 'What are you talking about?'

'He called your number. Your China Roses number. He found you via the website. But instead of getting down to business, he started asking questions about the girls. Where they were from, how they got here. You didn't want to deal with him, so you called Bill King, who took him away in his wife's flower van. Next day we found him shot in the head in an industrial unit outside Coventry.'

The stare hardly wavered, but now Gorman could see round the edges to the fear behind it. He thought some of this was news to Mrs Cassidy. Well, some of it might not have been accurate – he was surmising a little, filling in the gaps between what he knew with what he thought must have happened – but it was close enough that she knew how much trouble she was in. 'I don't know anything about anybody getting shot.'

'But you called Bill King. What did you think he was going to do?'

'I didn't think he was going to shoot him!' As soon as the words were out, Celine Cassidy knew she'd incriminated herself. Gorman saw the knowledge slide through her face like the final curtain of a three-act tragedy. She drew an unsteady breath and continued. 'I thought he might . . . you know . . . rough him up a little. We get trouble-makers from time to time. Every establishment like ours does. It's no use calling you people: either you don't come, or you arrest us! So we need someone to call. We call Bill. He can't always come in person – he travels a lot, you know? – but he can put the fear of God into someone over the phone.'

'But this night he turned up in person?'

The woman nodded. So far as Gorman could judge, she wasn't even trying to keep anything from him. 'I hardly had time to put the phone down. He was already in the area, see. Smelled lovely, he did, from all the flowers. He said he'd give the punter a lift back to Norbold. Well, I didn't believe that, and I don't think the punter did either. But I didn't know he'd got a gun! I didn't. They drove off, and I never heard any more.'

'You called him a trouble-maker. This punter. What kind of trouble was he making?'

'Asking questions, like you said. Mainly about some Vietnamese girl. We don't have a Vietnamese girl – haven't had one for months. I told him that. He said that was because she hadn't got this far. I couldn't make out what he was on about. I said we had plenty of other girls, nice girls, from China and Korea and one from Thailand, but he just got more and more angry. So I called Bill. He took the punter outside, and that was the last I saw of him. I haven't seen Bill since, either,' she added in a slightly puzzled tone.

'Were you expecting to see him?' asked DC Friend. Her face was set, her tone rigidly controlled. 'Had he another consignment for you?'

Now Mrs Cassidy's expression closed down. 'Don't know what you mean, dear.'

Gorman spelled it out for her. 'These nice girls from China and Korea and the one from Thailand: I want to see them. I want to see them all, and I want to see them now.'

They emerged from different parts of the building, in various states of dress and undress, reluctant and worried, eyes downcast, slim fingers clasped together. There were seven of them. The oldest was about twenty-two, the youngest might have been sixteen with a following wind. Not one could produce a passport, or visa, or work permit, or a rent book for accommodation, or evidence of a bank account where her wages were being paid.

Gorman nudged Emma Friend. 'You're on.'

Friend had been a police officer for seven years; she could still do her job even when she wanted to cry. She smiled at them and said, very slowly and clearly, 'We're not here to hurt you. We want to help you. You don't have to work here any longer. We'll look after you until we can send you home. Is that all right?'

The silence that followed went on so long that she began to wonder if any of them spoke English. She and Gorman exchanged a helpless glance.

Then one of the girls stepped forward. She was wearing what the purveyors of such things call a play-suit, her long dark hair falling in a sheet over her shoulders, and she looked about as playful as a whipping-boy. But she drew herself up to her full five-foot-nothing in front of Mrs Cassidy, and spat in her face.

TWENTY-FIVE

Rambles With Books had only just opened, and the only customer was Miss Hornblower. And Miss Hornblower left when she saw Hazel's expression.

Ash looked round from dusting his shelves, surprised to see her. Even when she wasn't working, she wasn't usually here much before tea-break. 'Hazel? Is everything all right?'

'Gabriel, *nothing's* all right!' she cried. He couldn't tell if she was more angry or distraught, but he could hear both in her voice. 'You told my boss that I withheld material information about the whereabouts of a murderer!'

Ash's deep-set eyes saucered. 'No, I didn't. Whoever told you that?'

'Dave Gorman. Are you calling him a liar?'

For a moment Ash was dumbfounded. He didn't for a minute think that Gorman had lied to her, or that Hazel was lying to him. He could make no sense of it. 'Hazel, I don't understand. Who are we talking about? You know who killed David? Then tell me, because I don't.'

Then, from total unfeigned incomprehension, he took a single step into complete and awful understanding. The blood drained from his face so fast that he gripped a chair for support. 'Oh dear God, I was right. I thought I was imagining it. I thought she'd hurt me so many different ways that now I suspected her of everything. But she *was* involved with the traffickers. She Who Must Be Obeyed.' He swallowed hard. 'She killed David? Had him killed? Are you sure? How do you know?'

It was Hazel's turn to be mystified. 'Who are you talking about?'

'Well – Cathy.' As if it was self-evident.

'So am I!' shouted Hazel. 'Gabriel, you told Dave Gorman she'd been staying in your house and I knew about it! He was ready to sack me!'

'Hazel – you *did* know about it. You saw us together. You said so.'

She was shaking with fury and exasperation. 'I saw two silhouettes at the bedroom window. I didn't know it was Cathy! How in hell was I supposed to guess it was Cathy?'

'Things you said,' he murmured miserably. He couldn't now remember exactly what they were, but he'd believed at the time – he'd believed until right now – that Hazel had recognised the figure she'd seen. It had been a misunderstanding; but the kind of misunderstanding that ruins lives. 'I thought you knew.'

'I'd have *known* if you'd *told me!*'

He tried to explain. 'I didn't *want* you to know. I didn't want to put you in the position of knowing, and having to either tell Dave and let me down, or not tell him and let *him* down. She turned up without a word of warning, she was there for three days, I never really knew why although she talked about a business deal gone sour, and then I told her she had to leave.

'At that time I had no reason to suspect she had anything to do with David and the case you were working. It was only afterwards – only when you and I were talking, and you said there was a woman high up in the organisation – that the pieces fell into place.'

His head rocked back and he stared blindly at the ceiling, where odd patches of old soot had shown through, staining the new paint. Then he looked at Hazel again. His cheeks were drawn, his eyes despairing. 'Did you find her? Do you have her in custody? Does Dave want me down at Meadowvale too?'

Hazel was almost angry enough to let him think so. 'Bloody Cathy! You've always thought everything revolved around Cathy, even after what she did to you. You're still letting her jerk your strings. No wonder you kept putting off the divorce – you're still secretly hoping that sometime you'll get together again!'

Ash was appalled that she might think so. 'Hazel – the only reason I allowed her in the house was to get her consent to the divorce. You were right, until I had that formalised I couldn't guarantee the boys' safety. Now I can. I told you that.'

'You didn't! You made some gnomic remark that seemed like an explanation but was actually designed to shut me up and shut me out. I accepted it because I trusted you. It never occurred to me that Cathy of all people had got you dancing to her tune again!'

'It wasn't like that,' he muttered. But perhaps it was. Cathy had never told him why she'd risked returning to Norbold. He'd guessed – it had taken no great leap of imagination – that she was involved in something illegal, and he'd known he should have alerted the police. If he'd done that right away, she'd have been in custody before David Sperrin went to Coventry to confront his ghosts. It might have made a difference. He said quietly, 'Have you arrested her?'

'Of course we haven't arrested her,' snapped Hazel, 'we didn't know she was here until she was gone, and we don't know where she is now.'

'But you said . . .' But had she? Or had he invested her words with meanings they had never been meant to convey? They'd been at cross-purposes so often, making assumptions instead of opening their minds and sharing their thoughts. He supposed that was his fault too, although perhaps not wholly. 'She Who Must Be Obeyed . . .?'

'That wasn't *Cathy*,' exploded Hazel. 'That was Mrs Kiang the florist. It was her van David saw. She and her husband were both involved. That was what David scratched on his knee – a bunch of flowers.'

'Not Cathy?' Ash swayed again, relief sapping his strength almost as much as fear had done. 'Thank God. I've been so worried. I know she's done some dreadful things before, but this . . .'

'So that's all right, is it? My friend is still dead, and Rose Doe is still dead, and there are Chinese and Korean and Vietnamese kids working in slave conditions all over the Midlands, and Dave Gorman's out looking for them now but Lord knows how many we'll be able to find and rescue. But we can all breathe a sigh of relief because Cathy Ash is in the clear this time!'

'That isn't what I meant . . .'

'Gabriel, that's *exactly* what you meant! When it comes right down to it, your first priority is the boys, which is fine, and after that – and not far after that – it's Cathy. You have no business filing for a divorce. You don't want a divorce. No matter what she did, no matter what's happened since, you want her back. If you don't know that, you're not being honest with yourself.'

'I never wanted to hurt you . . .' he whispered.

'Well, thank Christ for that,' she snarled. 'I hate to think what you'd have done if you'd been trying!

'Do you know what *really* hurts? You had a straight choice. That morning when David was missing – when I knew he was in danger and I thought there might still be time to find him – you had a straight choice between helping me and helping her. And there was never a moment, was there, that Cathy wasn't going to win.'

Her stare was a direct challenge. He had no answer for her. With all the misunderstandings there had been, all the confusion, he knew exactly what they'd both said that morning. It would be engraved on his conscience for ever.

It did nothing to assuage Hazel's anger, or salve her pain, that he didn't even try to deny it. She wouldn't have believed his denials, but she was obscurely certain that he owed her the attempt. For old times' sake. For what they'd meant to one another. Unless that too had been a conceit: a fantasy she'd conjured to please herself, and he'd been either too polite to disabuse her or too wrapped up in his own concerns to notice.

His eyes dropped. His voice was low. 'Hazel – please . . .'

She stepped back abruptly, as if he'd reached for her. 'Please? You really think you have the right to ask me for something? Anything? Then let me say this clearly, for the avoidance of all doubt. It's over. Whatever there was between us, it's history. I've wasted two years on something that I thought was real, and important, and it turns out I was wrong. Well, it's not the first mistake I've made and it won't be the last. But I'm damned if I'm playing second fiddle to a murderess! I've always thought that a dead wife was the only rival you couldn't compete with. It turns out I was wrong about that, too.

'I don't want to see you again, Gabriel. I don't want to hear from you again. If you phone me, I shan't answer. If you come to the door, I won't open it. Run back to Cathy or don't, whatever takes your fancy. It's no concern of mine any more.'

Tears were running down the seams of Ash's face, dripping off his chin onto his shoes. He made no attempt to stem them, or hide them. 'You don't mean that.'

'Try me.'

'Please, Hazel, can't we talk? In a day or two, when this isn't so . . . raw? I'll call you.'

'Don't waste your time.'

'Then will you call me?' he begged.

The look she gave him killed every last hope in his breast. It was cold, and aloof, and final. 'Not for help if I was dying.' She turned and left the shop, and didn't even slam the door behind her.

A dot appeared in the white northern sky. It grew quickly to an insect, then to a bird, finally to a light aircraft, a high-wing monoplane that circled the airstrip once before coming in to land.

The man was waiting, leaning against his car as the aircraft taxied to a halt. He shrugged up the collar of his coat against the icy slipstream. Normandy has a certain robust charm for much of the year; not so much in December.

The woman unfolded herself from the passenger seat and hurried across the tarmac, the chill breeze tugging at her hair. 'Have you been waiting long? I had to come the scenic route.'

'I heard. Things became . . . difficult. Did you achieve what you went there for?' They were speaking French, the woman with an English accent.

'Not really,' she said, rolling her eyes in weary exasperation. 'It wasn't a total waste of time – I saw my sons, which was important to me.'

'And your husband?'

'He broke my phone.' She laughed. 'I had the devil's job

whistling up my ride. Even then I had to come a roundabout way, via Ireland. I went to earth in Cork for a few days, in case the police were watching the Channel coast.'

'He could have done a lot worse than break your phone,' said the man severely. 'It was a foolish, unnecessary risk. Foolish and unnecessary.'

'It was my risk to take,' she pointed out sharply; and then, smiling, 'And look, here I am, safe and sound. I know him, you see. He was never going to betray me. He doesn't have it in him.'

'A weak man, yes?'

'Perhaps,' she conceded. 'In some ways.'

The man made a gesture, half disparaging, half dismissive, wholly French. 'But the main reason for your trip was less successful.'

A look of annoyance crossed the woman's face. 'I was too late. A week earlier I might have been able to salvage something. I'm afraid we'll have to start again. Fortunately, neither the supply nor the demand is likely to run out any time soon. All we need are some rather more reliable partners.'

'Partners!' The man snorted derisively.

'What word would you prefer? Representatives – agents? It doesn't matter what we call them. We need someone to do the bits we'd rather not do ourselves, the bits that can get you locked up. Do you want to drive a lorry through Customs twice a month? Then we need someone who will. Preferably, someone a bit smarter than the Kings.'

'They were unlucky.'

'Incompetent people always think they've been unlucky. She was smart enough, and careful enough. Bill's just a thug. He always thought with his muscles; when he started thinking with his gun, we were on a countdown to disaster. Maybe I'll make our associates pass an intelligence test in future!' From her expression, the man wasn't sure she was joking.

He watched her curiously. 'You're not concerned they could betray us?'

'The Kings?' The woman shook her head negligently. 'They don't know enough to. They couldn't pick either of us out at an ID parade. I could wear my second-best pearls and pretend to be a prison visitor, and neither of them would be any the wiser.'

They were in the car by now. The man turned up the heating.

'No,' the woman said then, slowly, thoughtfully. 'Weak isn't the right word.'

'Pardon?'

'You asked if my husband is a weak man. I think mostly he's . . . unrealistic. He expects too much, especially of himself. So he's always being disappointed.'

'More fool him.'

'No, he was never a fool. He's a highly intelligent man: what he lacks is a bit of low cunning. I wonder now what I saw in him.' She laughed again. 'Good earning potential, I think. I was very young. The prospect of living well in London appealed to me.' She cast the man a sidelong look. 'Unrealistic he may be, but he had me sign the divorce papers before he'd drive me to the airstrip.'

'Well, that's a good thing, isn't it? Now you've severed all legal ties to him, you're a free agent.' He gave a meaningful chuckle. 'Not that you allowed him to cramp your style very much, even before.'

She shrugged. 'I don't think I was cut out to be anyone's wife.'

'And now you're done with him, yes? Finally and for good. Aren't you?'

'Yes,' said Cathy Ash. 'Yes. Well, maybe . . .'

9 781780 298047